PRAISE FOR *Anything But Fine*

"With so much humor and heart, Tobias Madden shows that whether it's coming out, romance, friendship, school, or career ambitions, sometimes the biggest triumphs come from dancing into the unexpected."

—**JASON JUNE**, author of *Jay's Gay Agenda*

"Sincere, charming, emotional, and chaotic, *Anything But Fine* is an honest portrayal of how equally terrifying and beautiful figuring out who we are and who we can be is."

—**JONNY GARZA VILLA**,
author of *Fifteen Hundred Miles from the Sun*

"At its heart is such a fresh, diverse, heartwarming love story that anyone will love. *Anything But Fine* is such a fun, cute, and romantic read! I was cheering for Luca from the beginning and continue to cheer for him beyond the final page."

—**GARY LONESBOROUGH**,
award-winning author of *Ready When You Are*

"With a messy, swoony romance and an array of complex and evolving relationships, Luca's story is a lesson in realizing that the only misstep is not taking the next step, and the power that comes from within."

—**STEVEN SALVATORE**, author of *Can't Take That Away*

"*Anything But Fine* is a hilarious and moving portrait of what it means to reassess your life when your future suddenly looks very different from what you've always dreamed. Tobias Madden has created a queer love story that is fresh, romantic, and thoroughly entertaining."

—**ERIN GOUGH**,
award-winning author of *Amelia Westlake Was Never Here*

"*Anything But Fine* is a gorgeous story about love, loss, friendship, and hope—and about finding your true self after your one and only dream shatters into a thousand pieces."

—**FLEUR FERRIS**, bestselling author of *Risk*

Anything But Fine

TOBIAS MADDEN

PAGE STREET
PUBLISHING CO.

PAGE STREET
PUBLISHING CO.

Copyright © 2021 Tobias Madden

First published in the United States in 2022 by
Page Street Publishing Co.
27 Congress Street, Suite 105
Salem, MA 01970
www.pagestreetpublishing.com

Distributed by Macmillan, sales in Canada by The Canadian Manda Group.

26   25   24   23   22   1   2   3   4   5

ISBN-13: 978-1-64567-438-2
ISBN-10: 1-64567-438-X

Library of Congress Control Number: 2021937036

Cover and book design by Kylie Alexander for Page Street Publishing Co.
Cover image © Creative Market; Volodymyr Melnyk

Printed and bound in the United States

FOR MUM AND DAD, WHO TAUGHT ME
EVERYTHING I KNOW

One

THE SECOND IT HAPPENS, I know my life is over. I feel the bones break. I literally hear them crack into pieces. As soon as my body hits the floor, my whole world falls apart. My future collapses—dream by dream, goal by goal—right before my eyes.

One missed step and it's all over. It's as simple as that.

One missed step.

Scorching January sunlight pours in through the windows of the studio. It bounces off the wall of mirrors, making me squint as I dance across the floor. *Chassé, pas de bourrée, glissade, jeté.*

"Stretch that back knee in your *jeté*, Luca," Miss Gwen barks from her white plastic chair up the front of the room.

And again, to the left. *Chassé, pas de bourrée, glissade*—as I push off from the floor, I squeeze every muscle in my body, making sure my legs hit a perfect split in mid-air—*jeté.*

"Better."

Better, she says. Never *good*. No matter how hard I try in class, no matter how many competitions I win, nothing I do is ever *good* in Miss Gwen's eyes. To be honest, I don't think the word is even in her vocabulary.

I finish the corner progression and move out of the way as Talia darts across the floor behind me, her long legs sweeping effortlessly through the air as she jumps.

"Nice," I say to her when she joins me at the ballet barre beneath the windows.

"It was crap," she scoffs, pressing her hands against the wooden barre, stretching out her calves. "I'm so heavy today. I can't get off the floor."

And I mean, Talia legitimately has one of the most perfect *jetés* I've ever seen, and she couldn't be less "heavy" if she tried.

"You're ridiculous." I drag my palm across my forehead and wipe the sweat on my navy blue unitard.

"Come talk to me when *you*'ve had to haul your ass through *grand allegro* with your period."

I wrinkle my nose and walk off toward the back corner of the studio, ready to start the exercise again.

"Oh, I'm *sorry*," Talia hisses, following close behind, "does my period gross you out, Mr. I Have A Penis and Therefore Never Want to Talk About Anything Even Remotely Vagina Related?"

I snort. "Shut up and take the compliment. Your *jetés* are flawless, and you know it."

"Yeah, well maybe if Miss Gwen ever took her eyes off *you*, she'd notice how flawless my jumps are."

"Excuse me?"

Talia rolls her eyes. "Oh, please. We all know you're the favorite."

"Miss Gwen doesn't *have* favorites." I glance over at our ancient ballet teacher, sitting there in her chair like some kind of zombie vulture, waiting to tear us all to shreds if we don't point our feet properly. "She hates everything and everyone."

"Sounds like something the favorite would say."

"Why are you making this a thing?"

"I'm not making it a *thing*," Talia replies. "You're the one getting defensive, Mr. Favorite."

"I thought I was 'Mr. I Have A Penis,' etcetera, etcetera?"

"Whatever, bitch." She pushes in front of me and leaps across the studio, catching my eye in the mirror and flashing me her trademark *I'm the shit* smirk.

"God, I wish I had her legs," Abbey says from the line of girls behind me. She runs a hand over her bright red hair, which is slicked back into a bun so tight it's making her look permanently surprised. "And her hair."

"And her skin," Grace adds, milk-white hands perched on Abbey's slender shoulders.

"Slash, her Greek genes in general," I reply, turning back to watch Talia dance. "I'd kill to have some Mediterranean in me."

"Oh, I bet you'd *love* to have a Mediterranean in you," Abbey says, making her eyebrows dance.

"Oh my god," Grace says, covering her ears.

"Abbey, *stop*," I laugh, stepping forward into the space, my arms open wide.

I take a deep breath, lift my chest, and repeat the progression on both sides—*chassé, pas de bourrée, glissade, jeté*. It's such a simple exercise. I've been doing it in class like, five times a week since the dawn of time, but there's something about it that still makes me feel so . . . I dunno. It's kind of hard to explain. It's like . . . it makes me feel strong and super masculine (which, let's be honest, I'm not) but also graceful and delicate at the same time. Kind of like I'm showing every part of myself at full volume. It makes me feel lighter than air, like I could jump right through the roof and up into the sky. It makes me feel so . . . *me*.

I've been dancing at the Gwen Anderson School of Ballet since I was three years old. And not only is it by far the best ballet school in Ballarat, it's like my second home. Although, I don't know if I can really call it my *second* home when I spend more time here than at my *actual* home. And considering my mum died before I started dancing, Miss Gwen is the closest thing I've ever had to a mother. Which is kinda weird, because she's like, nine-hundred years old and possibly a vampire of some kind.

When I first started ballet, she was still in good-enough shape to demonstrate all the exercises in class, but, thirteen years later, she's lucky to be able to walk in and out of the studio. I mean, she really should be in a wheelchair by now, but she flat-out refuses. Too stubborn, I guess. Her daughter, Miss Prue, teaches all our classes now, but Miss Gwen still insists on coming in and screaming at us from her chair down at the front of the studio.

Yeah, it's about as fun as it sounds.

As I *jeté* past Miss Prue—stick-thin and kind of pinched-looking—she nods in approval. Miss Gwen might not be one to dish out praise, but Miss Prue is the exact opposite. "Beautiful, Luca," she calls out as I walk over to the side of the studio. "Just *beautiful*."

"She knows you're gay, right?" Talia says when I arrive beside her. She pulls a hairpin out of her jet-black bun, separates the metal prongs with her teeth and puts it back in at a different angle.

I roll my eyes. "Honestly, do you ever stop?"

"Just saying, she's barking up the wrong tree."

"She's like, forty," I reply, pulling the fabric of my unitard up the front of my thighs. "And married. And you're literally the worst person I know."

"You love me."

"Yeah, remind me why that is again?"

Miss Gwen claps loudly from where she sits beside the prehistoric stereo system. "All right, everyone. *Révérence*. And for god's sake, try to make it look like it's not causing you physical pain this time, will you?"

As a class, we move to the center of the studio and perform our carefully choreographed bows and curtsies, set to a gently tinkling piano track.

"Thank you, Miss Gwen," we say in unison. "Thank you, Miss Prue."

"Thanks, girls," Miss Prue replies, then smiles at me and adds, "and *boy*."

As we start to file out of the studio, Miss Gwen calls my name.

I stop and turn around.

"No . . ." Talia whispers as she slips past me, "she doesn't have favorites at *all*."

I ignore her and jog over to Miss Gwen, who stays in her chair, gripping its plastic arms with her wrinkled hands.

Miss Prue is fiddling with the stereo.

"This is a big year for you, Luca," Miss Gwen croaks.

I nod.

"ABS auditions are only—"

"Six months and thirteen days away," I say. "I know."

Miss Gwen exhales loudly through her nose. "You've got all the potential in the world, Luca, but that counts for nothing if you don't put in the *work*."

"Yes, Miss Gwen."

"I know what you boys are like." Her top lip curls up at the side. "I've watched it happen over and over. You turn sixteen and you lose focus. You lose your drive. You don't *like* ballet anymore. It's too girly. It's not *cool*. You start thinking with your penis. Suddenly, your biggest ambition in life is to have sex with any girl who'll have you."

I turn my laugh into a strangled little cough. I should probably remind Miss Gwen that having sex with girls is literally the last thing on my to-do list, but instead say, "I am one hundred percent focused, Miss Gwen."

She narrows her eyes and leans in closer, as if she's searching my face for lies. "I will not have you squandering your hard-earned talent and wasting your time with all that . . . hormonal nonsense, do you hear me?"

I nod again, biting my bottom lip to keep from smiling.

"We haven't had a student accepted into the Australian Ballet School since Laura Pearson, and that was . . . when was that, Prudence?"

"Uh . . ." Miss Prue looks up from the stereo as she slides the syllabus CD back into its plastic pocket.

"2014," I say, glancing over at a framed photo on the wall of Laura dancing as Coppélia in the 2012 recital. I smile, thinking of how she always used to call me "cutie."

"Too long for a studio like this," Miss Gwen sighs. "I used to send two girls off to ABS every year. This . . . *drought* is becoming embarrassing."

"Mum," Miss Prue says gently, walking over and holding her hands out to Miss Gwen. "Luca has enough pressure on him as it is."

"I am one hundred percent focused," I say again. "I promise. I know what it takes."

Miss Gwen grunts as she uses her daughter's hands to pull herself up to her feet. "Yes, but, *knowing* what it takes and *having* what it takes are two very different things," she says, her eyes drilling into mine. "Do you *have* what it takes, Luca?"

I clear my throat. "I do."

"Then you should know better than to talk in class."

"Sorry. I—"

"Don't be sorry, dear. Do better."

"Yes, Miss Gwen."

"You can go now." She dismisses me with a wave of her hands.

Miss Prue smiles apologetically as I trot off across the studio and out to the carpeted waiting area.

"What was that about?" Talia asks, already changed back into her green and white St. Tom's summer dress, her ballet tights still on but rolled up to her knees.

"Just your standard, horrifically awkward pep talk," I say, grabbing my bag and heading into the bathroom to get changed.

"You coming to Grill'd?" she says through the door.

"Obviously."

Since I'm the only boy at the studio, I don't get an actual change room. I get the bathroom, which also doubles as a cleaning supply closet. Super glam, I know.

I take off my ballet shoes and battle with my sweat-soaked unitard, eventually managing to yank it off. I slip on my grey school shorts and white shirt—minus my St. Tom's tie—and throw on a pair of flip-flops. I swing my textbook-filled bag over my shoulder with a loud *oof* and head back out into the waiting area. Talia is standing at the top of the staircase that leads down to street level, hands on hips, lips pursed.

"Are Grace and Abbey coming?" I ask.

"I don't know," she huffs, already bounding down the stairs two at a time. "Let's go. They can catch up."

By the time I start down the carpeted staircase, Talia's already out on the street.

"Luca?" Abbey calls from above.

"Down here, hurry up!" I say over my shoulder.

I only look back for a second. One second. But that's all it takes.

With my eyes on Abbey at the top of the stairs, I miss a step. My stomach swoops as my foot finds nothing but air, and I fall. The front of my left flip-flop catches on the carpet, and my foot twists beneath me on the step below.

The second it happens, I know my life is over. I feel the bones break. I hear them crack into pieces beneath the weight of my body. I feel the ligaments stretch past breaking point as my ankle buckles, and I tumble down the stairs, landing on top of my backpack in front of the glass door.

"Holy shit!" Abbey yells from the top of the stairs. "Luca!"

Someone calls out for Miss Prue.

I can't feel my foot.

Time blurs as I watch Abbey and Grace race down the stairs toward me in slow-motion, Miss Prue only a couple of steps behind them. Talia swings the door open and stands above me, swearing. The rest of the girls from class stare down at me from the top of the stairs, hands over their mouths, eyes wide.

"Luca? Are you okay?" It's Miss Prue. It sounds like she's under water.

Abbey grabs my hand, but I don't really feel it. Grace is crying.

"I'm . . ."

"Can you stand up?" someone asks.

I feel hands grasp my arms, my waist, my wrists. I'm lifted to my feet, balancing on my right foot.

Miss Prue, still under water, asks, "Luca, can you put weight on it?"

Mindlessly, I lower my left foot to the floor. Pain shoots through the arch of my foot and I cry out. The world suddenly tilts, and I feel like I'm falling again. Everything around me fades to black.

It's all over.

One missed step.

It's as simple as that.

Two

"I'LL BE BACK IN a few minutes to put a cannula in your hand, mate." The young nurse swishes open the blue curtain and turns back to me. "Is your dad still around?"

I nod once.

"Do you want this shut?"

I nod again.

The nurse smiles, his lips pressed tightly together, then closes the curtain behind him.

I look up to the ceiling, shut my eyes, and draw in a long, slow breath, trying as hard as I can not to scream. It's been less than twenty-four hours since I fell down the stairs at Miss Gwen's, and if one more person gives me the *look*—like they're staring down at some helpless, wounded animal on the side of the road—I'm going to absolutely lose my shit.

I've been weirdly calm throughout the whole thing so far. The doctor said I was in shock. But I just felt . . . I dunno, kind of *distanced* from the situation. Like it was happening to someone else. Like I was watching it on the news or something . . .

Dad carrying me to the car and driving to the hospital at three-hundred kilometers an hour.

Me lying perfectly still inside the MRI machine while the doctors and nurses fussed with charts and cables and computers.

Dad snoring in an armchair beside me while I lay there staring at the ceiling all night, a different nurse visiting every five minutes, for no apparent reason other than to give me the *look*.

Even worse than the *look*, though, is when the nurses ask me how I *am*. Like, as if they're expecting me to say, "Yeah, not too bad, actually," even though my left foot feels like I've shoved it into a bucket full of bull ants and the stench of antiseptic and old people is making me feel physically sick and everything I've worked so hard for my entire life has been suddenly ripped away from me.

The weird thing is, I haven't cried yet. And I usually cry a *lot*. I mean, I've cried at literally every movie I've ever seen, including *Zootopia* and *High School Musical 3*. Both of which are brilliant films, by the way. Just so we're clear.

Dad, on the other hand, has been crying pretty much the whole time. When the surgeon came to explain my injury to us this morning, Dad sobbed so much I thought he was gonna pass out. I guess it's not easy for him to watch his son go through something this messed up.

Because the thing is, this isn't just a "Rest, Ice, Compress, Elevate" kind of injury. I've sprained my ankle a couple of times and even tore my hamstring once. Every dancer gets injured. It's a part of life for us. But this isn't like that.

This is the real deal.

I can't remember what the injury is called, but it's apparently very rare, very severe, and very, very shitty. The surgeon, Dr. Khatri, showed us some scans and rattled off a bunch of medical terminology, but the only bit I remember—because how the hell could I not?—is that I snapped four ligaments, broke three bones, and dislocated the entire arch of my foot.

Translation: it's totally and utterly fucked.

By the time the words "it's unlikely that Luca will ever dance again" casually poured out of Dr. Khatri's mouth, I was completely numb to the world. Which is lucky, because if I wasn't, I'm pretty sure I would've thrown up all over the polished hospital lino.

Dad was still wiping away tears when she started explaining the surgical procedure itself, which sounded like something out of a '90s sci-fi film. She said that because my injury is so severe, they won't be able to just realign the joints and put in a couple of screws to hold everything steady. If that was the case—which the doctor said it is, like, 90-something percent of the time—I'd be able to make a full recovery. But *no*, for my especially awful injury, they'll need to fuse the bones together permanently, putting in plates and rods and screws to lock the whole arch of my foot in place. Which means they're going to turn my left foot into a completely useless hunk of metal. Which means no more ballet for me.

All I can say is that paracetamol is totally useless. I mean, sure, for a regular headache, it does the trick. But when you're sitting at home on the couch post-surgery with a splint on your leg, your foot looking like a freshly pounded piece of meat from the butcher, your whole body covered in bruises from falling down a flight of stairs? Yeah, not so great.

The only thing worse than the sting of the stitches and the constant burning *inside* my foot—which is exactly as painful as it sounds—is the boredom. I'm usually at ballet three nights a week and all weekend. And when I'm not at ballet, I'm avoiding doing homework by practicing ballet in my room. Sitting here on the couch for twelve hours a day watching Nutribullet and air fryer infomercials, not even having the motivation to reach over and grab the remote so I can change the channel, is *not* something I'm used to. I've never felt so useless in my life. And no amount of Insta-scrolling is going to make me feel any less pathetic, that's for sure.

I click into my messages and open a group chat called *Bunheads 4 Lyf*. Talia started the chat for the four of us when we were eleven, and none of us ever bothered to change the name when we realized how horrifically uncool it was. The funny thing is, the name is so *not* cool now, it's kind of vintage and cute. But I have to admit, reading the words "4 Lyf" makes my chest cramp up a bit.

Lu. Thinking of you. Hope everything is okay. Let us know if you need anything. Purple love-heart emoji, from Grace.

Abbey: **Hope you're ok Luca xxx**

Talia: **WTF Luca. Call me.**

Followed by a love heart rainbow from Grace, and rows and rows of kisses from Abbey.

The messages are from the morning of my surgery, which

was . . . Thursday? And now it's Monday. No—Tuesday—and I still haven't replied. I just can't bring myself to write back. And I know that probably makes me a horrible friend, but what would I even say? *Life over, brb?*

I *know* I should reply. I just . . .

I click my phone closed and toss it to the end of the couch, just as Dad pokes his head into the lounge.

"Lu, what do you want for dinner?" he asks.

He took time off work to look after me, which, you know, is great, because I probably would've starved to death if he hadn't been here to bring me food. He's also been piggy-backing me upstairs to bed each night, and back down in the morning. He fluffs my pillows and helps me get dressed. He has to help me shower, too—to make sure my leg stays completely dry—but I've been keeping my jocks on because this whole experience is already mortifying enough without Dad seeing my junk on a day-to-day basis.

I don't take my eyes off the TV. "Whatever."

"You want steak?" He walks in front of me. His blue flannel shirt is a blur, my eyes still focused on the TV behind him. "Spaghetti?"

I shrug.

"Stir-fry?"

Another shrug.

"Tacos?"

Half a shrug.

"How about a bowl of 'please just answer your dad before he goes insane talking to himself all the bloody time'?"

I glare up at him, my arms folded tightly across my chest.

"Sorry, mate," he says, pinching the bridge of his nose. "I'm just . . . I don't know. I wish there was some way I could help you."

"It's fine, Dad. There's nothing you can do. I'm beyond help."

"I'm not sure if you're being melodramatic for effect, or if that's how you really feel."

"Melodramatic?" I scoff. "There is nothing *melodramatic* about this." I gesture to my mangled foot like I'm the woman from the air fryer infomercial. "This is the definition of *actual* drama, Dad. This is totally messed up."

He scratches the top of his shiny, bald head and clicks his tongue. "Look, I know it feels like your life is over, Lu, but you're not dead. You'll—"

"What?" I snap. "Finish that sentence, Dad. What will I do?"

He sighs, shaking his head, and kneels down beside the arm of the couch. "I don't know, Lu. I don't even know what I'm saying. Your mum would've been so much better at this."

I soften instantly, feeling my frustration fizzle out inside my chest. Dad's eyes glaze over as he stares down at the floral carpet, clearly thinking about Mum.

I don't really remember her, but it's as if I've gotten to know her through Dad's eyes, through his memories of her. She died almost fourteen years ago, but he still has all her old clothes hanging up in his bedroom closet. Which is kind of sweet. And also kind of weird, I guess. But I can tell by the way his face lights up whenever her name is mentioned—one corner of his mouth curling up and his eyes crinkling at the sides—

that she must have been pretty damn incredible.

"Steak sounds good," I say, forcing a smile.

Dad clears his throat and looks up at me, his eyes a little watery. "Steak it is, then."

Three

THE BIGGEST MISTAKE I make during my two weeks of forced, total-bullshit couch rest is making Dad get the box of old ballet recital DVDs out of the shed.

"Are you sure?" he asks, tilting his head to the side, in that way parents love to do when they think they know better.

"When have I ever been *not* sure, Dad? Just get them. Please?"

"If you say so," he huffs, leaving me on the couch.

I take it right from the top. Tiny tots. And I won't lie, this video does make me smile, but only because I'm so terrible. I'm three years old, so I guess I can be excused, but I pretty much just stand there in my fluorescent ladybug costume, staring out at the audience, grinning. At one point, I sit down at the front of the stage and start waving at the audience when I'm meant to be galloping around in a circle, following the leader. I always hated doing that. It wasn't fair. *I* wanted to be the leader.

From recital to recital, I watch myself grow up on the screen. From a chubby little toddler with white-blond hair mucking around up the back as "Flowerpot Number Three"; to a stick-thin kid with an awful, mousy-brown bowl-cut partnering the older girls in complex *pas de deux*; to me now: a lean but strong sixteen-year-old with James Dean hair and eyebrows "made for the stage"—thanks, Dad—performing the insanely difficult solo variations from *Don Quixote* and *Grand Pas Classique*.

By the time I get to last year's recital—this one on a USB that I have to plug into my laptop—a heavy weight has settled on my chest, making it hard to breathe. This is so not fun anymore. This is absolute torture. My eyes prickle as I watch myself leap and turn all over the stage in my white tights and brocade jacket. My double *cabrioles* are absolutely textbook. My *grand jeté en tournant*: flawless.

Boiling hot waves of rage start to bubble up inside my throat, as if my whole body is going up in flames. And suddenly I'm falling again, tumbling down the stairs at the studio, my ribs crunching against the carpeted steps, my arms and legs flailing, my hands trying to grip onto nothing. I close my eyes, clench my jaw, and scrunch up my face until I see bursts of tiny green stars in the blackness all around me.

"Everything okay?" Dad asks, just as I'm about to throw my three-thousand-dollar MacBook—which we definitely couldn't afford to replace—across the room.

I gasp in a shaky breath and look up, finally letting tears spill from my eyes.

"Oh, Lu," Dad says, "I knew those DVDs were a bad idea."

"I'm never going to dance again," I say. And for the first time since my fall, those words hit me with their full meaning, a knife straight through my heart.

I'm never going to do that again.

Dad plonks down beside me on the couch. "You don't know that, mate. It's early days."

"The doctor said I wouldn't—"

"The *doctor*," he interrupts, "doesn't know everything." He puts his hand on my leg, which is stretched out in front of me, my injured foot balanced on the edge of the coffee table. "And she shouldn't have said that to you, not right before your surgery. People recover from all sorts of crazy injuries, Lu. Athletes, dancers, gymnasts. It's not easy, but they get through it."

I shake my head, wiping a little bit of snot from my nose with the back of my hand.

"It's true." He nods. "I dunno how they do it, but they do."

"This isn't like that, Dad. Even if I *do* have some kind of miraculous recovery and get the range of motion back in my foot, by the time that happens I'll have been left for dead by the other dancers my age. Ballet won't wait. It's now or never. You think the Australian Ballet School is going to accept me in, what, like, four years' time when I'm *twenty* and fully recovered?"

"Well—"

"No," I answer for him. "They won't. And I'm not going to *make* a full recovery anyway, so it doesn't even matter. It's over, Dad. It's done. The dream is dead."

I fold my arms and stare down at my swollen, useless foot, hating it for existing.

"We don't know that," Dad goes on in a quiet voice. "We just have to wait and see. I don't want you to give up, Lu. Not yet."

"I'm not 'giving up,' Dad," I say, throwing my hands in the air. "I don't have a fucking choice in the matter. You think I want to be sitting here like some kind of fucking—"

"*Luca,*" Dad growls. "You swear too much."

I roll my eyes.

He sighs through his nose, pressing his lips up toward his nostrils. "I just don't want you to lose hope, Lu. Don't count yourself out yet. Who knows, maybe this is the Universe's messed-up way of telling you you'd be incredible at something else? Maybe you'll become a famous ballet *teacher?*"

"Yeah, like *that's* the reason I've been slaving away in the studio every day of my life, so I can end up teaching a bunch of no-hopers how to *tendu.* No, thanks, Universe."

"A *tendu* is one of those big jumps, right?" Dad asks. "Where you do the splits in the air?"

"What? No." I scrunch up my face. "That's a *jeté.*"

He chuckles at himself. "You'd think I'd know all the lingo by now, wouldn't you? I was always abysmal at French."

I stare back at him. I know what he's trying to do.

"Did I ever tell you I failed my HSC French exam?"

I don't reply.

"True story," he says, stretching his mouth out like the awkward smile emoji. "I was *awful.*"

And because I can't help myself, I say, "Why the hell did you do French for your HSC if you were so bad at it?"

"To get the girl."

"What girl?"

"*What girl?*" Dad scoffs. "Who do you think? Your mum. She had all these vintage Italian postcards stuck up in her locker at school, and she used to talk about going to live in Tuscany one day."

One of Dad's all-time favorite stories is how he wanted to call me plain-old *Luke*, but Mum refused, saying that the Italian version, *Luca*, was much more alluring and interesting.

"I was planning on wooing her in Italian," Dad continues, "but they didn't offer Italian classes at our school, only French and German. So I figured French was close enough."

"That is the most ridiculous thing I've ever heard," I reply. "And also, no one says 'wooing' anymore. It sounds like something you'd do to a cow."

"Well, whatever you want to call it, it worked. It turned out she found my offensively bad French 'endearing'—her words, not mine." He grins, clearly still chuffed with himself, all these years later.

"So, what I'm gathering from this conversation is that you're saying I should try to fail even *more* subjects at school, in order to 'woo' boys?"

Dad pats me on the thigh and stands up. "That would be very bad parenting on my behalf, Luca. But if it means you bring a nice boy home to meet me sometime . . ."

"*Dad.*"

"I'm just saying. You're a teenage boy. Teenage boys like to . . . you know."

"No, Dad, I don't know, would you care to elaborate?"

"No pressure," he says, waving his hands in front of his face. "I just want you to be happy. You do you."

"Excuse me, but where on earth did you learn 'you do you'?"

He shrugs like a cartoon caricature of himself. "Your old man can be pretty *hip* when he wants to be," he says, proceeding to do this weird little '70s dance move.

"Nope. No, he can't." A laugh escapes me, and I shield my eyes. "Stop that, your dancing is offensive."

When I take my hands away from my face, Dad is staring down at me, smiling.

"What?" I ask.

"Nothing. I just . . . It's nice to hear you laughing," he replies, before plodding off into the kitchen. "You want a cup of tea?'

⁓

"How does it feel?' Doctor Khatri says, tracing her fingers down the length of my freshly set cast. Her office-slash-treatment-room is in this little house directly across the road from the hospital. It *looks* like someone's grandma's place—rose bushes and all—but it *smells* like the hospital. It's very weird.

"It feels like my leg has been swallowed by a giant hunk of plaster," I reply.

The bulky white cast starts just below my left knee and wraps all the way down over my ankle and foot. Only the tips of my toes poke out at the end. A faint memory of Mum playing 'This Little Piggy' on my toes swims into my mind, but when I blink, it disappears. Sometimes I can't tell if these patchy images are real, or if my brain just conjures up fake memories so I don't feel so shitty all the time about not having a mum.

"You'll get used to it," the doctor says, and it takes me a second to remember she's talking about my cast. "Now, the sooner we start your physical therapy, the better, so I've booked you in to see *the* best occupational therapist in Ballarat tomorrow. She's going to work with you once a week throughout your recovery."

My first thought is: *Thank god Miss Gwen's studio had insurance. Dad would never have been able to afford this on his own.*

"Your OT won't be able to work on the foot itself for quite some time," Doctor Khatri continues, "but she'll make sure you're using the crutches properly, and she'll do her best to discourage any compensatory patterns in the surrounding muscles. She's a real whiz with post-op recovery. I'm sure her sessions will make the time in the cast fly by."

I side-eye Dad. "Yeah, I'm sure it'll just *fly by*."

"Yes, I'm sure it will." He nods pointedly, widening his eyes at me in a way that I know says, *Please stop sassing Doctor Khatri.*

"Now," she says, "I would be remiss if I didn't remind you to expect a permanent deficit in the range of movement in your foot and ankle."

Like I could forget.

"It's always better to go into this kind of lengthy recovery process with realistic expec—"

"Yep," Dad says, cutting her off. "Got it. Loud and clear, thank you."

Doctor Khatri clasps her hands in her lap. "Of course."

"Are we done?" I ask, and Dad clears his throat loudly.

"Yes," the doctor replies, "I think that's it for now. Here is some information for you—" she hands me a colorful stack of pamphlets "—about Lisfranc fractures, taking care of the cast, and about the recovery period in general. Please get in touch if you have any queries, and, if not, I'll see you in about six weeks to remove the cast."

"Thank you," Dad says when I don't reply.

"I'll leave you to it." Doctor Khatri offers me a patronizing smile before sweeping out of the consultation room.

"Up we get." Dad helps me up to my feet and passes me my shiny new pair of crutches, one at a time, watching as I thread my arms through the elbow cuffs and grab the handles.

"You gonna be okay?" he asks, holding out his arms as if I'm going to topple over like a toddler taking his first steps.

"I'm *fine*," I say, and it comes out a lot more forcefully than I mean it to. "It's just crutches, Dad. I'm like, *highly* coordinated, remember?"

"Okay, just checking."

But by the time we make it outside to the car, my shoulders are on fire, my hands are absolutely killing me, and it feels like someone is screaming the words *permanent deficit* at me on repeat from inside my own brain.

Dad is looking at me like he knows, but I refuse to admit it.

"Do you need help getting in?" he asks.

"I'm fine, I got this." I awkwardly hoist myself into Dad's four-wheel-drive with one arm, holding my crutches in my other hand outside the door. It takes me so long to thread them both through the door one-handed, that by the time I get them inside, I'm about ready to snap them in half. And then I realize I've trapped myself behind the crutches and can't reach the door handle to pull it shut.

I slump down in the seat and glare at the glovebox.

Without a word, Dad jumps out of the car, jogs around to the passenger side, and shuts the door for me.

"You good?" he asks, sliding back into the car and turning the ignition.

"I'm *fine*," I say as we pull out of the car park, feeling literally anything but fine.

Four

THE WHITE WALLS OF the waiting room at Ballarat Allied Therapies are covered with photos of sportspeople. I don't recognize any of them—which is no surprise, because I know literally nothing about sport—but I'm guessing other people must know who they are, or their photos wouldn't be up on the walls. The pictures are signed in black permanent marker, most of them saying things like "Thanks, Sami" or "You're the best, Sami."

Apparently, Sami is one hell of a popular occupational therapist.

I've been to the physio plenty of times but never an "OT," as the doctor kept calling it yesterday. To be honest, I have no idea what the difference is, but unless the OT can send me back in time so I can *not* fall down a flight of stairs and ruin my life, I'm not sure what good she's going to be able to do.

I pull my phone out of my pocket and click into the *Bunheads 4 Lyf* chat.

Grace: **Lu, I'm getting worried now. Please write back.**

Purple love heart.

Abbey: **Just tell us you're okay.** Single tear emoji.

Way to be dramatic, Mr. Favorite. Talia, snarky as usual. **Message back, bitch.**

Then Grace again: **You know what, two weeks of radio silence is NOT FAIR, Luca. Miss Gwen and Miss Prue keep asking how you are but I have NO IDEA. Because you won't reply. You won't answer our calls. If you don't write back RIGHT NOW, I'm going to break into your house to make sure you're not lying dead on the kitchen floor.** Huffy-face emoji. Spy emoji. House emoji. **If you need space I totally get it but PLEASE JUST REPLY.** Three purple love hearts.

I'm sure if I didn't live on the complete opposite side of town to the girls, they would have already stormed over and broken down my front door. I'm surprised Grace hasn't alerted the authorities.

I start to type, **Hey . . . I'm sorry I haven't**—but I still can't think of anything to say, so I backspace and swipe out of the chat.

Just as I shove my phone back into my pocket, a guy around my age struts—and I do mean *struts*—through the automatic doors to the reception desk. I can't see his face, but from behind, he's straight out of a Nike catalogue. Broad shoulders, muscly arms, narrow hips. An ass that puts the peach emoji to shame.

"I've got an appointment with Mark at one thirty," he says to the receptionist. His voice is sort of deep, but . . . I dunno, playful? Kind of how I imagine a golden retriever would talk.

"Jordan?" the cheery receptionist asks.

"Yep."

"Take a seat," she says. "Mark is finishing up with another client. He shouldn't be too long."

"Cool," Jordan replies. "Thanks."

And as he turns away from the desk, my stomach does this sickening swoop. Holy shit. This boy is *stunning*. Like, forget the Nike catalogue, he should be in one of those cologne ads where the guy is half-naked and artfully dripping with water for no apparent reason. He has the most gorgeous tan skin, short, jet-black hair, golden-hazel eyes, and cheekbones the girls at ballet would literally kill for. And then there's his lips. I mean, lips like that should be illegal. Or it should at least be illegal for them to *not* be kissing someone at all times.

He furrows his brow, then smirks, and I realize I'm staring. As in, staring with my mouth open, staring.

I tear my eyes away from him and pick up a random magazine from the coffee table to distract myself. I can't help but notice that he sits in the chair directly opposite me, and I spend the next thirty seconds trying to convince myself that his choice of seat is not a deliberate sign from the Universe that he wants to marry me.

I so badly want to look up to see if he's looking at me, but I think I might actually pass out if he is, so I keep my eyes glued to the page. And even though I'm reading the words, not a single one enters my brain. It's way too busy making up elaborate sex fantasies about the beautiful Asian guy sitting opposite me in the OT waiting room.

I shift uncomfortably in my seat, feeling heat rise in my cheeks. Because here's the thing: I've always been useless around straight guys. Especially *hot* straight guys. And this guy is definitely hot, and I'm assuming he's straight, because it's Ballarat and *everyone* here is straight. Which makes being useless around straight guys kinda shit, to be honest. I just can't seem to be myself around them. And it's weird, because I'm not trying to hide anything. I'm not ashamed of being gay, and I'm certainly not a self-conscious person. But put me in an enclosed space with a hot straight guy and I literally lose the ability to speak. It's like my brain gets wiped clean.

So, of *course* the Universe decides Jordan is in a chatty mood today.

"Hey, man," he says, and I die a little inside.

I take a deep breath, pretending I'm so fascinated by what Meryl Streep wore to the 2007 Oscars that I don't hear him.

"What happened to your leg?"

Completely out of my brain's control, my eyes flick up to meet Jordan's gaze. He smiles and I'm officially dead. Deceased. Death by dazzling smile.

"Is it broken?"

That's two questions in a row, and I'm just sitting here like some kind of vow-of-silence yoga wanker.

His smile fades. "Are you okay, dude? You look a bit flushed."

Yes, Jordan, that's because I'm *mortified* that you're talking to me and I can't seem to think of a single word to say back to you. I'm surprised I can even *think* words right now.

I clear my throat.

I swallow.

I take another deep breath and . . .

"I broke my foot," I say, and I swear to god, cheerleaders start shaking pom-poms in my mind.

"Oof," Jordan replies with a grimace. "How'd you do that?"

"Fell down a flight of stairs."

Oh my god, I'm actually having a *conversation* with this guy. The cheerleaders start doing backflips all over the place.

"Must have been a pretty good stack," Jordan says, wincing as if he can feel my pain.

"Well, I'm a perfectionist, so . . . if I'm going to do something, I'm going to do it right."

Jordan chuckles.

Wait, was that . . . was that a *joke*, Luca?

WINNING.

"I respect that," Jordan says, still laughing. "I'm the same, plus I'm majorly competitive. I might need to start avoiding stairs completely, just in case I try to outdo you."

And suddenly it's five hundred degrees in here. Sweat pricks on my palms and—oh, god, *really?*—I start to get hard in my trackies.

Seriously, penis? *Seriously?* He said "outdo" me, not *do* me.

I can't cross my legs properly because of my cast, so I clasp my hands over my crotch, praying to the awkward erection gods that Jordan doesn't notice.

"How long do you need to have the cast on?"

"Six weeks," I reply, trying to avoid looking at any part of Jordan that will make me harder than I already am.

News flash: that is *any* part of him.

"I broke my leg when I was six," he says. "It was balls."

Oh, for the love of god, please don't talk about balls right now.

"Yeah, it's not great so far," I manage to say, pressing my

hands down a little harder. "I don't know how I'm gonna last six weeks. My leg itches like crazy, and I only got the cast on yesterday."

"I used to stick my school ruler down mine so I could scratch my leg. The doctor told me not to, but it felt *so good*."

He laughs again and I never want him to stop. Like, *ever*.

"What are you here for?" I ask.

"Ah, just this rotator cuff thing I've had for a while," he says, reaching around with one hand to massage his shoulder. "The doctor said I've got bursitis, but I'm pretending I didn't hear that. We're smack bang in the middle of rowing season, so I can't afford to take any time off."

Of course he's a rower. I bet he plays football, too.

"And then we go straight into footy season, so there's no time to rest."

Told you.

"It's my last year," he says with a sigh, "so I gotta make the most of it, you know."

"You're not gonna play next year?"

For some reason, this makes me think about the girls at ballet moving on without me. Learning the Advanced 2 syllabus without me. Doing their exams without me. Performing in the recital without me. Talia probably getting into ABS without me. I suddenly feel a deep ache in my chest and have to actively stifle the urge to cry.

At least I can finally take my hands away from my crotch.

After a moment, Jordan smirks, and says, "I don't think they let you play for the school team once you've, you know, finished school."

"Oh," I say. "You're in Year Twelve?"

"Yep. Home stretch."

"I'm only in Year Eleven. I've still got an eternity to go."

"It goes so fast, trust me," Jordan says, running a hand through his shiny, black hair. "Soon you'll be wishing you had more time."

I snort. "I don't know about that. School's never really been my thing."

"What school do you go to?"

"St. Tom's."

"Cool, cool," he says. "Great rowing squad."

"Yeah, they're awesome," I reply. I don't know much about rowing, but what I *do* know is that the St. Tom's boys always win. I also know that they look like a bunch of Captain Americas in their zoot suits, which is always a plus. "How 'bout you?" I ask. "What school do you go to?"

"Jordan?" A man says from beside me. I turn to see a tall, blond, ex-AFL-looking guy poking his head out of one of the treatment rooms.

Jordan jumps up from his chair and walks over to the man, greeting him with a handshake. Before he walks into the room, he turns and shoots me a heart-stopping grin.

And for a second—just one—I completely forget about my mangled, piece-of-shit foot.

I forget about the whole damn thing.

"Luca Mason?" A woman's voice pulls me sharply—and disappointingly—back to reality.

I look up and see a tall woman with dark-brown skin and super-short black hair standing in the doorway to one of the treatment rooms. She's wearing a crisp white blouse, tapered navy pants, and brown leather heels. A chunky gold necklace sits across her delicate collarbone, and bright-green earrings dangle from her ears. I literally have to stop myself from applauding her outfit.

"Yep," I say, scrambling to pick up my crutches and get to my feet—well, *foot*.

I hobble over to her, and she says, "I'm Samiya, but you can call me Sami. It's lovely to meet you, Luca."

So, this is the fabled "Sami" from the sportspeople wall of praise. Her smile is broad, her chestnut eyes warm and strangely soothing. I follow her into the treatment room, past the electric massage table, stopping when I notice a framed photo on her desk: Sami's face squished up against the blushing white cheeks of an adorable blonde woman, both mid-laugh. There is something so genuine, so infectious about the photo, that I involuntarily chuckle out loud.

"That's Julia," Sami says, sitting down at her desk. "My girlfriend."

And here I thought I was obsessed with her before.

"She's beautiful," I say, as Sami motions for me to sit.

"That photo doesn't do her a *shred* of justice. She's the best person in the world. It's a scientifically proven fact."

I smile, feeling weirdly giddy. I think I have a crush. A lady-crush. (It's totally a thing.) Not an I-want-to-see-you-naked crush, like I get with boys, obviously. It's the kind of crush where I want to like, take a girl out for a picnic and get to know every little thing about her. And gush about the people we like, and, I dunno, braid each other's hair and stuff. Like in one of those tacky teen movies from the '90s.

"So," Sami says, tilting her head slightly, "how are you feeling?"

"Do you want the 'you're a stranger, so I'm going to be polite' version, or the actual truth?"

"Actual truth. Always."

"I feel awful," I say, and Sami laughs. But not at me. It's like she instantly gets me.

"Awful how?"

"Aside from the fact that I'm never going to be able to do the one thing I love ever again?"

"Aside from that," she says. "For now, anyway. I meant how are you feeling *physically*?"

"Also awful."

We both laugh. I haven't felt this light since before my fall.

"My foot has this horrible ache, like, twenty-four-seven," I say. "It wakes me up in the middle of the night sometimes."

"That's a healing pain," Sami replies. "I know it's uncom-fortable, but that's honestly a good sign. What else?"

And because, for some reason, I already trust this woman with my life, I tell her everything. I tell her how every muscle in my entire body hurts, not just my foot. I tell her how I feel like a complete waste of space, like I'm useless without ballet, like it's not worth existing anymore. I tell her how Dad's been piggy-backing me upstairs at home every morning and night, and how it makes me feel like a five-year-old, but that I literally can't bring myself to climb up the stairs on my crutches.

Sami, who's been tapping away at her keyboard, making notes, looks up. "That's how you broke your foot, right? Stairs?"

"Yeah." I nod. "And I know it's ridiculous, but I just suddenly have this full-on phobia of stairs."

"That's not ridiculous," Sami replies. "That's totally normal. More than that, it's a basic survival instinct. You'd be silly *not* to be wary around stairs after an injury like this."

"Then I think I must be a total genius."

Sami smiles her hundred-watt smile, and I feel like I'm breathing in helium. "Now," she says, "as lovely as it is that your dad has been helping you move around the house, you need to start doing everything for yourself again. Not only for your physical recovery, but for your mental health, too. It's crucial that you feel capable and independent during this time."

I nod.

"Does that make sense?"

"Totally," I say, before adding with a smirk, "but I can still use my cast to get out of doing chores, right?"

"Oh, obviously," Sami says, with a flick of her wrists. "That's a given."

We both laugh again, and I think I actually blush this time.

Lady-crush. It's absolutely a thing.

Five

WHEN THE PRINCIPAL OF a fancy private school like St. Thomas's College calls you into their office for a meeting on a Sunday morning, it's either because you've won some kind of incredibly prestigious award, or because you've majorly screwed up. Neither of those things seems remotely likely right now, so I have no idea what's going on when Dad and I are ushered into Mr. Sandhurst's office.

"Thanks so much for coming in," he says. "I know weekends are precious."

It's so strange to see him wearing anything other than a suit and tie. He doesn't hold quite the same level of authority in his chino shorts and blue polo shirt. And why is it that middle-aged men have such creepy-looking shins?

"No worries," Dad replies.

I smile at Mr. Sandhurst, trying to get my crutches to balance on the wooden arm of the chair as I lower myself to sit.

"So, Luca," my principal says, fingers tented in front of his mouth, "how are you feeling?"

It's funny, because when Sami asked me the exact same question yesterday, I knew she really wanted to know. That she actually cared what my answer was. Coming out of Mr. Sandhurst's mouth, the words feel empty and . . . I dunno, just for show.

"I'm okay," I reply. "I started my physical therapy yesterday, and my OT is amazing. So, I'm feeling a lot better than when I was stranded on the couch."

Mr. Sandhurst chuckles, and even that feels kind of empty. "Well, that's a start, I'm sure. And tell me, what is the prognosis, in terms of your recovery?"

"Six weeks in the cast," Dad says in a weirdly deep voice, like he's trying to sound more manly than he really is. "And then another couple of months in a moon boot."

"I see."

"And then a lifetime of not dancing," I add, with an awkward laugh. I can't help myself. It's way easier to joke about my fate than actually accept it.

Mr. Sandhurst knits his brow. "The doctors don't think you'll make a full recovery?"

"Nope."

"What Luca *means*," Dad says, still in his not-Dad voice, "is that there's a long road ahead, and the eventual outcome is a bit unclear at this stage."

Mr. Sandhurst nods. "Right. But you think it's unlikely he'll be able to dance in the foreseeable future?"

I'm not sure why I've suddenly been excluded from the conversation, since it's *my* injury and *my* life we're discussing.

"Well, we're not—" Dad begins, but I cut him off.

"It's *very* unlikely I will ever dance again. I'll be lucky if I can even walk properly."

Dad sighs deeply, pinching the bridge of his nose like he always does. I know he hates me talking like this, but what's the point of giving myself even the tiniest bit of false hope? The doctor—the woman who screwed the plates and rods *into my bones*—said I wouldn't dance again. I'm pretty sure if anyone knows, it's her. And sure, I could be all *miracles happen* and *mind over matter*, but it's not going to fix my shattered bones. Nothing will. That's the whole point.

"Well," Mr. Sandhurst says slowly, "that puts us in a bit of a difficult position, I have to say."

"What do you mean?" Dad asks, looking up.

"Luca's grades are far below the standard we expect from our Year Eleven students." Mr. Sandhurst's eyes flick between Dad and me.

"We know his grades have always been a bit low," Dad says, "but that's never been a problem before. He's doing his best." He pats me on the leg. "Aren't you, Lu?"

I nod, starting to feel physically ill. I know where this is going, even if Dad doesn't.

"I'll admit," Mr. Sandhurst replies, "we've been very lenient with him in the past. But Luca is here at St. Tom's on a scholarship, and the conditions of that scholarship are very clear."

"But it's not an *academic* scholarship," Dad says, his voice rising. "So why do his grades matter?"

Mr. Sandhurst takes in a deep breath. "As Luca won't be able to dance for some time—"

"I'll no longer meet the criteria for the performing arts

scholarship," I blurt out before I realize I'm talking out loud.

"What?" Dad asks, his neck starting to turn bright red.

"They're taking away my scholarship," I say, half to Dad, half to myself.

This can't be happening right now. It just can't.

"Yes," Mr. Sandhurst says. "I hate to say it, but that is correct. And, unfortunately, since Luca is ranked at the bottom of all his classes—except dance, of course—he does not qualify for any of the school's other scholarships, academic or otherwise."

"So you're kicking him out?" Dad asks, standing bolt upright and moving around behind his chair, knuckles gripping the wooden backrest as if he's trying to snap it in half. "Because he's *injured*?"

"No," Mr. Sandhurst replies, way too calmly. "Luca has been a valued member of our school community since he came to St. Tom's in Year Seven, and I would never ask him to leave. All I am saying is that he will no longer qualify for any kind of financial assistance."

My heart is beating a thousand miles an hour. "But we can't afford th—"

"Luca," Dad warns. He turns his attention back to Mr. Sandhurst, who is sitting there as cool as a cucumber. "My son has a horrible accident and loses the ability to do what he loves the most, and you're going to *punish* him for that?"

"We are not punishing any—"

"You're kicking him out!" Dad yells. "You're expelling him because he had an accident and doesn't meet your elitist standards anymore. This is not happening. The school board is going to hear about this."

"It is the school board who makes these stipulations," Mr. Sandhurst says. "It's out of my hands."

"That is ridiculous!" Dad shouts.

"Please don't raise your voice at me," Mr. Sandhurst replies, his own voice still low and annoyingly calm.

"I'll raise my bloody voice if I want to. This kind of treatment is—You know what, I've never liked this school. You treat kids like they're nothing but exam scores."

"Dad," I say quietly, my cheeks burning.

"As I already explained," Mr. Sandhurst says, "we are *not* expelling Luca, nor asking him to leave. All I am saying, is that we are unable to provide financial assistance to a student who does not satisfy any of the scholarship requirements."

"We can't afford to pay the full fees, and you know it," Dad growls. "Without that scholarship, Luca would have been down the road at North from the start. Which means you wouldn't have been able to use him on all the posters for your precious performing arts department for the last four years. You've promoted this school on the back of Luca's achievements *outside* school. You've used him. He's been your little mascot this whole time, helping you poach all the most talented kids from all the other schools in Ballarat, and now—when he needs you—you're giving him the flick. You need to let him stay. You *owe* him."

"We don't *owe* Luca anything," Mr. Sandhurst says firmly. "We have provided him with a first-class educational program for four years, even though he has shown no inclination to work on his academic shortcomings. If you cannot afford to pay the full fee amount, then everyone at St. Thomas's College will be very sad to see Luca go. He has been a valued member—"

"Of the school community, yeah, yeah," Dad interrupts. "This isn't right. He's just a kid. You really want to take this away from him right now? His school, his friends? Everything he knows? When he's clearly already lost so much?"

Mr. Sandhurst purses his lips. "As I said, my hands are tied, Mr. Mason. Either you pay the full fees, or Luca will need to find another school."

"Fuck you," Dad snaps, and I've never—and I mean *never*—heard him say that to someone before. "You think I'd let my son stay at a school that treats its pupils like this? Come on, Luca, we're going."

"But—"

Dad grabs my crutches and holds them out to me. "Please, mate. Just . . ." His face is bright red, and his eyes are starting to get watery.

I push myself up from the chair on one foot and grab my crutches, slipping my arms through the elbow cuffs as Dad wrenches the door open. Without another word, I hobble out of the office.

Mr. Sandhurst follows us to the door. "I really am very sorry, Mr. Mason," he says. "But my han—"

Dad slams the door in his face.

No mum. No ballet. No school. No friends.

To be honest, the rest of my teenage existence is looking pretty grim.

Dad's been on the phone in the kitchen for the last two hours, so I shut myself in my room upstairs to avoid all the yelling.

I flick open Spotify on my phone and scroll through playlist after playlist until I find one called "Life Sucks." I flop down onto my bed on my stomach and let the depressing music wash over me, my tears making little wet patches on the sheets.

How can I possibly start all over again at sixteen?

I sit up, wipe my cheeks and open the *Bunheads 4 Lyf* chat.

Hey, I type, and before I've even thought of what to write next, three dots appear below, with Grace's tiny blonde DP next to them.

LUCA. HOW ARE YOU. WHAT THE HELL IS GOING ON WITH YOU?

Okay all caps, I reply.

Don't you dare, she writes. **You've been ignoring us for weeks. I'm allowed to all-caps your ass.**

Fair call.

Then a reply from Abbey, who's DP is a bikini photo from her trip to Port Douglas over the summer. **OMG LU. You're back! How are you? We miiiisssss yoooouuuuu xxx**

I'm fine, I write. **Well, not really. Everything is pretty fucked tbh.**

What do you mean? Grace asks.

Where do I even start?

Abbey writes: **How's your foot? When are you coming back to ballet?**

I sigh. **That's the thing . . . I'm not.**

Not what? Abbey replies.

Coming back.

Grace: **WHAT?**

Abbey: **???**

Grace: **Ever?**

Ever.

Six rows of crying emojis from Grace.

Broken heart emoji from Abbey.

Awkward smile emoji from me.

Lu, I'm so sorry, Grace writes.

What did you do to your foot? Abbey asks.

I broke it. In like a million places. It's full of metal now. I won't be able to point my foot. Or jump. Or do anything required for ballet. Face-palm emoji. Crying emoji. Coffin emoji.

Abbey: **Holy shit.**

Grace: **I am so sorry, Lu. I don't know what to say.**

For a moment, I just sit there, staring down at my phone. How the hell am I meant to tell them I'm not coming back to school either?

Yo bitches. Talia, finally joining the chat. **Mr. Favorite has come crawling back I see. What did I miss?**

Scroll up, Grace says.

I wait. Three dots appear, then: **WTF**

Yep, I write. **I'm so sorry I didn't say anything to you guys sooner.**

Grace: **Don't be sorry, Lu.** Purple love heart.

A line of kisses from Abbey.

Umm ... I type. There's something else.

Abbey: **What?**

Grace: **What??**

Talia: **...?**

I'm not coming back to school.

There is total silence for like, a full minute. And by silence

I mean no messages. No three dots. Nothing.

Then Talia calls me.

"Hello?" I say, expecting screams from the other end of the line.

"Are you serious?" Talia asks. Her voice is quiet. She sounds nothing like her usual self.

"Yep. I got kicked out."

"What the actual fuck?"

"They took my scholarship away because I can't dance anymore. And . . ." I've never really talked about money with the girls, but it's not like they don't know.

"Luca," she says, "this is seriously messed up."

"I know, but what can I do?"

"I dunno . . . take the bastards to court?"

"And say what? I practically failed every subject last year. I don't have a leg to stand on. No pun intended."

"Not funny, dickhead."

"Sorry," I sigh. "I just don't know what to do, you know? I don't even know what to feel. My whole life has turned into a literal nightmare. Like, wake me up, someone, *please*."

"I'm gonna get my mum to look into it."

"Doesn't your mum only do divorces and wills and stuff?"

"Yeah, but she's still a lawyer. She knows her shit."

"Well, I doubt she'll be able to help," I say. "Unless we kill Mr. Sandhurst and need to split his assets."

"That can be arranged."

I laugh. "Don't. My life is in ruins, I can't be laughing right now."

"So where are you going to go to school?"

"I don't know. I think Dad's sorting it out now."

"As long as you don't go to North."

"I don't know if there's any other option," I say, picturing myself getting dunked in a toilet at North Secondary. "CHGS is obviously out of the question, and I'm not Catholic, so that rules out like, all the other private schools in Ballarat."

"It's meant to be the four of us for life, Luca. What the hell am I going to do without you? Grace and Abbey are so annoying."

"Yeah, because this is all about you, Talia."

"I have to go," she says. "Dinner. Message me updates."

"I will."

"Sorry, Lu."

"Not your fault."

"Screw Mr. Sandhurst and his precious fucking school."

"*Your* precious fucking school," I correct.

"Whatever. Bye."

Six

"**DO YOU MIND IF** I drop you off here, mate?"

Monday morning. Dad pulls into a park about three blocks away from my new school.

"I don't want to get stuck in the drop-off traffic," he says. "I'll be late for school myself."

Dad's a primary school teacher. Everyone always assumes he's a plumber, or one of those old policemen who doesn't leave his desk anymore and just does pile after pile of paperwork. But when you've seen him playing "The Floor is Lava" while teaching long multiplication to a room full of eleven- and twelve-year-olds, it suddenly all makes sense. His school is on the other side of town—the nice side of town—near St. Tom's. North Secondary is on the not-so-nice side of town, and we live somewhere in the middle, which means Dad now has to go completely out of his way to drop me off.

"Sure," I reply, feeling physically ill. I keep telling myself there's nothing to be nervous about, that it's just *school*, but my stomach does not agree.

"I hope it goes well," Dad says. "Just be yourself. They'll love you."

"Or they'll hate me."

"No one's ever hated you." Dad laughs. "Don't be so dramatic."

I lean over and kiss him on the cheek. "Bye, Dad. If I don't survive, give all my things to charity, okay?"

Dad rolls his eyes. "Bye, Lu. Have a great day."

This is the first time I've had to walk more than a block on crutches, and my school bag certainly doesn't make it any easier. Every second step is dangerously wobbly, the combined weight of my body and nine-hundred kilos of textbooks balancing on two spindly metal poles.

I carry on—very slowly—down the footpath toward Ballarat North Secondary College, which I soon discover is the complete opposite of St. Thomas's College in every single way. St. Tom's was all clock towers and science wings and lecture auditoriums. North Secondary is a bunch of portables laid out in a big square with a gymnasium and an oval on one side. Gone is the café, the oak trees, and the gleaming performing arts center, replaced with a run-down canteen, some eucalyptus trees up the back of the oval, and a classroom with a cracked mural out the front that says DRAMA.

I eventually find my way to the office, which seems to be the only building in the school—besides the gym—that's attached to the ground. When I push open the door, a pretty, round-faced girl is perched on a chair in the waiting area, smiling gleefully up at me. She's wearing a navy North blazer over a blue plaid dress and black tights, with a bright turquoise headscarf covering her hair.

"Luca Mason?" she asks, jumping out of her seat.

"That's me," I reply, forcing a grin.

"My name's Amina Ahmad. I'm your official North welcoming committee!"

"Oh. Hey."

"Welcome!" she says, literally beaming. "It's so lovely to meet you! Mr. Fennell asked me—oh, sorry, he's the principal. He asked me to show you around and help you settle in. Are you nervous? It must be *full on* to move schools at a crucial time like this."

I'll tell you what's full on: this kind of chirpiness at 8:55 a.m.

"Umm, yeah," I say. "It's . . . a lot."

"Well, you don't need to worry about *anything*, because I'm here for you. Okay?"

And it's weird, because this girl seems like, genuinely excited to help me. Which means she's either desperate for friends or . . . I dunno, that's all I got. But I guess *I'm* desperate for friends too, so I can't exactly tell her to leave me alone, can I?

"Thanks," I say. "That's . . . lovely of you."

"I've got your timetable here," she says, holding out a piece of paper. I slip my left arm out of my crutch, letting the metal rest against my side, and take the timetable from her. The subjects have been highlighted in different colors.

"Did you . . ."

"I just thought it would be easier for you to read if it was properly color-coordinated, you know? I can get someone to print you out a new one if you want."

I can't help but chuckle. "No, no, it's fine. Don't worry about it."

"Oh, *yay!*" Amina smiles, and I've never seen anyone so happy about highlighters and timetables in my life. "We have a couple of subjects together, which is awesome. Psychology and biology. You've missed quite a bit of content already, but I can totally catch you up. We have double biology after lunch. So fun, right?"

I feel like this girl has somehow got the wrong impression about my interests.

"Totally," I reply, looking down at my timetable. "Super fun."

I ended up with all the same subjects at North—except dance, obviously. And I know I couldn't actually *do* dance, even if it was offered here, but to have to replace it with *biology?* Kill. Me. Now. Although I'm assuming the textbook will have those cross-section diagrams of the male reproductive system that kind of weirdly turn me on, so that's not nothing, I guess.

"You're going to love it here," Amina says, nodding encouragingly. "I know it's not as fancy as St. Tom's, but North has a really great heart. I promise."

I've heard a lot about North—kids smoking weed in the bathrooms, boys punching each other in class, girls ditching for three days straight—but no one has ever mentioned its "great heart."

Amina insists on walking me to maths ("You're in General and I'm in Methods with the Year Twelves, but the rooms are right next door to each other. Do you want me to carry your bag?"), and by the time I finally hobble into class, the teacher is already writing equations up on the whiteboard in green marker.

"Sorry," I say to him, a little out of breath.

"Luca, right?" he asks. He's probably in his mid-twenties, a bit of a jock, not bad looking.

"Yep."

"Just take a seat, mate. I won't make you do the awkward introduction thing."

"Thanks, sir."

He laughs. "Mr. Jones is fine. Most of the kids call me 'Jonesy'."

Nicknames for teachers? That would *not* fly at St. Tom's.

"Thanks, Mr. Jones."

As I turn to face the class, I realize there are only two seats left: one right up the front, and one up the back. I head straight toward the back of the room, because not only would I never be caught *dead* sitting in the front row, but the seat up the back is on the end, which means I won't have to squeeze my way through the crowded aisle.

But when I lean my crutches on the edge of the table and go to pull the chair out—balancing on one foot—the guy sitting in the next seat turns to me and says, "What are you doing?"

He kind of looks like a ginger gorilla—big and bulky with a white face full of freckles.

"Sitting down," I reply.

"Uh, I don't think so." He turns to the boy next to him, laughing and muttering something I can't make out.

I go to sit, but he whips back around and wraps one of his muscly monkey arms around the chair, glaring at me from under thick red eyebrows.

"I said, I don't think so."

"Sorry," I say, noticing that a few girls in the next row have turned around to watch. "Is someone sitting here?"

"No," he replies, as if I've missed something.

"Then, can you please let me sit down."

He stares back at me.

"Look, mate," I say, putting on my "straight guy" voice, "just let me sit down. I'm already here. What's the big deal?"

"The big *deal* is that I don't want a poof sitting next to me."

Heat rises in my face. Word travels fast, apparently.

"Scott," Mr. Jones says from the front of the room. "Language." He glares at both of us—as if *I've* done something wrong too—then turns back to the whiteboard.

That's it? *"Language"*? This jerk calls me a poof in front of the whole class and that's all he gets?

"Fine," I whisper to Scott, pretending like I'm not absolutely dying inside. "I wouldn't want you to catch my *gayness* anyway."

"Fuck off, faggot."

"*Scott*," Mr. Jones says. "Don't make me ask you again."

My face burning, I awkwardly hop my way to the front of the class and down the aisle to the seat smack-bang in the middle of the front row. The mousy-looking girls either side of me glance my way, then back to their textbooks. Neither of them says anything. Not "Scott is a homophobic asshole, don't worry about him," or "I promise not everyone at North is such a wanker." Not even "Hi."

And suddenly, I've never felt more out of place in my life.

I can't find Amina at recess, so I go and sit in a cubicle in the boys' bathroom for the whole fifteen minutes, scrolling through Instagram.

Just as the bell finally rings, a message from Grace pops up: Purple love heart. **I hope Day One goes well, Lu!** Purple love heart.

Then Abbey: **Good luck babe!!! xxx**

And Talia: **Don't get stabbed, k?**

I reply with a bunch of fingers-crossed emojis, which doesn't really make sense, since I've already had one horrific class, but whatever. The girls don't know that.

Picturing Scott's sneering, freckled face makes my stomach churn. No one at St. Tom's ever gave me shit about being gay. Well, a few of the boys teased me a bit when I first came out in Year Eight, but Year Eight boys are kind of wankers, so that doesn't count. And after a couple weeks, my sexuality was old news. Mainly because Susan Myers and Ross Chan had sex in one of the practice rooms in the performing arts center (allegedly involving Ross's trumpet in some way, but you didn't hear it from me) and got expelled. After *that*, no one cared one bit about me being into guys.

I flush the toilet to make it look like I wasn't just sitting in here hiding the whole time and drag myself to my next class: English. It's probably my least-hated school subject, aside from dance. I say "least-hated" because I still don't exactly *like* it, but it's not nearly as painful as everything else. Words make a hell of a lot more sense to me than numbers do, that's for sure.

At the end of the lesson, I sit and wait for the other students to pour out of the portable, laughing and shoving each other, and then hobble out onto the pavement. Standing there waiting is Amina, holding a bright purple lunchbox with magazine cut-outs of the One Direction boys stuck all over it with clear contact. She follows my gaze and giggles.

"I used to be a bit obsessed with them," she says, spinning the lunchbox around to give me the full effect. "And by 'a bit,' I mean a lot. And by 'used to be,' I mean I totally still am. Harry is my everything."

"Fair enough," I laugh. "I don't think I've listened to a One D song since I was like, twelve, but Zayn will never stop being ridiculously hot."

Amina's smile falters, just for a split second, and I can instantly tell it's because she's never met a gay guy. But then her grin spreads wider. "He's definitely beautiful, but he also sparked the beginning of the end, so I'll never forgive him for that. Anyway, let's go. I'll show you where we sit for lunch."

She walks me through the campus, and I can't help but notice how she automatically slows her pace so I don't have to rush. Dad tends to instantly forget—and then *keeps* forgetting every thirty seconds—that I can't move at my normal pace now that I'm on crutches. He ends up five meters ahead before he realizes he's talking to no one. But Amina paces along right beside me, telling me about the time she held a pretend wedding ceremony for her and her life-sized cardboard cut-out of Harry Styles.

Eventually, we arrive at a little courtyard nestled between two portables at the edge of the concrete quadrangle. There are two girls sitting at opposite ends of a wooden bench.

"Hey, guys!" Amina says, as overly cheerful as ever.

"Hi," says a petite Asian girl, barely looking up from her sandwich.

"Hey, Amina," says the other, a curvy white girl with an absurdly long brown plait hanging over her shoulder.

"This is Luca," Amina announces. "It's his first day. Luca, this is Alicia and Bree."

"Hi," the girls say in unison, neither of them looking me in the eye.

Amina whispers in my ear, "They're a bit shy, but they're super nice once you get to know them."

We sit on the bench opposite Alicia and Bree, who are officially the quietest girls I've ever met. Amina talks basically the whole lunchtime, monologuing about Alicia's "mad crochet skills" and Bree's fondness for fractions. I happily sit and listen, glad to have someone else doing all the work. When she asks me about my hobbies—as if she's interviewing me for some kind of cheesy game show—I just shrug and say I haven't found anything I'm that into yet. I don't know why I don't tell her I'm a dancer. I guess because I'm *not* anymore. I could say I *was* a dancer, but that's a million times worse. How can I be sixteen and already have a *was* in my biography?

Luckily, the bell rings before I start to cry—like I do the second I picture myself in ballet tights these days—and Amina shows me to our biology class. She automatically heads for the front row, but I hop toward the second row and she follows me, even though I can tell it absolutely *kills* her not to sit up the front.

And even though she's nothing like my friends at St. Tom's—and I mean, they're literal chalk and cheese—it's nice to have someone to sit next to. But then I wonder what Amina was doing *before* I arrived at North this morning. Does she usually sit by herself in class? Does anyone actually talk to her? She seems so sweet, but like, where are her friends? I *guess* you could call Alicia and Bree her friends, but they don't seem close. At all. They seem like three completely separate people who just happen to sit on the same benches at lunchtime. I doubt Amina and those girls have a Nerds 4 Lyf group chat. Which kind of makes my heart ache for her a little bit. Because I doubt Amina has a group chat with anyone at all.

Seven

THE REST OF MY first day at North is fine. I say "fine," but what I mean is "frustrating in every single way you can possibly imagine."

It's funny though, I never realized how useful the word "fine" was until now. Not only has it gotten me out of having to explain to Dad just how much my body aches every minute of every day, but it also means I don't have to admit to Amina how I really feel when everyone's whispers and sniggers are so purposely *not* hidden behind my back. (The students circulated the news of the "gay dude on crutches who got kicked out of St. Tom's for being too poor" like their lives depended on it.)

My classes are "fine" too. I spend the whole of biology asking Amina questions that are apparently so basic she thinks I'm asking them just to amuse her. And there's not a single penis diagram in sight.

In short, the day is not "fine." It's awful.

And then Talia messages me when I'm waiting for Dad to pick me up.

How was day one, loser?

Fine.

See. There it is again.

Did you make any friends?

Obviously.

Names?

Amina. And I know the other girls didn't actually talk to me, but I add **Alicia** and **Bree** for effect.

Are they prettier than us?

Omg Talia. Superficial much?

That means they ugly.

I shake my head at the screen. I know Talia has always been a bit of a bitch, but it used to seem funny. Like it was all part of her prima-donna-ice-queen act, but she didn't really mean it. But now . . . I dunno. Maybe I just don't have time for her usual bullshit after spending the day with Amina, who literally could not be nicer if she tried. After biology, she got down on the ground and tied my shoelaces in double knots for me because I couldn't lean over with my crutches and she was worried I'd trip on the cracked pavement on the way back to our lockers. I mean . . . Talia purposefully closes elevator doors on people because she doesn't want to get "claustrophobic."

Gotta go, I write. **Dad's here.**

(Dad is not here.)

You coming this weekend? Talia asks.

Coming where?

Coffee. Saturday. After ballet.

I go to write *Some of us don't have ballet on Saturday anymore, Talia* but there's no point starting a fight.

Sure, I reply. **See you then.**

Bye bish.

I roll my eyes and shove my phone in my pocket.

⌒

Day Two at North is just as "fine" as Day One.

I sit with Amina and Alicia and Bree at lunchtime again, but I'm not really *there*. I just stare down at the quad, watching all the other students. Some tiny Year Sevens—who honestly look like six-year-olds to me now, and I can't believe I was ever that small—are playing a game of handball that quickly turns into an actual punch-up. A couple of Year Twelves are leaning against the wall of the portable opposite us, kissing and feeling each other up in possibly the most NSFW public display of affection I've ever seen. Then a group of girls—Year Elevens, I think, as I'm pretty sure two of them are in my maths class—strut past, their skirts hemmed *way* shorter than would have been allowed at St. Tom's. They're laughing and putting on lip gloss and flicking their long, shiny hair over their shoulders, and I can't help but feel like these are the people I should be hanging out with, not . . .

I glance back at the girls on the benches beside me: Bree is—no joke—reading her maths textbook; Alicia is taking these tiny, mouse-like bites out of her sandwich, glaring at the pavers like she's plotting a murder; and Amina—who is wearing this super-cute pink floral headscarf today—is rambling about how much homework she already has from chemistry.

By the time I turn back to the quad, the group of girls is gone. And that's when I see him. Strolling across the concrete with three other guys.

It's the boy from the OT waiting room.

Jordan.

I choke on my sandwich.

"Are you okay?" Amina asks, patting me gently on the back.

"Yeah, yeah, fine," I reply, swallowing hard and waving Amina off. "Who is that?" I point to the boys, who have stopped to talk to a very tall, very leggy blonde girl.

"Which one?"

"The buff Asian guy."

"Oh," Amina says, her voice dripping with longing. "That's Jordan Tanaka-Jones. Everyone calls him TJ. He's in Year Twelve. He's our School Captain."

Jordan Tanaka-Jones. At North Secondary. My heart has suddenly decided it's in some kind of marching band.

"I went to primary school with him," Amina says. "He's . . ." But she stops herself.

"What?"

"Well, you know, everyone's a bit . . ."

"In love with him?"

"I was going to say, 'pathologically obsessed,' but sure, 'in love' works too."

I laugh and the other girls flinch at the sound.

I turn back to Jordan, and it's only then that I realize one of the boys he's with is everyone's favorite homophobe, Scott. "Who are the rest of those guys?"

"They're the Boys' Firsts rowing squad," Amina says. "Minus their cox, Tom. He's only in Year Ten, so he doesn't really hang out with them."

"But Scott's only in Year Eleven," I say. "He's in my maths

class. Why does *he* hang out with them?"

"You mean Gibbo? The redhead?" Amina rolls her eyes. Apparently, I'm not the only one who doesn't like him. "He's supposed to be in Year Twelve, but he got held back in Grade Six. Him and TJ have been best mates forever. Their mums grew up together."

"I see." I can't imagine Jordan being friends with someone like Gibbo. Not that I really know anything about Jordan, I guess. "And the other ones?"

"The tall white boy's name is Andrew, but everyone calls him Horse—I have no idea why—and the shorter guy with black hair is Macca, Peter McKenzie. You've probably met his grandpa, David? He facilitates some of the Waddwurrung cultural sessions for schools."

But all I can think about is Jordan. His school shirt fits him perfectly—unlike mine, which is at least three sizes too big—and his bum is as peachy as ever in his grey school shorts, which is saying something, because these shorts are not cute. His grey socks are pulled up to his knees, his navy tie loosened ever so slightly, his top button undone.

"Who's the girl?" I ask, jealousy creeping into my voice. "Is she a rower too?"

"No, that's TJ's girlfriend. Rhiannon."

And just like that, my life is over. Again. Twice as over. Super over. *Blown up into billions of pieces and flushed down the toilet* over.

"They've been together since the Boat Race after-party last year."

With Boat Race—Ballarat's annual "Head of the Lake" all-schools rowing regatta—on the horizon again, that means they've been together for almost a year.

"TJ and Rhiannon are North royalty," Amina adds, sticking another dagger in my heart without realizing.

I actually feel sick. Is there a worse feeling than finding out there is no chance whatsoever of your crush liking you back? And I mean, of *course* I should have known better than to fall for a guy like Jordan. Especially after the Lincoln Van de Berg debacle of Year Nine, when I swore I'd never fall for a straight guy ever again. It's just not worth putting all that energy into someone who has zero chance of ever liking you back because of, you know, *biology*.

Amina must have been talking this whole time, because she says, "And that's kind of ridiculous right? Would you be with someone who did that?"

"Um, sure," I reply, still in a bit of a daze.

"What?" Amina sounds appalled. "Really?"

"No," I say, tearing my eyes away from Jordan, "That's . . . awful."

"Right?"

Bree and Alicia stand up beside us.

"We're going to the library," Bree says, in this kind of bored tone that implies the library will be way more fun than talking about boys.

"Okay, bye," Amina says, smiling. "See you in chem."

"Bye," I call out as the girls disappear behind the portables.

When I glance back over at the quad, my heart skips a beat and then squeezes three beats into one count, like it's forgotten the choreography and is trying to catch up.

Because Jordan is walking directly toward us. Toward *me*.

"Hey, man," he says when he reaches the benches. He looks kind of puzzled. And maybe I'm imagining this, but also like, happy to see me? "Hey, Amina."

She lets out a strangled little squeak that I think is meant to be a "hi."

"Hey," I reply, wondering why the hell people evolved with the ability to blush.

"What are you doing here?" Jordan asks. "I thought you went to St. Tom's?"

I laugh awkwardly. "Yeah, well, *slight* change of plan."

"Is everything all right?"

"Yeah," I say, feeling like someone's choking me, "totally."

"Cool, cool. Well, welcome to North, I guess. I'll see you 'round."

"Yeah. Totally. For sure. Cool."

Jordan smirks. "See ya, mate."

"See ya."

He turns to Amina, who—I kid you not—has literally not moved this entire time, and says, "Love your hijab today, Amina. Pink really suits you," and then struts off toward the lockers.

As soon as Jordan is past the portables, Amina explodes into a fit of giggles.

"What?" I ask.

"Oh—my—*gosh*," she says, short of breath. "Jordan Tanaka-Jones just gave me a compliment!"

"Well, it's—"

"And ex*cuse* me, but are you going to tell me how you know TJ, or are we pretending that's not a thing?"

I clear my throat. "I mean, I don't *know* him, know him."

"But . . .?"

So, I tell her about the magical world of the OT waiting room—a place where beautiful jocks like Jordan actually talk to dancer boys like me, and she gasps in all the right places.

"I still can't believe he knows my *name*," she says, smoothing down the bright, floral material framing her face.

"Didn't you say you went to primary school with him?" I ask. "How could he not know your name?"

Amina scoffs. "Oh, come on," she says, staring at me like I'm an idiot. "You know how it goes. People like me fly under the radar. We're easy to forget. I'm just 'the nerd in the hijab.' Most of the kids at North wouldn't know my name."

"I don't know if that's true."

"I'm serious," she presses. "Yes, I may have gone to school with TJ for the last twelve years, but he's the year above me, and he's popular and beautiful and he plays every sport under the sun and I'm . . . well . . ."

"You're what?"

"Look, put it this way: when everyone was having sleepovers in Grade Six, I was giving myself extra homework. Legitimately *making up* assignments for myself and getting my parents to mark them for me."

I laugh. "Well, when everyone was having sleepovers in Grade Six, *I* was—" but I stop myself.

I was going to say: *I was at ballet. I was getting screamed at by Miss Gwen for not pointing my feet hard enough. I was traveling to Melbourne and Bendigo and Warrnambool with Dad every other weekend for competitions. I was locked inside my room for hours at a time with foot stretchers and turning boards and balance balls and foam rollers and spiky balls and TheraBands.*

I've never been like other kids my age. I'm focused. I'm driven. I have a goal.

Well . . . *had* a goal.

"I didn't go to any sleepovers either," I say eventually. "And you're not easy to forget."

"Shoosh," Amina replies, her tan cheeks flushing pink.

"It's true! Jordan—TJ, whatever—knows your name, and I'm sure everyone else does too. You're like, a total genius, you're super nice to everyone, and you're weirdly obsessed with One Direction, which is actually kind of adorable for some reason and I'm not really sure why."

She giggles, covering her mouth with her hand.

"And you're funny and pretty and—"

"Oh, now you're just making fun of me," she protests. "I am not *pretty*."

"Um, firstly, you *are*, so don't be ridiculous and pretend like you're not. And secondly, you are absolutely rocking that floral hijab right now and we both know it."

She slaps me on the leg. "Stop," she says with a chuckle. "*You're* the one who's being ridiculous."

"Like, it's cute to be modest, Amina, but you also gotta know when to flaunt what you got."

"Oh my goodness," she says, standing up. "We are not having this conversation!" She grabs my crutches and holds them out to me. "We need to go get our books for psych."

I take my crutches from her and hoist myself up. "Relax, the bell hasn't even—" But just as I say it, the electronic bell sounds around the quad.

"See?" she says, one eyebrow raised, before marching off

toward our lockers.

For a second, I watch her walk away, and then I call out, "Yes, Amina! Work it!"

And she doesn't turn around, but I swear she grows two inches taller.

Eight

"**MISS PRUE RANG AGAIN** today," Dad says when he drops me off at Ballarat Allied Therapies after school. "Don't you think it's time you gave her a quick call? Just to tell her you're okay?"

"Why can't you tell her?" I reply, unbuckling my seatbelt.

"I think she'd probably like to hear it from you, mate."

"I dunno," I say. "Maybe."

"And I haven't seen Talia and Grace and Abbey for a while. Why don't you invite th—"

"Dad, I gotta go." I open the car door to show him this conversation is over. "Can we not do this now?"

He sighs and says, "Fine. I'm off to Coles. You need anything while I'm there?"

"How 'bout a new foot?"

"Very funny, Lu. I'll see you in an hour."

When I walk into the waiting room, my heart stutters: my prince is there.

Waiting for me.

Naked.

(Not really, but let's just picture that for a minute, shall we?)

"Take a seat, Luca," Shelby the receptionist chirps as the automatic doors *whoosh* closed behind me. "Sami will be with you shortly."

"Thanks."

As I make my way into the waiting area, Jordan looks up, locks eyes with me and smiles, and I literally have to stop walking for a second because I can't remember how to coordinate my arms and legs and crutches.

"Hey man," he says, with one of those reverse nods that straight guys always do to their mates. He's wearing a blue polo shirt and tight, black footy shorts—his PE uniform, I guess. It's . . . a lot.

"Hi," I reply quietly.

My stomach twists into a pretzel when I realize my future happiness with Jordan now depends solely on my choice of seat in the waiting area. I can't sit *next* to him, because that would be like admitting I'm in love with him, (which I am, but that would be coming on *way* too strong, considering I met him like, three days ago). And I can't *not* sit next to him, because then it'll look like I'm avoiding him, which would clearly be interpreted as me not being remotely interested, which would ruin our chances of ever getting married and growing old together.

He furrows his brow, and I have this awful swooping feeling that I just said that entire inner monologue out loud.

"You good?" he asks, adding, when I don't reply, "Do you need help sitting down?"

"No, I'm okay. I was just . . ." I trail off, unable to think of a way to finish that sentence without explaining my Choice of Seat vs. Marriage dilemma.

To be safe, I take a seat against the wall with Jordan, but with a one-seat safety buffer. I figure this tells him I'm casually interested, but not that I have a pathetic school-girl crush on him (aka the truth).

Who knows, maybe I'm overthinking things. Wouldn't be the first time.

"So, when did you actually start?" he asks. "At North."

"Yesterday."

"I wondered why I hadn't seen you before."

Wait, what? He *wondered* about me?

"How you finding it?" he asks.

"School?" I shrug. "Fine." (There it is again.)

"Cool."

I try not to look like I'm sitting here frantically thinking of something interesting to say, but Jordan saves me from my own awkwardness. "And how's your foot?"

"Well," I reply, "it's still broken, so . . . you know. Not the best."

He smiles with one side of his mouth.

"How's your shoulder?" I ask.

"Yeah, not great." He reaches up to squeeze it. "But I'm sure I'll survive. Just wanted to make sure it's okay for Boat Race."

I nod, and silence falls between us again.

"You coming?" he asks.

"Where?"

He chuckles. "Boat Race."

Boat Race is probably the biggest sporting-slash-social event of the school year in Ballarat, and the whole thing is absolutely *next level* at St. Tom's. There are extra assemblies, a specially elected costume committee, whole-school war cry rehearsals. I mean, it is completely extra in every single way, but it is *everything*. I've been in the official, invitation-only St. Tom's cheer squad with the Bunheads every year since Year Seven—which is a way bigger deal than it probably sounds. And the thing is, I can't picture myself in the crowd at Lake Wendouree with anyone but the Bunheads, cheering for anyone but St. Tom's. But then I glance over at Jordan, and all I can see is his perfect chest in a skin-tight, bright-blue zoot suit. And suddenly the idea of being at Boat Race with a North banner in my hands doesn't sound so bad, after all.

"Of course I'm coming," I reply. "I love Boat Race."

"Nice," he says with a nod. "We'll need all the support we can get if we want to beat those St. Tom's boys. They're absolute *beasts* this year"

And he's not wrong. The St. Tom's boys all have legs as thick as my torso, and most of them can already grow beards.

"Make sure you cheer nice and loud for me," Jordan adds.

"Oh, don't worry, I'll be screaming your name."

He laughs, and every inch of my body turns to lava.

"Appreciate it, man," he says, still chuckling.

I stare down at my cast, wishing I *was* made of lava so I could melt right through this chair and disappear into the ground.

Jordan must follow my gaze, because he says, "Hey, how come no one's signed your cast?"

"I like it pristine," I reply, because I'd rather die than tell Jordan no one has asked to sign it yet. "It's like a new pair of white shoes. Worthless as soon as they've got a single mark on them."

"Jeez. Don't ever look in my closet, then. Not a 'pristine' shoe in sight."

"I won't judge." (Are you inviting me to your bedroom?)

He smirks. "I'm *pretty* sure you just called my whole wardrobe worthless. So . . ."

"Well, one man's trash is another man's treasure, right?"

"So now my clothes are *trash?*"

"Don't worry," I say, "garbage-chic is totally in right now."

Jordan stares back at me, shaking his head. For a second, I'm worried I've offended him, but then he says, "You're funny, you know that?"

And obviously I'm dead. A compliment from a crush is pure kryptonite.

"Here," he says, getting out of his chair.

"What?"

He reaches over to the coffee table and grabs a texta from a cup filled with pens and pencils and crayons.

"You don't have to—" But he's already kneeling down in front of my cast, making his mark right down at my ankle. I lean over to see what he's writing, but his hand is in the way.

"Wait. Sorry, mate. I just realized I don't know your name." He looks up at me, a sheepish grin on his face.

"Luca," I say, hypnotized by his hazel eyes. "L-U-C-A. It's Italian. But I'm not Italian. My mum just . . . it doesn't matter."

He returns his attention to my cast, scribbling away in blue texta. When he's done, he stands and grins down at his handiwork.

"What does it say?" I ask, craning my neck down to see, but I can't make it out from this angle.

He shrugs, just as Sami calls my name from across the room.

"You better go." He hands me my crutches and settles back into his chair.

I glance over at Sami, who is smiling her heart-melting smile, hands clasped in front of her body.

I side-eye Jordan in a way I hope comes across as flirty and not salty, and say, "*Fine*. But if you drew a cartoon dick on my cast, there'll be hell to pay."

He laughs, and I walk over to Sami, praying to the Universe—and Jesus and Buddha and anyone else who'll listen—that Jordan is watching me leave.

"So, how's the new school?" Sami asks once we're sitting down. Today she's wearing this bright yellow top tucked into black jeans, and earrings in the shape of little rainbows. I mean, she's literal sunshine.

"Um . . . polite version or actual truth?"

She chuckles. "You already know my stance on that."

I sigh. "It's . . . kind of shit, really. But, I guess that's to be expected."

"Why is that to be expected?"

"Well . . . I dunno." I look down, pulling on the hem of my school shorts. "I've only been there for two days, so I guess I shouldn't judge it too soon. But . . . I dunno."

"Have you made any new friends?"

"I have made exactly *one* friend." Unless I can include Jordan in that statement. *Can* I include Jordan in that statement?

"Better than none, right?"

"Of course," I reply, "but it's just so weird to go from having this amazing group of friends at St. Tom's, who I've known like, forever, to suddenly being a total nobody."

"But your friends from your old school still exist. They're still your friends."

"Yeah, but they're not *there*, you know?"

Sami nods slowly.

"And I'm so *sore*," I say, keen to change the subject. "Why did no one tell me that using crutches would hurt more than shattering my foot?"

Sami laughs. "You have a very dark sense of humor, Luca."

"I'm just being honest," I say.

"I wish everyone was that honest. It's a great quality."

I smile, feeling myself blush.

"All right," Sami says, hopping up out of her chair. "Let's get you on the table, I'll have a look at all those problem areas."

"But do you know the worst thing?" I say, as Sami massages my thigh—well, *pummels* is probably a more accurate word. "I blame my foot for all of this. I actually *blame* my left foot for turning my life to shit. Like, as if it's my *foot*'s fault that I fell down the stairs. That I'm never going to dance again. That I had to change schools and suddenly became a total loser overnight. I *hate* my foot. I can't look at it without feeling like I want to just cut it off and be done with the whole thing. I mean, how messed up is that? That can't be normal."

Sami looks down at me with her lips pressed lightly together, tiny crinkles appearing around her eyes.

"Well, for starters," she replies, "what is 'normal'? And secondly, I'm not going to tell you how to feel. If you want to hate a bunch of tiny bones and tendons wrapped up in a nice little parcel of skin, go ahead and hate your foot. If that helps you deal with this massive life change you're going through, then blame your foot all you like." She digs her thumbs into my quad, and I can't help but groan in pain. "Sorry, is that too much?"

"No, it's good," I say through gritted teeth.

"But if blaming your foot gets you bogged down in the past instead of helping you figure out what you can do *right now* to feel better, then maybe you should try focusing on something else. But it's up to you. This is your journey."

And I know she's right. I know I need to focus on "right now." But there's a pretty huge hole in my life "right now," and I need to fill it with something. And anger and awkward jokes have been working pretty well for me so far, so . . .

"Am I allowed to stop hating my foot tomorrow?"

"Luca," she replies, "you can do whatever you want. Whatever makes you happy. That's the end goal, isn't it?"

"You know," I say, watching Sami's rainbows shake from side to side, "you should start charging extra for life advice."

"Don't I know it."

"Oh," I say, only just remembering, "can you tell me what that message on my cast says? Down at the bottom?"

"Sure." She stops massaging and leans over to look at my ankle. "It says . . . 'Luca—Honored to be your first.'"

I spend the whole car ride home trying to interpret the underlying meaning of Jordan's message. I mean, yeah, he could have meant it literally, meaning he's honored to be the first person to sign my cast—which is still adorable, by the way—but he also could have meant other things. Sex things.

I know he's straight, and I'm probably getting carried away here—doesn't sound like me—but it seems like flirting. Like, the double meaning is way too clear for him not to have used it on purpose, right? Or am I seeing it the way I want to see it because I'm desperate and a loser?

Being the only gay kid in school makes me look for hidden meaning in every interaction I have with other guys. One time at St. Tom's, Paul Sanderson asked me for a pink highlighter—specifically pink—and I legitimately thought he was trying to come out to me in code. I was obsessed with him for months.

(P.S. Paul was super cute. And totally not gay.)

I stare down at my cast: *Honored to be your first.*

Maybe Jordan was being sarcastic? Or maybe it's one of those things where footy boys like, slap each other on the ass during a game. You know, a *bromance* kind of thing.

Ugh, I dunno. Sometimes I don't think straight guys realize how much they mess with my emotions. Or maybe they do it on purpose for the ego boost. All they have to do is say one nice thing to me and suddenly I'm in love with them. Why do I let myself get attached so easily? And to people who will never feel anything for me? Am I that desperate to be with someone that I'll fall for literally any boy who'll talk to me?

Because the thing is, I might be gay, but I've never been like, *actively* gay. As in, I've never had sex with a guy. I've never done anything with a guy. I haven't even *kissed* a guy.

And I know I'm only sixteen, but my birthday is less than ten months away, and then I'll be a seventeen-year-old virgin.

And soon I'll be an eighteen-year-old virgin, because as far as I know, I'm the only gay guy my age in Ballarat, and no amount of jerking off to gay porn is going to make me *not* a virgin. And then I'll finish school and move to Melbourne and finally be surrounded by gay guys—I'm just assuming there will be like, thousands of them in Melbourne—but none of them will want to have sex with me because I'll be That Virgin Guy.

So, the answer is yes. I am *that* desperate.

Nine

THE SEQUINS AND DIAMANTÉS on Talia's tutu sparkle under the bright lights of the stage. She's like a turquoise disco ball. Which is not ideal when I'm partnering her in one of the most difficult *pas de deux* I've ever danced in a competition.

"Careful," she says to me through a painted-on smile as I lower her down from a lift.

"What?"

"You're not putting me on my leg." She *chaînés* away from me, toward the front of the stage.

I stride forward in time with the music until I'm right behind her again. "I *am* putting you on your leg. You're just *off* your leg today."

She flourishes her arms and prepares for a *pirouette.* "As if."

Rising up onto the tip of her toe, she turns and turns *en pointe* with my hands wrapped loosely around her tiny waist. When her momentum starts to slow, I grasp her hips and stop her in place as she extends into a gloriously high *arabesque.*

"How's that?" I ask.

I take her silence to mean "Much better, thank you, Luca."

Talia is a ruthless partner. But she's the best. And together, we're unstoppable. She's been my duo partner since Under 8s, and we've never lost a section. Not one. Ever.

She comes down from her *arabesque* and glides across the stage to my right. I follow, waiting for her to land her *glissade* before I grab her by the hips again and lift her high above my head. As I bring her back down to the floor, her sequins flash in my eyes, momentarily blinding me. It's only a tiny lapse in focus, but that's all it takes to mess up a lift. The wooden tip of her pointe shoe stabs into the top of my left foot. I cry out in pain and drop her onto the stage in a crush of blue tulle.

"What the hell, Luca?!"

I look down at my foot, which has instantly ballooned inside my ballet shoe. Deep red blood seeps through the white canvas and starts to pool around my foot.

"No, no, no, no, *no!*"

I try to take a step but the bones in my foot crunch under my weight, making a sound like cracking ice. Pain shoots all the way from my toes up into my skull, making stars burst behind my eyes. I fall to the floor, landing face-first on the cold, hard stage.

I scream and my eyes snap open.

"Holy shit," I say to myself as I sit up in bed, completely out of breath and drenched with sweat.

It was just a dream.

I pull the wet sheet off me and toss it onto the floor, revealing my chunky white plaster cast. My chest tightens and I gasp in a breath. Tears fill my sleep-crusted eyes.

It was just a dream, but I've woken up in a nightmare.

I'm supposed to meet up with the Bunheads on Saturday when they finish ballet, but Talia bails—something to do with a fight with her mum—and Abbey has to go to her cousin's surprise bridal shower, so it ends up being just me and Grace.

"Well," she says, after ordering us both flat whites at our favorite cafe down the bottom of Sturt Street. "Tell me everything."

So, I tell her about my surgery and the nurses and the *look*. I tell her about Mr. Sandhurst and Sami and the dreams. I tell her about North and Amina and my new teachers. And the whole time I'm talking, she just sits there stirring her coffee and doing her very best to not make eye contact with me.

"Are you okay?" I ask eventually, interrupting my own story about the first time I met Jordan at the OT.

She exhales loudly and starts re-braiding the end of her already-perfect plait. She does that when she's uncomfortable.

I fold my arms across my chest. "What? Just say it."

"Say what?"

"I dunno. Whatever it is you want to say. Something's obviously bothering you. You're not even listening to me."

"I am," she says, flipping her hair back over her shoulder. "I'm just . . ."

"Just what?"

"I'm mad," she snaps, finally looking up. "At you."

I lean back in my chair, feeling my chest cramp.

"You completely ignored us," she says, her bright-blue eyes wide. "For like, two weeks. Do you have any idea how worried we were?"

"I know," I say, "but you have to understand—"

"No, I *don't* understand, Lu, that's the point. If I'd hurt myself, I would have wanted my friends there by my side. Or, at the very least, I would have told them what the hell was going on. And then you drop this bomb that you're not coming back to ballet *or* St. Tom's and we're just supposed to, what, pretend you never existed?"

"No, that's not what this is," I say. "I was just . . . overwhelmed and angry and upset and . . . I'm not good at this kind of thing, you know that."

Grace huffs. "Not good at sending *one* text message to your best friends in the world to tell them you're okay?"

"But I'm *not* okay!" I say, suddenly furious at her. "How could I possibly be okay? You have no idea what this is like for me."

"No, because you didn't include us."

"I don't have to 'include' you, Grace. This isn't *about* you."

"Of course not," Grace says, "because everything is about you, Luca. It always is."

"Are you serious? I'm never going to dance again, Grace. Me. Not you. *My* life is over, not yours. What part of that *isn't* about me?"

"The part where I'm losing one of my best friends!"

It's like a slap in the face. I take a deep breath. Grace is crying now.

"You're not losing me," I say quietly.

"But it's not going to be the same, is it," she replies, wiping little bits of mascara from under her eyes.

And maybe she's right. How could things possibly be the

same? Ballet brought the four of us together. It's the glue that kept our friendship so strong all these years. And now it's been taken away from one of us.

Grace picks up her cup and takes a sip of coffee. Surely it's cold by now.

I'm silent for a long moment, just sitting there biting my bottom lip, staring out the window.

"I dunno," I sigh, eventually.

"You don't know what?"

"Anything," I say flatly. "I don't know anything anymore."

"I'm sorry, Lu. That this happened to you. It's really awful."

"I'm sorry for being a dick."

"A *total* dick."

We both laugh, but it feels kind of hollow, like we're forcing it.

And I think in that moment we both know, deep down, that Grace is right.

It's never going to be the same.

Ten

AS SOON AS I walk through the school gates on Monday morning, I can feel it: Boat Race is in the air. With less than a week to go, it's now the only topic of conversation at North.

Can anyone take the coveted boys' Head of the Lake title from St. Tom's? (We've basically won for the last century.)

Does anyone stand a chance against the St. Margaret's girls?

And, much more importantly: *Who is going to hook up at the after party?*

"I'm so excited to have a Boat Race buddy this year!" Amina says on our way to last-period psychology on Monday.

"A *what?*" I ask.

"A Boat Race buddy." She's in such a good mood today that she's practically skipping along beside me. "You know, someone to go to Boat Race with?"

"Won't the whole school be going?"

"Yes, but this year I can actually go *with* someone. It's different."

"Oh," I say slowly, "you mean *me?*"

"No, I mean Gibbo," she says. "Of course I mean you!"

"Do Alicia and Bree not go to Boat Race?"

"This might come as a surprise to you, Luca, but sport isn't really their thing."

"Sport isn't really my thing either, but I still go. Although, to be fair," I add as we arrive at the classroom, "I'm only there for the sightseeing." I raise one eyebrow and Amina rolls her eyes.

"Well, *that*," she says, opening the door for me, "is obviously not their thing either."

We take our usual seats in the middle row.

"So, who do you normally go with?" I ask, sliding my crutches under the table.

"Oh, you know. Whoever." She does this weird little shrug and then turns to face the front, which is Amina code for "It's time for class, you can shut up now," but I feel like there's something she's not saying.

I stare up at the empty whiteboard, a weird knot tightening in my stomach. How can I go to Boat Race and cheer for a school I've only been at for like, two weeks, when I went to St. Tom's for four whole *years*? It just doesn't make sense.

Amina nudges me with her elbow, and I turn to see this huge grin on her face.

"What?" I whisper. It must be something incredibly important if she's decided to not pay attention in class.

She leans over and writes two words on the blank page in front of me, followed by a big, curly question mark:

Matching T-Shirts?

I smile up at her, even though I'm totally dying inside.

The next day, I forget that Boat Race even exists, because there's only room in my brain for one very important thought: *I get to see Jordan at the OT today.*

All morning in drama, I daydream about what he might be wearing this afternoon. I spend double English trying to brainstorm interesting topics of conversation that won't leave me looking like a complete awkward loser like last time. At lunch, I want to ask Amina where Jordan's locker is—so I can "accidentally" bump into him and say something casual but cool like, "Catch you later at the OT, yeah?" But I can't think of a way to ask without sounding like a creepy stalker. And besides, whenever I mention Jordan, Amina launches into a ten-minute monologue about something adorable he's done (that in no way actually *involved* her, but that she knows every single detail about anyway), and I do not have mental energy for that right now.

But when I finally walk into the waiting room at Ballarat Allied Therapies at 4:00 p.m., Jordan isn't there. For some reason, the fact that he might have had a different appointment this week—or not had one at all—never occurred to me. I kind of thought waiting-room chats were going to be our thing, that Tuesday afternoons at the OT were going to be for *us*. Not that there is an "us," considering I've only spoken to him for a total of like, eleven minutes, and he is not only *straight* but has a super-hot *girlfriend* and honestly, *What the hell is wrong with me?*

After dinner on Boat Race Eve (aka Friday night), my phone buzzes. I'm sitting on the couch with Dad watching last night's *MasterChef*. He's all misty-eyed over someone making the perfect pavlova, and I'm pretending like I'm interested, for his sake.

Talia: **Luca. Stop ignoring us, you shady little bitch. We need to talk plans for tomorrow.**

I won't lie, I've been completely avoiding the girls' messages about Boat Race. They've been talking about it constantly in the group chat all week (costumes, parties, boys, drinks—it's a full thing), so I just let them debate all the key topics (knee socks vs. leggings) and join in as soon as they've moved onto something else. Because the thing is, I honestly have no idea what I'm going to do.

It's not like I can turn up at the lake with the Bunheads and pretend like I *didn't* get kicked out of St. Tom's. But I know the girls will hate me if I don't go, and they'll hate me even more if I *do* go, but with the wrong people.

Amina has been so excited all week about having a Boat Race Buddy with a capital B, and it would be a major dick move to ditch her at the last minute, even though I never actually *said* I would go with her. And the thing is—and trust me, I'm as surprised as anyone—I really enjoy hanging out with her.

And then there's the fact that I already told Jordan to his face that I'd be cheering for *him*—for North—and I really do want to be there to support him, even though that's ridiculous because he probably doesn't give a shit whether I'm there or not.

What plans? I reply to Talia, because it's just so much easier to act innocent sometimes.

Talia: **Tell me you're coming to Boat Race with us and not your new bogan friends.**

Grace: **Please, Lu. We need you!**

You have to come! Abbey writes. **Jonno is having a MASSIVE after party at his place on the lake. It's gonna be LIT!** followed by about nine-hundred flame emojis.

I don't know . . . I write back, and I instantly know I've said the wrong thing.

What do you mean YOU DON'T KNOW? Talia says. **It's BOAT RACE. It's tradition. Would you rather come to Jonno's Lake Wendouree mansion or slum it in some westy crack den with the North losers?**

And now I'm angry.

Don't be such a snob, Talia. You don't know anything about North.

Chill, guys, Grace writes.

Yeah . . . Abbey says. Snowman emoji.

I groan, and Dad says, "You good?"

"Yeah, fine."

"Boy trouble?" he asks, sounding hopeful.

I snort. "Girl trouble."

He laughs, as if I'm kidding, and turns back to the TV.

I don't know what I'm doing yet, I say. **I'll message you tomorrow.**

Talia: **See you there in green and white or you're officially dead to me.**

And even though I know she's being dramatic, I also know she's one hundred percent *not* kidding.

Eleven

WHEN I WAKE UP the next morning, I feel like I'm gonna throw up. I don't know if Dad's chicken casserole was a bit funny last night or if I'm nervous about what the hell I'm going to do about Boat Race today, but I do *not* feel good.

I grab my phone. When I open Instagram, there's a new follower waiting for me. I click on the profile, and there's Amina's adorably round face smiling up at me from her little DP.

I click Follow Back and my phone buzzes almost immediately. **Good morning, Luca!** Squinty-eyed-enormous-grin emoji. **It's Amina from school. How are you?**

I chuckle. **Amina from school? Thought it must have been that other Amina I know who looks exactly like you haha. I'm good. Just woke up. You?**

I'm great, obviously! It's Boat Race! Are you excited?!

My stomach gurgles. *Ugh*, definitely not Dad's chicken, then.

Totally! I lie. **Can't wait to see some boys in zoot suits!** Peach emoji. Eggplant emoji.

OMG! Luca, stop! Is that all you think about?

(Yes.)

Come on, I write. **Don't tell me you don't dream about TJ in his rowing gear.** Monkey covering its mouth emoji.

You're a terrible influence, Luca Mason.

Or am I the BEST influence?

I'm going to have breakfast, Amina says. **See you at 9am at the lake? (P.S. I painted our T-shirts last night, they're so adorable!)** Love-heart-eyes emoji.

I bite my lip and take in a deep breath.

Perfect. See you there.

Dad makes me eggs and bacon for breakfast, but I can't stomach it. I just sit there in the kitchen, shifting my food around my plate until he asks, "You okay, Lu?"

"I don't feel great."

"Why don't you go lie down? You've still got a while before you have to leave for Boat Race."

My stomach turns again at the mention of it.

"I don't know if I'm gonna go."

"What? But you love Boat Race. And it'll be a great chance for you to see all your friends in one place."

"Please don't remind me," I groan. I finally give up on breakfast and push my plate away. "It's just . . . it's really complicated this year, okay?"

"Complicated?" Dad grabs the plate and takes it over to the bin, getting rid of my untouched brekky.

"You have no idea."

"Come on, mate," he says, scrubbing our plates in the sink, "It can't be *that* bad."

But what Dad doesn't understand is that this one decision

could possibly ruin the rest of my high school existence.

"You know what?" I say, throwing my hands in the air. "I'm not going. No matter what I do, people are going to end up hating me, so what's the point?"

Dad laughs as I let my head plonk down onto the table. "Sorry, mate," he says, "I shouldn't laugh. But don't you think you're being a *little* dramatic? No one's going to hate you just because you decide not to go to a rowing race."

I scoff through my fingers. Dad doesn't know Talia like I do.

"Well," he carries on, "you're welcome to stay home and help me with my marking. I've got a whole pile of Grade Six short stories to read."

I look up. "Yeah, or I could crawl into a hole and die."

"Gee, *thanks*."

"Not because of *you*," I say, rolling my eyes. "Because in a few hours I'm going to have no friends."

"Then stay home," Dad replies. "It would be pretty exhausting for you on your feet all day with your crutches, anyway."

"Oh my god, Dad," I say, relief washing over me like cold water, "you're a genius! No one's gonna hate me if I blame my *foot* for not being able to go! I'll just say I'm in heaps of pain today, so I have to book an emergency appointment with my OT."

"Well, you don't have to *lie*," he says. "Just say you're not sure if you could stand up for that long on the grass."

"No, no, no. The lie is *heaps* better."

I pull my phone out of my pocket and send a message to the Bunheads:

I am so sorry, but I'm not going to be able to come today.

I'm in so much pain, and Dad said he doesn't want me standing out on the grass all day. He booked me in for a last-minute appointment with my OT at 10am. Tears-streaming-down-its-face emoji. I'm SO sorry. Make sure you cheer extra hard for me!! Go St. Tom's!

I almost forget to change the last bit to **Go North!** when I copy and paste the message and send it to Amina.

Grace replies first, as usual. **We'll miss you.** Purple love heart.

Single-tear emoji from Abbey.

Talia: **Whatever loser.**

I roll my eyes.

My phone pings again, and it's Amina.

That is totally fine, Luca. I'm so sorry you're not feeling good. Is there anything I can do to help? Have you got anti-inflammatories etc?

Ugh, why does she have to be so damn *nice* all the time?

But it's too late. I've made my decision. While the rest of the high school population of Ballarat is at Lake Wendouree having the best day ever, I'm going to be stuck inside on the couch all day with Dad and his Grade Six short stories.

That is what my life has come to.

———

Amina sends me a message at exactly 10:30 a.m.

How did it go at the OT? I hope you're feeling a bit better x

I haven't moved from the couch since she messaged me two hours ago.

Thank you! Hugging emoji. **I'm okay. Glad I went.**

I feel awful for lying, but what am I supposed to do? It's too late to change my story now.

How's Boat Race? I ask. **I'm so jealous!**

So much fun!

Me: **How are the races so far?**

Three dots . . .

Good! Thumbs-up emoji.

And I mean, I know I only met her a couple of weeks ago, but that is the most un-Amina reply I could possibly imagine. I was expecting a blow-by-blow update on all the races so far with an in-depth description of everyone's costumes and a detailed verdict on which school has the best war cry and why, not one word and a half-hearted emoji.

Something is wrong.

I decide to wait a couple of minutes—in case she's constructing an essay-length reply in her notes—but nothing else comes through.

Does the St. Tom's cheer squad look amazing? I ask. **(You can tell me, I can take it)**

The St. Tom's theme this year is "superheroes," which is basically just an excuse for the girls to wear booby tops and tiny skirts that would never be allowed at school on any other day of the year. But it also means boys in tights and capes, so it's not like I'm complaining.

The three dots appear . . .

And then disappear.

Then appear again . . .

Then disappear.

And oh my god. I stare down at my phone, feeling kind of

queasy. Because I'm ninety-nine percent sure Amina is sitting at home right now, with two hand-painted T-shirts crumpled up on the couch beside her, *pretending* to be at Boat Race. And I'm one hundred percent sure I'm a terrible person.

The three dots appear again, but I click on the video call icon at the top of the chat before Amina has a chance to reply.

"Hello?" she answers softly, her face filling half the screen.

"You didn't go?"

"It's fine, Luca. I didn't—"

"It's *not* fine," I cut in. "You were so excited."

"I know, but . . ." She sighs. "I just felt weird going without you."

Stick a dagger through my cold, lying heart, why don't you?

"You know what," I say, "I actually feel heaps better now. I think we should go."

"You're just saying that because you feel bad."

"I'm not. I swear."

"I don't know, Luca . . ."

"Come *on*," I plead. "It's Boat Race. It's Jordan in a *goddamn* zoot suit. We *cannot* miss that."

Amina makes a humming noise that sounds like it's about to turn into a big fat *"No."*

"We have to go," I say. "Are we Boat Race Buddies or not?"

Suddenly, her video goes dark.

"Amina?"

"Sorry, I'm still here," she replies, through what sounds suspiciously like a sniffle. "But . . . Luca, are you sure? If you're going to be uncomfortable, or if you're not going to enjoy it because you're in pain . . . I mean, there's always next year, right?"

"Amina," I say, in a voice that sounds so much like Dad it shocks me. "We. Are. Going. I'll see you there in fifteen minutes. And you better not forget my T-shirt."

Twelve

DAD DROPS ME OFF in front of St. Margaret's, right across the road from Lake Wendouree. The school is nowhere near as fancy—or as outrageously expensive—as St. Tom's or CHGS, but it's the only campus in town with waterfront views, so that's something. Talia always used to joke that to go to Maggie's, you had to be either A.) bitchy, B.) a virgin, or C.) a bitchy virgin. Which I now realize is probably the same as her saying everyone at North is a violent, weed-smoking criminal.

It's a six-kilometer walk around the lake—I only know that because we were forced to do it weekly in Year Ten PE—on a thin, sandy gravel path. There are playgrounds dotted all the way around, as well as food kiosks, fountains, gardens, even a "wetland reserve" (which is actually just an old boardwalk in the middle of a bunch of reeds). I've spent very little time at the lake unless forced to, but even I have to admit, it's pretty damn stunning on a day like this.

There are thousands of people—students, teachers, parents, family, friends, ex-rowers, news crews—spread out along the banks of the lake opposite St. Margaret's. From this distance, the school chants and war cries and whistles all blend into a dull roar that hangs in the air like static. The official cheer squads are across the other side of the rowing course on a skinny finger of land called "the Spit" with perfect race views. The Spit is the only place I've ever watched the races from, and where I can't help but feel like I should be right now.

As I cross the road, I notice Amina leaning up against a tree, just off the path, wearing a bright blue T-shirt. She sees me, stands bolt upright, and waves, literally jumping up and down on the spot. I smile back at her, hands on my crutches. She reaches down into a blue backpack at her feet and pulls out another bright-blue T-shirt, shaking it in the air above her head like a Mardi Gras banner.

"What is *that?*" I say as I hop up over the curb onto the grass.

"Your T-shirt!" she replies, beaming.

"I can see that. But what's on the front?"

"It's us!"

"It's *what*, sorry?" I squint to try to make out the details, praying that she's kidding.

"Us," she laughs. "You and me."

But when I reach the shade of the tree, I see she is definitely *not* kidding. Painted almost identically on the front of both T-shirts is a cartoon version of me and Amina in blue and white North zoot suits, oars in hand, rowing our very own boat together.

"When you said 'paint our T-shirts,'" I say, stopping in front of her, "I thought you meant some cute stripes or polka dots like everyone else, not a full Picasso."

"Picasso was a cubist," she replies, dropping her arms down by her sides. "This is Japanese manga style."

"Amina, I don't know what any of those words mean," I say, and she rolls her eyes melodramatically. "Also, I think you've made my nose a bit big. Just saying."

"But wait," she says, like my favorite lady from the air fryer infomercial, "there's more." She flips the T-shirt around, and it says BOAT RACE in perfect, white block letters on the back.

"How did you get the letters so neat?"

"Stencil," she replies, clearly very proud of herself. "And then on *mine* . . ." She turns on the spot to show me her back, and I feel my eyes grow so wide it almost hurts.

Painted across the back of Amina's T-shirt—in the same crisp, white letters—is the word BUDDIES.

"Get it?" she asks, turning back around with a massive, cheesy grin on her face.

"Oh, don't worry, I got it." I try to laugh, but it sounds more like choking.

"Now *everyone* will know!" She does a little golf clap. "You just have to make sure to stand to my left all day."

And I mean, I've seen some pretty embarrassing Boat Race costumes in my life (including in Year Eight, when one of the senior boys went commando in a white morph suit and it rained and everyone could see his, you know . . . *everything*) but this has gotta be up there in the top ten.

"Aren't they cute?" Amina asks.

"They're definitely . . . *something*," I reply, forcing a smile.

"Quick, put it on, put it on!"

I slip the T-shirt on over my perfectly respectable, perfectly plain T-shirt, and we join the crowd huddled around the banks of Lake Wendouree. Amina manages to get everyone to clear a path for me and my crutches, and we slowly make our way toward the front to the crowd. And even though I can hear people sniggering about our T-shirts the whole way ("Oh my god, Cassidy, look . . ."—"Nerd alert!"—"Boat Race Buddies? What are you, like, five?"), I actually couldn't care less. I'm obviously not trying to impress anyone at North—except Jordan, of course, but he's not here, thank *god*—so who cares what they think. And Amina is so happy she basically has sunshine and rainbows shooting out of her face like that old Snapchat filter. Which almost makes the whole thing worth it.

When we finally make it right up to the edge of the water, Amina slings off her backpack, pulls out a piece of rolled-up blue cardboard, and opens it with a dramatic flourish.

North Is Oarsome it reads, in the same white block letters as our T-shirts.

I can't help but chuckle, even though it's a total dad joke. "Very punny, Amina. Well done."

"I was going to make you one too," she says, "but I thought it might be a bit hard for you to hold with your crutches. We can share, if you like?"

"It's fine." I lift one of my crutches high up into the air. "I'll just wave this thing around. Totally does the trick."

As the first set of boats glide past, Amina screeches "GO NORTH! YOU GOT THIS!" directly into my ear, while I stare out across the water at the Spit. The school cheer squads are lined up in clumps the whole way along the narrow bank, in the exact same order as always. St. Tom's has the number-one spot, of course, with a perfect view of the finish line and a cute little green marquee set up for shade if it gets too hot. Next to St. Tom's is CHGS in their ugly burgundy and gold, then all the Catholic schools in a neat row, then East High in red and black, and then, *all* the way down the far end of the Spit, is North.

To be honest, I didn't even know North *had* a cheer squad, so yay for them—I mean, *us.*

It's not like I can make out anyone's faces from this distance, but even seeing the St. Tom's marquee and hearing the faint echo of their chants drifting across the lake is enough to make me want to dive into the murky water—fully clothed—and swim over to take my rightful place with a pair of green and white pom-poms.

My phone starts buzzing in my jeans and I fish it out to see a bunch of new messages in the Bunheads chat.

Talk about timing, Universe.

Talia: **Abbey, where are you?**

Abbey: **Just went to the bathroom.**

You've been gone for ages, Talia replies. **You're missing all the races.**

Abbey: **Not feeling well.**

Eye-roll emoji from Talia. **If you're giving Jonno a BJ on the playground, we are so not friends anymore.**

I shove my phone back into my pocket and glance over at Amina, who has just joined in with one of the North war cries. She grins at me as she chants, waving her NORTH IS OARSOME sign in the air like her life depends on it. And suddenly, my desire to launch myself into the lake and swim over to the Spit seems to disappear.

The first time the words *"Go North!"* fly out of my mouth, it feels like I'm cheating on St. Tom's. Or like I'm breaking some kind of unspoken rule, like the first time I said "shit" at school in Grade Five and I legitimately thought Dad was going to jump out of the bushes and ground me for swearing. But after a couple of hours, it starts to feel almost normal.

Amina turns to me after one of the Year Nine girls' races, with this look on her face like she's stepped on a nail.

"What?" I ask, over the cheering around us. "Are you okay?"

"I need to go to the bathroom," she says, chewing her bottom lip.

"Oh," I laugh. "Let's go, then."

"But we'll lose our spot! We have such a good view from here. Maybe you should stay and hold our place?"

"I'm not staying here by myself. Someone will push me into the lake."

"They will *not.*"

"I need to go too," I reply, which is actually not a lie, now that I think about it. "And it's going to take way too long if we go separately."

"But—"

"We got through the crowd once, I'm sure we can do it again."

"There are twice as many people here now," Amina groans.

"We'll be *fine.*"

She hops up and down on the spot with her knees pressed together.

"Amina, come on. What's the alternative? I *refuse* to be arrested for public urination. I do not have enough self-esteem to survive something like that right now."

"Fine." She bends down to grab her backpack. "Let's just go."

But when we make it back out through the crowd, I go to turn left, and Amina turns right.

"Where are you going?" I ask. "The bathrooms are this way."

"Those ones will be *so* busy," Amina replies. "It will be much quicker if we go to the ones near the playground."

And she's definitely right. The closest public bathroom will have a line so long it wraps all the way around the lake. But the bathrooms Amina wants to go to—back down to St. Margaret's, around past the Spit, and almost all the way up to the enormous wooden playground (aka the quickest way to get a splinter in town)—will take us *directly* past the St. Tom's cheer squad.

"Those ones are so much further," I argue, but Amina is already striding down the path toward the Spit like she's in a race of her own. Which means I have no choice but to hop along behind her and try to keep up, unless I want to lose her in the crowd and spend the rest of the day by myself. Which is *so* not happening.

By the time we reach the old Olympic rings statue—which stands at the solid-land end of the Spit—I'm completely out of breath. The rings have been there since the fifties or whatever, when Melbourne hosted the Olympics, and all the rowing events were held on Lake Wendouree. It's probably Ballarat's proudest moment in history. The statue is literally *meters* from the St. Tom's marquee, which means if any of the Bunheads happened to look in this direction at this exact moment, they would definitely be able to see me. And if Talia sees me here at the lake with Amina—wearing *this* T-shirt—I am totally and utterly screwed.

I turn my face toward the statue—and more importantly, *away* from the Spit—and notice a flash of orange and green and white.

Oh, you have *got* to be kidding me . . .

Standing in the shadow of the rings—with her back to us, thank god—wearing a long, emerald-green cape and white short shorts, furiously making out with Jonno, is Abbey.

"Shit," I say under my breath, ducking my head.

"What?" Amina asks.

"Nothing," I say, my eyes glued to the gravel at my feet.

Please, please, *please* let Abbey be too focused on Jonno's tongue right now to notice me . . .

"Is something wrong?" Amina asks. "Do you need to stop? Let's stop for a second."

But I can't stop. I'm surrounded on both sides.

"No, no, no," I say, "I'm fine. Come on, I thought you were in a hurry."

I speed off along the sandy path—which is a hell of a lot harder than it sounds on crutches—and this time, Amina has to jog to keep up with me.

This was a terrible idea. Why the hell did I come here today?

See you there in green and white or you're officially dead to me.

And not only am I here wearing the brightest bright blue

T-shirt Ballarat has ever seen, I also have a fucking cartoon of myself wearing a bright blue zoot suit painted across my bright blue chest.

"Luca, why are we running?" Amina pants from beside me.

But I don't reply. And I don't slow down until we're all the way around the corner, with a solid wall of trees between us and the Spit.

I'm pretty sure Abbey didn't see me—because she would have chased me down to get photo evidence if she did—but what if she's still there with Jonno on our way back? Or what if I bump into *anyone* from St. Tom's on the way back? They'll run straight back to tell Talia.

Before I know it, Amina and I are standing outside the red-brick bathrooms opposite the playground.

"I'll be back in a sec," she says as she trots off to the ladies' on the other side.

"What the hell am I doing?" I say to myself, shaking my head up at the cloudless sky.

There's no way I can walk back past the Spit. It's way too risky. But it takes an hour to walk around the lake—again, I only know this because of the awfulness that was Year Ten PE—which would take me like, two and half hours on crutches. Which is so not an option right now.

I need to go home.

"Hey, gayboy," a deep voice says from behind me, and I almost jump out of my skin. I turn to see Gibbo walking out of the men's bathroom, flicking water off his hands. At least, I hope it's water.

"Shouldn't you be getting ready for your race?" I reply.

"Or, I dunno, learning how to use a pair of tweezers?"

"Ha *ha*, dickhead," he says, pulling a face that makes him look even more annoying than he usually does. "We've still got hours before our race. Not that I owe you an explanation for taking a piss."

Then, two more boys follow him out of the bathroom: Jordan's friend Macca, and the little Year Ten guy from their rowing crew. Tim? Tom?

"Looks like Luca heard we were in the bathroom," Gibbo says, elbowing Macca in the ribs, "and he's come to sneak a peek."

The other boys laugh and I roll my eyes.

"Isn't that right, princess? Gay guys love public bathrooms, don't they?"

"Cruising isn't really my thing, Gibbo, but you certainly seem to know what you're talking about."

His smile fades and his bushy red eyebrows meet in the middle. "You wanna say that again?"

He takes a slow step toward me, but just as he does, Jordan walks out of the bathrooms behind him. He's wearing a baggy white T-shirt over his blue zoot suit, with sunnies pushed back on top of his head. My heart flutters, even though I'm probably about to get punched in the face.

"Who are you t—" He stops when he notices me. "Oh. Hey, mate," he says, with one of his trademark upward nods.

"Hey, mate"? We've gone from *"Make sure you cheer nice and loud for me"* to *"Hey, mate"*?

His eyes drift down to the cartoon on the front of my T-shirt, one corner of his mouth curling into a faint smirk.

"I think we've got a stalker, bro," Gibbo says to Jordan, his infuriating grin returning to his infuriating face.

Jordan scoffs and shakes his head.

"I'm tellin' ya," Gibbo goes on, "he's gagging for a piece of this." He grabs Jordan's ass and Jordan shoves him away with a laugh.

The rest of the boys all chuckle, and I look straight at Jordan, waiting for him to say, *Give it rest, Gibbo,* or *"Leave Luca alone, he's actually pretty chill."*

But he doesn't.

He meets my eye and I stare back at him, my pulse surging through my body.

Say something.

He keeps his eyes on mine for a second, his expression unreadable, then turns away and starts off down the path back to the Spit.

"Come on, boys," he calls over his shoulder, "we're missing all the action."

Gibbo bumps me—hard—with his shoulder as he walks past. "See ya, princess," he says in a high-pitched voice, which is apparently the funniest thing Macca and Tim/Tom have ever heard.

I glare after the boys, my face burning, my eyes filling with tears.

I need to get out of here. Now.

I pull my phone out of my pocket and call Dad, who answers after half a ring. Like he was expecting my call.

"Lu?"

"Can you come pick me up?"

"Is something wrong?" he asks. "You sound upset. Are you okay?"

"I'm fine," I reply, "I'm just . . . tired from all the standing."

But what I really mean is, *"No, Dad. I'm not okay."*

I'm not okay at all.

Thirteen

DAD WAS HALFWAY THROUGH *Toy Story 3* when I called him from the lake, so I join him and his Grade Six short stories on the couch as soon as we walk through the door. I definitely don't want to talk about what happened, but I kind of don't feel like being alone, either. I try to focus on the movie, but no matter how hard I try, my mind keeps drifting back to the lake . . .

Why didn't Jordan say something to Gibbo? Where was the sweet guy from the OT waiting room when I needed him? Where was the cute boy who signed my cast and said I was funny? Maybe I've been completely wrong about him this whole time.

I start mindlessly scrolling through Instagram when a message pops up from Amina: **Did you get home all right?**

Yep, I reply. **How's it going over there?**

I told her there was no way she could let that punny poster go to waste, so she decided to stay at the lake by herself. Which is a pretty big deal for her. I mean, for anyone, really.

It's good, she writes. **St. Tom's is basically winning everything, of course.** Eye-roll emoji. **No offense.**

None taken. Send me updates, please!

"How's it all going, Lu?" Dad asks, after the scene where Woody tries to hang glide out of the day care center.

"All what?"

"All everything." He takes his reading glasses off and rests them in his lap. "School. Your foot. *You.*"

"I don't really want to talk about it," I reply. "I think I need to pretend this is just a normal Saturday on the couch, you know?"

Dad nods. "Can do. You hungry? I can whip us up some Bolognese?"

"Sounds good."

He slides out from under his mountain of short stories and heads into the kitchen.

My phone buzzes. I pick it up, expecting to see an update from Amina, but it's the Bunheads chat.

Talia: **Abbey. Seriously. WTF. Where are you?**

Chill, Talia, she replies. **I just went to get coffee.**

You are the worst cheer squad member since the dawn of time, Talia writes. **You know that, right?**

Abbey: **Well I'd be even worse if I wasn't cafinated.**

It's "caffeinated", babe. Grace adds. **Just hurry back. Not long till the firsts' races.**

I swipe out of the app and put my phone face down on the arm of the couch, feeling restless and annoyed all of a sudden. Why do they have to keep messaging each other in the group chat? Can't they start a St. Tom's 4 Lyf chat for the three of them so I don't have to read a minute-by-minute update of their day?

Dad brings back two steaming bowls of pasta, and we eat

while the toys are swept along the conveyor belt into the fiery trash incinerator. By the time we finish our meal, the credits are rolling.

"Christ, I always forget how sad that one is," Dad says, wiping tears from his cheeks.

"You say that every time."

"It's meant to be for kids. It should have a happier ending."

"Not all kids get happy endings, Dad," I reply, and I'm not talking about *me*, but then I realize I *am* talking about me. About my friends. About Jordan. About ballet.

I'm not going to get my happy ending.

Dad frowns and sighs loudly. "Are you sure you're okay?"

Suddenly, I feel smothered. Anxious. Claustrophobic.

I feel like I need to get out of here.

But I can't.

"Lu? Are you all right?"

"I'm *fine*." We've had this conversation too many times. I'm sick of this conversation. I *hate* this conversation.

"You can talk to me, Lu."

"I already said I don't want to talk about it."

"I know," Dad says. "But I also know what it's like to grieve something. When your mum died, I—"

"This isn't the same," I snap. It comes out with more bite than expected, but it feels good to be angry. Like, *really* good. "You still don't get it, Dad. Ballet isn't something I've lost. Something I'm missing. It's *me*. It's all of me. And it's gone. And I'm trying to be happy, but I don't have a fucking clue who I am anymore and nothing is working out the way it's supposed to."

"I thought you'd been doing okay lately? You've seemed

more like yourself the last couple of weeks."

"But I'm *not* myself," I say, my emotions dangerously close to the surface. "Can't you see that? If I was, I'd be at Boat Race right now with my friends. I'd still go to St. Tom's. I'd still be able to dance."

"I know, Lu, but—"

"No, you *don't* know. How can I ever be happy when I'm living someone else's life? When I'm in a nightmare I'll never wake up from? Don't you see, Dad? This isn't my life!"

"Then you'll find a different path," he says quietly, slowly, as if he's trying to defuse a bomb inside my chest that is clearly about to blow. "You'll make a new life for yourself."

"I don't want a new life!"

"Luca, just—"

"What about *your* new life, Dad?" I yell. "Mum died like, fourteen years ago. Your closet is still full of her old clothes. You haven't gone on a single date. You talk about her as if she's still here. She's dead, Dad. You're the one who needs to get a new fucking life!"

For a moment, he just sits there in silence, his lips pressed together, his eyes filling with tears. And then he gets up, walks to the front door and slams it on his way out.

I burst into tears as soon as he's gone. I don't know why I said it. I didn't even mean it. I'm a horrible person. I'm an awful son. I sit there for what feels like hours, crying so much my stomach starts to cramp. Eventually, my phone buzzes.

Amina: **St. Margaret's won the girls' Head of the Lake! And St. Tom's won the boys'. But North came second in BOTH! It's the best result we've had in fourteen years! YAY!**

I drop my phone onto my lap and slump down into the couch.

Jordan will be celebrating with the boys in his crew right now. Kissing his beautiful girlfriend. Getting lifted into the air by the cheer squad, everyone chanting his name. He'll be on top of the world. And he won't notice I'm not there. He won't even fucking care.

The suns sets. Dad's still not home.

I feel sick to my stomach every time I picture his face. The way the color drained from his cheeks. How his chin started to shake.

Shit.

Still sitting where he left me, my cast propped up on the coffee table, I let out a groan and drop my head into my hands. My stomach grumbles in reply. I should eat something. It's been hours since we had that spaghetti.

I make my way to the kitchen and make a cup of two-minute noodles—cooking has never been my thing. To be honest, nothing has ever been my "thing." Except ballet.

I've never really thought about it before, but there are so many things I missed out on because of dancing . . .

Learning to cook.

Learning to ride a bike.

Having time to do homework.

Going on school camps.

Going on holidays.

Free time.

Junk food.

Parties.

Being a kid.

The list goes on and on and on.

Suddenly, I'm furious again. But for the first time, I'm not angry that I fell down a flight of stairs and broke my foot. I'm angry at ballet. At the fact that I gave up my whole childhood so I could be the best dancer I could possibly be. And for what? If I hadn't broken my foot, I *still* might not have made it as a dancer. There was no guarantee I'd get accepted into the Australian Ballet School, no guarantee I'd end up making a career out of ballet. And even if I *did*, how long could it have possibly lasted? Dancers get maybe twenty years at the absolute most. And then what?

Either way, I would have ended up with nothing.

So, you know what? I'm done. Fuck ballet.

I pull out my phone and open Instagram, keen for something to distract me from the shitstorm of emotions I'm feeling right now. The first story at the top is Talia's. I click on it and my screen is filled with St. Tom's kids' faces, drinks in hand, shouting and singing and dancing. It's from an hour ago. Talia's next story is a selfie of her and Grace and Abbey with the caption *Bow down to the ballet bitches*. The next one shows Jonno stripping down to his jocks and jumping into his enormous infinity pool. After that is a super-blurry selfie of some guy kissing Talia's neck. Then a boomerang of a bunch of girls cheers-ing their pre-mix vodka sodas.

My blood starts to boil, and I exit Instagram, only to be greeted by more messages in the Bunheads chat.

Talia: **Damien wants me to go home with him. Thoughts?**

Eww! Abbey says. **No way you can do SO much better**

He's super rich and his parents are away . . . Shrugging-lady emoji.

Grace: **Talia, absolutely not. We're all staying at mine. End of story.**

Abbey: **Guys where the f are you? I haven't seen you since the boys did the nudie run around the pool**

I'm in the cinema room downstairs, Talia writes.

I'm still in the kitchen, Grace replies.

COME OUSTIDE, Abbey says. **You're missing all the fun. Jonno just ordered 200 pizzas not even kiddingggg**

Coming.

Coming. Purple love heart.

Abbey: **BSET NIHGT EVER**

I lock my screen and hold my breath, having to seriously stop myself from chucking my phone at the wall.

Of course they're having the best night ever. Of course they're all as happy as fucking Larry. Of course they're not giving a single thought to the fact that using our group chat when I'm stuck at home by myself would make me feel like absolute shit.

But my phone just keeps on buzzing in my hand. Message after message in the Bunheads chat. And every time it vibrates, I want to scream. Every message is like a slap in the face. A stab in the back.

I know what I need to do.

My stomach twists as I open the chat, click on the group name and scroll through the settings. In between Hide Alerts and Photos are the words Leave this Conversation, in bright red text.

I take a deep breath and exhale slowly through tight lips, my heart thumping in my throat.

And I click Leave this Conversation.

It's weird, because all I did was tap my screen, but it feels just as harsh—just as deafening—as when Dad slammed the door on me this afternoon.

Fourteen

"LU? ARE YOU AWAKE?"

I roll over to see Dad poking his head through my bedroom door. Yellow sunlight is seeping through the cracks around the blinds, shining a thin, rectangular spotlight on his face.

I hum a croaky "Mmm" in reply. It's still early—heaps earlier than I planned on getting up. I kind of wanted to sleep all day so I wouldn't have to think about Boat Race or Jordan or the Bunheads or Dad, but the magpies woke me up hours ago. Of course.

"Can I come in?" Dad asks, and I nod.

He opens the door and steps into my room, his eyes cutting to the empty mantelpiece opposite my bed. He tilts his head to the side, with this look on his face like he's trying to remember where he put his car keys. "When did you take your trophies down?"

I sit up in bed and a memory flashes behind my eyes. . . . Me. Tears streaming down my face. Throwing all my ballet trophies into a cardboard box. Shoving them up the back of my closet behind my winter jackets.

"Last night," I say, rubbing the sleep from my eyes.

We both stare up at the mantel for a while, like, as if we look at it for long enough, my trophies will all magically reappear, and my life will go back to normal.

Eventually, Dad clicks his tongue and says, "You hungry? I just started cooking breakfast."

"Yep," I say. "I'll come down in a sec."

By the time I make it downstairs, Dad's laid out a full breakfast buffet on the kitchen table. I'm talking eggs, bacon, tomatoes, beans, toast, juice, a pot of coffee—the works. I take a seat opposite him and say, "This looks amazing," but he doesn't reply. So we both just sit there in literally *the* most awkward silence I've ever been involved in in my entire life. It's so tense that it feels like there's someone else in the room, shouting out all the things we're both not saying to each other.

"I'm sor—" I start, but Dad says, "Look, Lu—" at the same time, and we both stop.

Silence.

"I shouldn't have left yesterday," he says after a long moment. "I just knew that if I stayed, I would've said some things I really didn't mean. And you're already going through enough as it is without copping an earful from me."

"It's okay, Dad, you—"

"No, no," he says, shaking his head, "it's not okay. I'm your dad. It's my job to look after you, not the other way around. No matter what you say to me. I'm the adult. I shouldn't have left. It was irresponsible and . . . and unforgivable. I'm sorry."

"Dad, it's not your fault," I reply, shaking my head. "I was *horrible* to you. *I'm* the one who should be sorry. I shouldn't

114

have said those awful things. I didn't mean it. Any of it. It all just . . . came out."

"I know, mate. I know."

He spoons some beans onto his plate, and I pour some coffee into my mug.

"But you know what?" he says, offering me the plate of bacon. "You were right."

I take the bacon and start picking out the crispiest bits. "About what?"

"Now, I'm not saying I ever want you to speak to me like that again—Christ knows where you get that temper from, and *please* stop swearing so much—but I think, in a way, I needed to hear that."

"You mean, about Mum?"

"Yeah," he sighs. "About Mum. It's been almost fourteen years since she passed away, and you're right. I haven't let her go. Not even a little bit."

He loads his fork with toast and egg and beans.

"But . . . you loved her," I say.

He puts his fork down and smiles his lopsided smile, his eyes crinkling at the sides. "I did. I do. I think I always will. And all I ever wanted was for her to be a part of your life, you know? But . . . as much as I want her to be here, she's not. And . . . I don't know. The thought of getting rid of her things, it just—I feel sick to my stomach even *thinking* about it."

"You don't have to do that," I say. "I didn't mean any of what I said. I was just angry because . . . Everything is just . . ."

"I know, mate," he says. "I know. And I'm not saying I'm gonna chuck all of Mum's clothes in a Salvo's bin this afternoon.

But I'm . . ." He pauses and takes in a slow breath.

"Dealing with it?"

He lets out a long sigh. "Dealing with it."

Jordan isn't at school on Monday.

I promised myself I wouldn't think about him, but by lunchtime, I've already played out so many different versions of the scene from Lake Wendouree in my head—including one where Jordan punches Gibbo in the face and kisses me in front of everyone, but also one where Jordan punches *me* in the face and pashes his girlfriend to celebrate—that I can barely remember what actually happened.

As soon as Amina and I sit down at our benches, she launches into one of her usual lunchtime monologues, and I let the words wash over me, weirdly comforted by the sound of her voice.

It's just us these days. Alicia and Bree have started hanging out on the steps outside the library. (I think I might have accidentally scared them away with my gayness. Whoops.) So, I let Amina work her way through an endless series of conversation topics while I just sit there, staring down at the quad. At the complete lack of Jordan. I want to ask Amina if she knows why he isn't here, but if I bring him up, I know she'll figure out that something is wrong. And then I'll have to tell her what happened at the lake, and I definitely don't have the energy for that right now.

I'm just so exhausted. I feel kind of empty and deflated, like I've run out of fuel. I can't be bothered talking. I can't even be bothered eating my sandwich. I just . . . can't be bothered.

Because here's the thing: ballet left a huge hole in my life. And I don't think I realized until last night that I accidentally filled most of that hole with Jordan. Thinking about Jordan. Talking about Jordan. Planning what I'd say to Jordan if I saw him. Dreaming about Jordan. (I had to secretly wash a couple of pairs of boxers without Dad noticing after some of those dreams.) But Jordan was never an option. And deep down, I obviously *knew* that. Which is the most ridiculous part of the whole thing.

And it makes no difference to *him* whether I like him or not. He's one of those people who has everything going for him, you know? And it's the same with Amina. Because she has school. She has her ridiculous brain. Her family. Her faith. They both have so many things. So much that makes them *them*.

And without ballet, without the Bunheads, without my nonexistent chances with Jordan . . .

What the hell do I have?

Fifteen

JORDAN IS BACK AT school on Tuesday. I try not to notice the way his shoulders slump as he makes his way across the quad. I try to ignore the fact that he doesn't stop and talk to a million different people on his way to the canteen like he usually does. Something doesn't seem right. His strut is gone. But his strut is none of my business anymore. If something is bothering him, he can talk to Rhiannon and Gibbo about it. I don't care. I am actively *not* caring about Jordan Tanaka-Jones.

But when I walk into the OT waiting room that afternoon for my weekly appointment, and Jordan is sitting there in his North uniform, hunched over, staring at the carpet, it takes literally all of my willpower to *not* care about him.

I take my usual seat beside Jordan—with a one-seat buffer, of course—because the last thing I want is for him to know how upset I was after what happened at the lake, and he glances up straightaway.

He looks different. Confused. Sad.

"Hey," he says. His voice is kind of dry and cracked.

"Um, *hi*." I fold my arms across my chest.

"Mate," he says, turning in his seat. "About the other day. At Boat Race. Gibbo and the boys . . ."

I raise my eyebrows and don't reply.

"That was . . ." He takes a deep breath. "I didn't handle that the way I should have. The way I wanted to. I'm sorry."

"You didn't seem very sorry at the lake."

"I know," he sighs, shaking his head. "It was . . . And I don't want to make excuses—because it was a total dick move—but I just didn't want to start something with Gibbo right before our race. There was already some shit going down, and I really needed the crew to be on the same page, you know?"

"And what page was that?" I ask. "The homophobic one?"

Jordan scrunches his eyes shut and rubs his temples like he's got a massive headache. I can't believe how different he seems. He's usually the most outwardly confident and friendly person I've ever met. But there's no warm smile today. No jokes. He has dark rings under his eyes, and his hair is all squashed on one side, like he slept on it funny and didn't shower this morning. Actually, it looks like he hasn't slept for days.

"I'm sorry," he says again. "Boat Race is a huge deal, and my shoulder was playing up, and I . . ." He trails off, looking like he's been wounded.

And for some reason, all I want to do is give him a hug and tell him everything is going to be okay.

"I'm sorry," he says, one more time. "I just wanted you to know that."

We're quiet for a minute, and I watch as he reaches up to massage his shoulder.

"Is it okay?" I ask. "Your shoulder?" I'm not sure why I ask, because it's obviously not okay if he's here at the OT. It's like when the nurses asked me how I was feeling when I broke my foot and I wanted to punch them in the face.

"Not really," he replies. "I twinged it the day before Boat Race. But we still came second, so . . ."

"Yeah, I heard. Congrats."

"You didn't see the race?"

"No," I reply. "I had a . . . thing. In the afternoon."

The way his head droops when he looks back down at the floor tells me there is so much more to this than him hurting his shoulder. And I can either let it go—I *should* let it go, because I don't care about Jordan anymore, remember?—or . . .

"Are you okay? I ask. "Not your shoulder. I mean like, are *you* okay?"

Without realizing I'm doing it, I place my hand on Jordan's back. My fingers tingle and I get so nervous that I want to pull my hand away, but then he breathes into my touch, so I leave my hand where it is. He starts to shiver, even though it's not even remotely cold in here, and it takes me longer than it should to realize he's not shivering. He's crying.

"Hey," I say gently, rubbing his back.

A patchy image flickers before my eyes . . . Sitting on the curb with a scraped knee, bawling my eyes out, Mum kneeling beside me rubbing warm little circles on my back, telling me it won't hurt for much longer . . .

Jordan sucks in a shaky breath, and I blink the memory

away. I pull my hand back and hold it to my chest. He covers his eyes with his hands and lets his head lean back and hit the wall behind us.

"Jordan, what's wr—"

But before I can finish, he's up and out of his seat, heading for the door. As quickly as I can on my crutches—I'm a lot faster now, after practically sprinting around the lake with Amina—I follow Jordan outside, where I find him leaning against the metal railing that runs along the ramp in front of the building. Even with his back to me, I can tell he's still crying.

I move closer—but not too close, in case he needs a bit of space like Talia does when she's upset (which isn't very often, because she usually refuses to show any kind of human emotion).

"Jordan," I say quietly.

He wipes his eyes and then slowly turns around.

"Sorry," he croaks.

"You don't need to be sorry."

"I fucking hate crying."

"Really?" I ask sort of cheerfully, trying to lighten the mood. "I kind of love it. I always feel so good after a big cry. It's like, totally liberating."

"Yeah, well, we're not all . . . you know."

He makes this weird face, and surely he doesn't mean what I think he means.

"We're not all *what?*" I ask, my stomach clenching. "Gay?"

He turns away from me, pushing his hips into the railing and lifting his face to the sky.

"You think I'm allowed to cry because I'm gay, but you're

not because you're straight?"

"Forget it," he says, without turning around.

"Is that really what you think?"

He groans in frustration, and I know he's upset, but there's no way I'm letting that go.

"Tell me," I press. "Is that what you think?"

"Yes," he snaps, whipping around to face me again. His eyes are bloodshot, his cheeks wet. "That's what I think. You can do whatever the hell you want, because you're already different. The rules don't apply to you. But for some of us, the rules are still rules. And for *some* of us, there are a lot of rules."

"What the hell are you talking about?"

He kicks a loose stone off the concrete ramp. "Look, we don't need to do this. This isn't your problem. I'm sorry if I offended you or whatever, but just . . . go back inside, okay?"

"It kind of *is* my problem if you're going to say shit like that. Especially after what happened at the lake."

"I said I'm sorry, all right? About all of it. Just go inside. You're gonna miss your appointment."

"And you're gonna miss yours."

"Who gives a shit."

I don't know why—because I should just go back inside—but I take a step toward him. "You're allowed to cry, Jordan. I don't care what anyone else has told you, or whatever like, *rules* you think you have to follow. You're allowed to cry."

"It's not that simple."

"It *is*. It really is. Do you know what my dad says?"

Jordan folds his arms across his chest, and I try not to notice how hot he looks right now because I'm supposed to be angry with him and he's clearly upset and the last thing I should be doing in this particular moment is checking him out.

"What does he say?"

"He says that we come into this world crying, so why should we ever stop?"

"That's super depressing, man," Jordan replies, his brow crinkling.

I can't help but chuckle. "He doesn't mean it like that. He just means, why should we ever stop ourselves from crying if that's what we feel like doing? It's totally natural. It's like, an instinct. If we feel something, we should let ourselves feel it, right? The same goes for all the good stuff, too."

Jordan stares back at me, the muscles in his jaw pulsing. I hop another step forward. I have the urge to reach out and put my hand on his shoulder, but I stop myself. For a second, he keeps glaring at me, his hazel eyes burning into mine, and then he crumbles. His perfect face cracks and he drops his head into his hands.

And he cries.

And cries.

And I just stand there, feeling strangely connected to this boy I hardly know.

Eventually, he clears his throat and looks up, wiping some snot from his nose. "Sorry."

"Don't be sorry."

"Then, I dunno," he says with a sad smile. "Thank you?"

The automatic doors *whoosh* open behind us and someone calls out my name. I turn to see Sami standing just outside the building, waving like she's trying to say, "Remember me?

The reason you're here?"

"Sorry," I say, "I'm coming! I'll meet you inside."

"Hurry up," she says in a surprisingly parental voice, before disappearing inside.

I turn back to Jordan, who's using the collar of his school shirt to wipe his cheeks. "Will you be okay?"

"Yep," he replies with a sniff. "I'm all good. You go."

There's not a single part of me that wants to go, but I say, "Okay," and force a little smile. I make my way back up the ramp to the automatic doors, and just as I'm about to walk through, I turn to say goodbye, but Jordan is already gone.

Sixteen

I SPEND THE MAJORITY of double English on Wednesday morning thinking about what could have possibly upset Jordan so much. I spend the rest of the class kicking myself for not asking. I desperately want to talk to Amina about it, but I know I can't. It just doesn't feel right. There's no way Jordan would want me telling her that he broke down in front of me—even though Amina and I clearly don't talk to anyone else at school, so it's not like word would travel very far.

"Did you hear?'" she asks in a whisper as soon as we sit down at our benches at lunchtime. "I only just found out."

"Hear what?" Those words—*Did you hear?*—were basically the start of every conversation I've ever had with Abbey. Rumors were her thing.

"TJ and Rhiannon broke up at the Boat Race after party."

"What?" I say, almost breathless. "Why?"

Amina shakes her head slowly, looking repulsed. "She cheated on him again before Boat Race."

My stomach drops and my heart leaps up into my throat in

this weird combination of shock and sadness and relief and joy and guilt, all wrapped up into one totally sickening feeling. How could I possibly be *happy* that Jordan had his heart broken?

"With who?" I ask.

"Horse."

I literally gasp. "From his rowing crew? The tall guy?"

"Yep," Amina says, giving the *p* a good pop.

Which explains why Horse wasn't with Jordan and the boys when I saw them at Boat Race, and why Jordan said there was shit going down that day, and why he didn't want to start a fight with Gibbo.

"Was it just like, a one-time thing?" I ask.

"Apparently it'd been happening for a while."

"What?"

"I know, right?" Amina scrunches up her face in disgust. "Who could *do* that to someone? How could Rhiannon go behind TJ's back like that?"

"And how could Horse lie about it to Jordan?"

"It's too awful to comprehend."

"I'm surprised it wasn't Gibbo," I add. "Seems like something he'd do."

"Yeah, but as if Rhiannon would get with *Gibbo*. Gross."

We both start to laugh, just as someone says, "Hey" from behind me. Amina freezes like she's seen a ghost. I turn to see Jordan standing there, leaning on the wall of the portable behind the bench.

A very attractive ghost, then.

"Hi," I reply. I want to swing my left leg over the bench so I can turn around properly, but I'm stuck because of my cast.

Still almost a month to go, trapped in this ridiculous thing.

Amina is still sitting there completely frozen, like one of those creepy wax figures from Madame What's-Her-Name's.

"Amina," Jordan says, and she snaps out of her daze, "do you mind if I talk to Luca for a sec?"

"Um, sure," she replies, standing up. "I was just . . . the library . . . to . . . yeah."

Jordan smiles. "Thanks."

"I'll see you in biology," Amina says to me, with a very serious and not-at-all subtle *We'll be analyzing every single word of this conversation later* look.

"See you there," I say, giving her a *You can go now* look in return.

She trots off toward the library and Jordan says, "Can I sit?"

I nod, and he steps around the bench and takes a seat beside me. And of *course* my heart starts beating a million miles a second, even though it *knows* I'm meant to be moving on.

At least I don't get hard.

"So, um," Jordan says, fiddling with his school tie. It's so weird to see him acting kind of shy. Weird but also like, totally adorable. "I just wanted to thank you again for last night."

"That's okay," I reply. "It was nothing."

"It wasn't nothing. And I'm sorry if I offended you. I didn't mean, you know, what I said about . . ."

I shrug. "I know. It's all good."

"I just thought—after what happened at Boat Race, and then *that*. I didn't want you to think I have any kind of problem with . . . Because I don't. At all."

And I'm not exactly sure why, but I really do believe him.

"It's fine," I say. "And I'm . . . um . . . sorry about Rhiannon. I only found out like, five seconds ago."

"Thanks," Jordan replies, twisting his mouth to one side. "It's . . . Well, it is what it is, you know?"

I don't know, but I nod anyway.

"Well, I'm sorry," I reply. "And I'm glad I could help. *If* I helped."

"You helped a lot." He smiles, and I practically melt right through the cracks in the bench. "I hope I can, uh, repay the favor sometime."

I scrunch my eyebrows, and he adds, "Not that I hope I *need* to, just . . . because . . . yeah, I'm gonna go now."

He stands up and runs a hand through his hair. His perfect, shiny black hair.

"I'll see you 'round?" he says, and it sounds like he actually hopes he'll see me around.

"Cool," I reply, trying to stay at least semi-chill about the whole thing.

And then he struts off toward the lockers. I stare after him, hoping with every fiber of my being that he'll glance back over his shoulder to give me one more smile, but then he disappears behind the portables and I'm left alone at the benches.

Just me and my stupid crush.

"I want you to teach me things," I say to Amina at lunch the next day, looking up at the cloudless sky. Now that it's March, the summer sting is gone from the sun. No more forty-degree days, that's for sure. Before we know it, Ballarat will be one gigantic fridge again, just like it is every winter.

"What?" she asks through a mouthful of meat pie. She's been talking about these "life-changing pies"—*Garlo's* I think she said?—for the last twenty minutes, saying how amazing it is to be able to buy halal pies at Woolies. I don't know what that means, but she seems super excited about it, so I'm guessing it's a big deal.

"I need to focus on the present."

Amina looks lost. "What are you talking about?"

"So . . ." I turn to face her and she does the same, putting her One Direction lunchbox on the bench between us. I feel like we're ten-year-old girls about to exchange friendship bracelets. "I'm going to tell you something that no one else at North knows about me, okay?"

"You don't talk to anyone else. How could they know anything about you?"

"Um, okay, *sassy*," I reply. "Where did you learn to talk like that?"

"Oh, I *wonder*," Amina giggles, slapping me gently on the arm.

"You're only meant to sass *other* people," I say, pretending to be hurt, "not me."

"Sorry."

"*Anyway*," I carry on. "Just promise you won't tell anyone, okay? Everyone already thinks I'm a freak as it is."

"Fine. I promise." There's something about the way Amina lowers her voice, and the way her expression hardens, that tells me she doesn't take promises lightly.

"I . . . used to be a ballet dancer."

Amina blinks at me, and I blink back at her, waiting for some kind of response.

"Oh," she says, "is that all?"

I scoff. "No, that's not *all*. I spent my whole life doing ballet. And I was really, *really* good. Like, not to brag or anything, but I was kind of incredible. I was going to go to the Australian Ballet School and become a professional ballet dancer."

"So why did you stop?"

"Because I fell down a flight of stairs and shattered all the bones in my foot." I lift my leg into the air beside us, pointing at my chunky white cast.

"Oh, this is recent? As in, you giving up ballet?"

"It's been just over a month." I lower my leg back onto the pavers at our feet. "And just to be clear, I didn't give up. I had no choice."

"I'm so sorry, Luca." She puts her pie down and grabs both of my hands like we're about to say grace. "Why didn't you say anything before? Are you okay?"

The way she asks reminds me of Sami.

"To be honest, it was pretty awful for a while," I reply. "I don't really know who I am without ballet." It feels so good to say it out loud to someone who isn't getting paid to help me. "But I had a massive fight with Dad on Boat Race night and we . . . well, I kind of realized that I can't keep living in the past. And as much as it kills me, I'm—" I take a deep breath, like I'm about to admit some kind of deep, dark secret "—I'm not a dancer anymore. That part of my life is gone. But that doesn't mean I can't be happy. I just don't know what else is out there that will *make* me happy."

I ignore the annoying voice in my head that starts chanting, *Jordan! Jordan will make you happy!*

"Of course you can still be happy!" Amina says.

"I know," I reply, nodding. "It's just . . . I missed out on a *lot* of things growing up. Ballet was literally my whole life. And now it's gone."

And the hole is still there. It hasn't miraculously disappeared overnight—if anything, it's bigger than ever. But I'm choosing to fill it with better things. Healthier things. I'm choosing to fill it with Amina. With school. With Dad.

"So," I say, "I want you to teach me things."

Amina's eyes light up, and I just know she's been waiting her whole life for someone to say those words to her. "Like what?"

"Well, for starters, I'd love if you could help me with my homework. Because I'm the absolute *worst* at school."

"You're not the—"

"*Secondly*," I interrupt, since I don't need her to lie to me about my terrible grades, "I want to learn to cook. I want to be able to make dinner for Dad sometimes. He does way too much for me at home."

"Oh my gosh, that is such a cute idea!" Amina claps her hands and bounces on the bench. "Do you know what, you can come over to my place and Papah can show you how to make some Indo dishes! His gado-gado is out of this world!" She stops, and her face flushes red. "I mean, if you want."

I get the idea that Amina hasn't had a friend over in a *long* time.

"Totally," I reply, "I'd love that!"

She grins, her round face glowing.

"This is probably a silly question," I say, "but what's gado-gado?"

"Oh, sorry. It's an Indonesian salad. My family is Indonesian. We do eat Aussie stuff, too," she adds, as if she feels the need to apologize. "But I love it when Papah cooks Indo food."

"Sounds delicious," I say. "I'm totally down for Indonesian."

"Okay, yay!"

"I was also wondering if you could teach me how to ride a bike?"

Amina's expressions drops. "Actually . . . I don't know how."

"What?" I ask. "I was sure I'd be the only sixteen-year-old in Ballarat who couldn't ride a bike."

"My parents couldn't afford to buy me one when I was little," Amina explains. "My tante and om got me one for my thirteenth birthday, but I never rode it. Not once. I gave my parents this silly excuse about not having time because of all my homework but, honestly, I just didn't want to draw any extra attention to myself. It was only a few months after I started wearing hijab and—" a memory flickers behind her eyes "—well . . . I'm sure you can imagine."

I don't know what to say. Amina and I have never talked about her faith or how it affects her. And it's not like I'm against it—at all—I just . . . I don't want to say the wrong thing, you know? Offend her by using the wrong term or something. I know people can be really touchy about religion, so I usually try to avoid the topic altogether. Like, I always tell Amina how cute she looks in her different-colored hijabs. But that's just like saying someone's wearing a cute hat, or a nice top, isn't it?

I dunno. I'm just so awkward with stuff like this.

Maybe this is how some people feel around me? Like there's a big gay elephant in the room and they don't want to step on its big gay toes. Or maybe *I'm* the elephant. I dunno.

Wait . . . Do elephants even *have* toes?

Seventeen

WHEN WE FINISH LAST-PERIOD psych on Monday, Amina says we should go back to hers so we can begin my "re-education," which she is taking *very* seriously. There are already flashcards and folders and flowcharts—all color coordinated, of course. It's actually perfect timing, because we have a psych SAC coming up, and I have literally no idea what a "measure of central tendency" is, let alone how to figure one out. Amina, on the other hand, remembers every single word of every textbook she's ever read. Her brain is like a giant, nerdy sponge.

My brain is *not* a sponge. Mine is a fucking colander.

But just as we're about to walk out the gate after school, her dad sends her a text. "Papah says he's having an old friend over tonight." She sighs like she's just been told the world is ending. "Which means I can't have you over."

"That's okay," I say, "I'll just come another night."

"I've been *so* looking forward to tonight, though."

"Well, why don't we go get a coffee instead?" I ask, and her face lights up. "I'll take you to my favorite cafe. We'll have to get the bus, but it's so worth it."

"Oh *yay*," Amina says, clapping her hands.

We get off the bus opposite Big W and walk around the corner onto Sturt Street. Sometimes I forget how pretty our main street is, with its big line of trees all the way down the middle. And the further you go up the hill—the closer you get to Lake Wendouree—the nicer the street gets. Way up the top is where St. Tom's and all the other private schools are, with their fancy metal gates and clock towers. It's also where all the doctors and lawyers live in their ridiculous mansions with their BMWs parked out the front. And it's not like me and Dad live in the slums, but there are certainly no sports cars parked on our street.

The second we arrive at the cafe, I realize what a horrible mistake I've made. Sitting at our usual table at the window in their green and white blazers, sipping their skim flat whites, are Talia, Grace, and Abbey. It's Monday, which means they don't have ballet today, which means after-school coffee instead.

When I see them, I try to turn around, but Amina is right behind me and it's impossible to turn around quickly on crutches, and then it's too late. Talia locks eyes with me through the glass and slaps Abbey on the arm. Abbey and Grace turn, and the three of them stare out at us on the street.

"We need to leave," I hiss at Amina, but the girls are already outside.

"Well, well, well," Talia says, her arms folded across her chest. "If it isn't our long-lost friend, Luca Mason."

Abbey raises one perfectly-penciled auburn eyebrow. Grace just stands behind them, looking down at the ground. Talia takes a step forward, her face like stone. Her hair is slicked back into a high pony. Her cat-eye eyeliner is *sharp*. She's like a Greek Ariana Grande, only twice as tall.

"So . . ." she says.

"So . . ." I reply awkwardly.

"Is there anything you want to say to us?" she asks, pouting her glossy pink lips.

"Like what?"

"Let's just go," Amina whispers from beside me, and Talia shoots her daggers.

"I dunno, Luca—" Talia cuts her eyes back to me "—maybe you'd like to tell us why you've turned into such a little bitch?"

"Oh, *I'm* the bitch?" I laugh. "Why don't you ask Abbey and Grace who the real bitch is, Talia."

"Just answer the question," she snaps. "Why are you *such* a little bitch?"

I know Grace is hating every second of this. She avoids confrontation with Talia at all costs. I try to catch her eye, but she's fidgeting with the end of her plait, staring down at the pavement.

"Okay," Talia says slowly. "Let's try another question, shall we? How was Boat Race, Luca?"

My stomach flips and I glance over at Abbey, who sneers back at me, a look of complete triumph on her face.

"I go to North now," I reply. "What was I supposed to do?"

Talia shrugs one shoulder. "Fine. Then why don't you tell us what kind of 'friend' would lie about being in too much pain to go—even though you broke your foot like, over a month ago, and we all know you couldn't possibly be in that much pain anymore—and then, on the *same day*, leave an incredibly important group chat without saying anything?"

"Oh, come *on*," I groan. "It's just a group message. It's not a big deal."

Abbey scoffs. "*Just* a group message?"

"You're right," Talia goes on, "I can totally see how it's 'not a big deal.' It's not like it's a group chat you've had with your three best friends since Grade Six or anything."

"*Ex*-best friends," Abbey says, flipping her long, red hair over her shoulder.

"Oh, grow up, Abbey," I snap. I'm not in the mood for her sass right now. And why isn't Grace saying anything?

"You may as well have slapped us all in the face, Luca," Talia shouts, and I know she's not playing. "First you ghosted us for weeks when you broke your foot. Then you told us you were leaving St. Tom's and quitting ballet in the *same message* and expected us not to be upset at all, because *you're* the only one who's allowed to be upset. Then you start giving us attitude because we still go to St. Tom's, as if we should all just leave school because you got kicked out. And you have the balls to be mad at us for still being able to dance, like it was only *you*—Mr. Fucking Favorite—who ever loved ballet in the first place. Then you ditch us at Boat Race—which has always been *our thing*, and we were nice enough to invite you even though you got kicked out of St. Tom's—and straight-up lie to our faces about it. And *then*, as if you haven't already been a big enough dick about everything, you unfollow us all on Instagram and leave our group chat like it means *nothing* to you. Well, fuck you, Luca, why don't you just—"

"Shut up!" Amina yells. "Just leave him alone, all right?"

"Oh, go back to Afghanistan where you belong," Talia snaps, and I can feel Amina freeze. Grace looks up, her eyes wide. Even Abbey looks shocked.

"What the *fuck*, Talia?" I say. "Are you fucking kidding me?" I turn to Amina, whose face is glowing red. "Come on," I say quietly to her, "let's get outta here."

We turn and start making our way up the street as fast as I can manage. After a few steps, Amina turns back and yells, "I'm not from Afghanistan, you Islamophobic cow. I'm *Indonesian!*"

I stop in my tracks, shocked by the sudden power in Amina's voice.

"Yeah," I call back to Talia, who flips her hair over her shoulder and starts to walk away, "and she's a better friend than any of you ever were!"

———

I take Amina around the corner and up a little street leading to the stage door of Her Majesty's Theatre. It's a street I've walked up god knows how many times on my way to performances and competitions and recitals, and my feet kind of just take me there. We don't say a word until I sit Amina down on the wooden bench right between the stage door and the theatre loading dock.

"I can't bel—"

But as soon as I open my mouth, Amina bursts into tears. I sit beside her, letting my crutches fall to the asphalt at our feet. I slide closer and draw her into a hug. I can't imagine what she must be feeling right now. I cannot *believe* Talia would say something like that. People don't actually *think* shit like that, do they? I know Talia can be a bitch sometimes, but *that* . . . that is just a whole other level of awful.

"Years—ago—" Amina chokes out through her sobs, "I told—myself—that I'd never—cry—in front of—people—like *that.*"

My eyes prick with tears, and I have to bite my bottom lip to stop myself from crying. It's not my place to be upset. And it's clearly not the first time someone has said something like that to Amina. I rub circles on her back and let her cry.

After a while, my phone buzzes. I pull it out of my pocket, expecting to see a message from Talia apologizing for being such a racist dick—or at the very least, a message from Grace apologizing for not telling Talia to shut the hell up—but it's Dad.

Hope ur having fun at Amina's! Let me know if u need a lift home.

We ended up going for coffee instead, I write. **Forgot to tell you!** Face-palm emoji. **Can Amina come to ours for dinner? We'll get the bus back.**

Sure! See u soon.

"Come over tonight," I say to Amina.

She sits up, wipes her cheeks, still sniffling. "Really?"

"Of course! Your dad is having his friend over, right? So, I'm sure your parents won't mind if you come chill at mine. Dad's gonna cook us dinner."

"I don't know . . ."

I'm not sure if she feels like she'd be intruding or if she really doesn't feel like coming, but I don't care. She needs company tonight. She needs a friend.

"Come *on*," I say, giving her a nudge with my shoulder.

"We can lock ourselves in my room and listen to One Direction all night."

Amina lets out a snotty giggle. "A bit of Harry Styles never goes astray."

"*See*," I laugh. "It'll be cute. And we can talk about what Talia said or we can *not* talk about what Talia said. It's totally up to you. Whatever you need. We can just put on some trashy TV and eat ten buckets of ice cream if you want. I'm up for anything and everything."

She attempts a smile. "Are you sure you don't mind hanging out with me when I'm like this?"

"What do you mean, 'when you're like this'? This is exactly when you're supposed to hang out with your friends. Besides," I add with a shrug and a smirk, "we're besties now, so you're stuck with me. Sorry."

Amina's eyes get a little watery again, and I worry I've said the wrong thing.

But then she says, "Thank you, Luca. For everything."

"You don't need to thank me."

"I do. Nobody has ever stood up for me like that before."

"I mean, I think you did a pretty good job of standing up for both of us."

"Well, thank you anyway. It means more than you could possibly know."

I smile back at her. "I know."

I always say that coming out was easy for me, and I guess it was, compared to some of the messed-up stories I've heard about other kids who've been kicked out of home and stuff like that. But if I wear a pink T-shirt to school, at least one person will call me gay to my face. And I'm *proud* to be gay, but when people use the word as an insult—even when guys say things like, *Oh man, that's so gay*—it makes me feel like shit. Because, when it comes down to it, some people still think being gay is a bad thing, or at the very least, second best to being straight.

And I know that's not the same as people saying Amina doesn't belong here just because of what she believes in—and I guess I'll never really understand what that feels like—but the point is, we both get treated like we're different. *Bad* different. And that is not okay. Because Amina is literally the nicest person I've ever met, and she deserves to be treated like nothing less than a fucking queen.

Eighteen

THE NEXT FEW WEEKS follow a predictable—but like, *nice*—pattern:

School. OT. Weekend study sessions with Amina.

Autumn in Ballarat couldn't be colder, so the girls all ditch their short summer dresses and start wearing their long woolen "kilts," throwing on knitted jumpers and scarves at lunch so they don't freeze to death outside. The boys at North apparently have some kind of unspoken code of conduct that forbids them from wearing long pants, so they all keep wearing their summer shorts. I, on the other hand, do *not* want to freeze my balls off, so I rug up in the grey North school trousers, navy knitted jumper, blazer and scarf. To be honest, though, I'm kind of glad Jordan keeps wearing his shorts, because his calf muscles look so good with his socks pulled up to his knees like that.

Not that I care what his calf muscles look like . . .

Then, all of a sudden, Term One at North is over. Which is awesome because it means no school. But it also means no OT, because Sami is going away with her girlfriend for the holidays.

Which means I won't see Jordan *at all* for two weeks.

Amina and I have actually seen him quite a bit at school since he visited our benches that first time. Nothing as *in-depth* as that, but he always says hey when we walk past him in the quad or in the canteen or wherever. I can tell his mates are like, "Why does TJ keep saying hello to those two absolute losers?" but who the hell cares? Ever since Jordan cried in front of me, I feel as if we have this weird little secret bond. Like, when he says hello, it feels like he's giving me some kind of imaginary high five. And as much as I'm still kind of in love with him—I swear I'm trying not to be, but he is just so damn beautiful in every way—it's awesome to think that we might be *mates*.

I've never had a "mate" before. Ever. Seriously. My friends have always been girls. Every single one of them.

After my last OT session, he gave me one of those "bro hugs" where you shake hands and hug each other with one arm. It's kind of more like a pat on the back than an actual hug, but I swear I was hard for like, two hours afterward.

So, yeah . . . Maybe it's a good thing that I don't see him for a while.

When I got home from the hospital after my foot surgery, I drew a big red circle around the eleventh of April on the calendar on the back of my bedroom door. Staring up at it now from under my doona, I really should be relieved. But I just feel sick.

After breakfast, Dad drives me to the hospital, where Doctor Khatri greets us warmly and says it's great to see me, even though I'm sure she doesn't mean that, since it's not like

I was a barrel of laughs the last time I saw her. She takes an X-ray of my cast to make sure the bones and plates underneath look good, then gets me to sit up on a bed with my legs stretched out in front of me. She pulls out this weird little circular saw and makes a big, long slice down the outside of my cast, all the way down to my toes, cutting right through Jordan's message. She does the same on the other side, and then—without even asking if I'm ready—pulls the top half of the cast straight off.

I literally have to bite my lip to stop myself from crying in front of everyone. My left leg is pale pink from the knee down and the hairs are weirdly dark and stuck to my skin, which looks kind of scaly and gross. It also stinks, but I guess that's probably normal, since I've been showering with a garbage bag over my leg for two months. My foot is still a bit swollen and has two long white scars running from my toes to my ankle. But the thing that shocks me the most is how *skinny* my leg is. Like, way too skinny. Doctor Khatri said my muscles might deteriorate a bit, but I had no idea how much my calf muscle would waste away in only six weeks. It's basically half the size of my right one now. It honestly looks like someone else's leg has been surgically attached to my body.

"It looks good," the doctor says, and I think she must be trying to make a joke. "The swelling in the foot should go down now that the cast has been removed. And the scars look great."

She makes me point my foot and roll my ankle, which doesn't exactly hurt, but it feels gross. Like I shouldn't be doing it, like my body doesn't want me to.

"The range of motion is much better than I expected," she says, and again, I have literally no clue what planet she's on, because my point—if you can even call it that now—has completely disappeared. I used to pride myself on having great feet. They're perfect for ballet: long and slender, with a super high arch, meaning my foot makes a beautiful curve at the end of my leg when I point my toes. The girls were always so jealous. Now, trying to point my left foot makes me want to bawl my eyes out.

I'm silent as the nurse fits my new "moon boot" to my foot. It's not one of those massive ones that goes all the way up to the knee, just a short one that stops above my ankle, almost like a snow boot. She pulls the Velcro straps and I must make a face because she says, "Too tight?" but I shake my head.

She tells me to stand up and put weight on it, but I just . . .

Doctor Khatri says, "Give it a go, Luca, it's safe. The bones have healed. The titanium plate is incredibly strong."

But I can't.

They both keep telling me to just take a step, just put my foot on the floor, just give it a go, just *do it*, but it feels wrong, and I can't, and all I want is to tell them both to fuck off and leave me alone.

"All right," Dad says, jumping out of his chair and handing me my crutches. "Let's just back off for a second, shall we? We'll give it a go later. He doesn't need to do it right this second, does he?"

Doctor Khatri clicks her tongue. "It's important that he starts putting weight on it immediately."

"I'm right here," I say, fuming. I hate it when they talk like I'm not in the room.

She turns to me. "You need to start putting weight on your foot as soon as possible or the muscles will continue to atrophy, and it will make your recovery very long and very painful.'"

I glare back at her. "Like it hasn't already been *very long* and *very painful*?"

"Yes, doctor," Dad says. "We just need a minute, okay?"

I don't know what I expected from this day, circled on my calendar for so long in thick red texta, but it certainly wasn't this.

———

Amina and I pretty much live at each other's houses over the holidays. She's still wholeheartedly dedicated to my "re-education," so we spend a lot of time getting me up to speed with psychology and biology, which are the two classes I have with her, and my worst subjects by far. And I can't believe it, but things actually start making sense.

Her house is tiny and cluttered, but it's the good kind of clutter that makes a house feel like a home. It's always warm inside, and a little dark, and smells like spices. It's the *complete* opposite to Talia's place, which is enormous and empty and cold, and everything's made of marble and steel and glass. Being there always used to make me feel bad about my own house, even though I love where I live. Plus, Talia's mum was always shouting at people on the phone or arguing with Talia, so it wasn't exactly cute vibes.

Amina's parents, on the other hand, are too adorable for words. They're both shorter than me (and I'm not tall) and literally the sweetest people on the planet. Her mamah is basically just an older version of Amina, with a gentle smile, and soft, welcoming arms. Her papah—who says I should call him "Om," which means uncle in Indonesian—teaches me how to make three different dishes, and I cook one of them for Dad at home from a recipe scribbled on a sticky note. I can't say that I *nail* it—I'm pretty sure I use double the amount of clove and half the amount of coriander I'm supposed to—but Dad tells me it's delicious anyway. I think he's just happy to see me putting my mind to something. And he adores Amina.

The one thing we can't even attempt to tick off my "to-learn" list is riding a bike, because a) neither of us owns one (her parents sold hers a couple of years ago), and b) I'm still on crutches. Against everyone's advice, I decide to keep using them until I can see Sami after the holidays. And I know I'm making things worse for myself, but I just have this awful feeling that my foot is going to shatter like glass as soon as I put weight on it. I don't know if my body is trying to tell me that there really is something wrong, or if my anxiety is just messing with me, but I flat-out refuse to walk on my left foot until Sami is there to tell me it's okay.

When we hang out at *my* place, things are a little more relaxed. Okay, a *lot* more relaxed. We study a bit, but I always make sure we balance out all the homework with a healthy dose of trash TV. One night, we're chilling on the couch after dinner—Dad's famous roast beef, which I quadruple-check is halal before I let him serve it to Amina—and I put on *The Bachelor*. As soon as I turn it on, Amina gets weirdly stressed and pretends she thinks it's ridiculous, but then halfway through she starts saying things like, "Why would he take Lisa on a date when he *clearly* has a real connection with Jodie," so I figure she's enjoying it.

"Have you never seen *The Bachelor*?" I ask, muting the TV in the ad break.

"No, of course not," she replies, as if I asked her if she regularly deals marijuana to kindergarteners.

I laugh. "Really? You're lying."

"I'm not," she says, her eyes wide. "Papah would never let me watch something like this."

"Why not?'

"He says reality TV is a complete waste of time."

"Well, I think 'complete waste' might be a bit dramatic."

"He says that if I want to get into medicine, I can't waste a single second on 'mind-numbing television.'"

"Wait, you want to be a doctor?" I ask. "How did I not know that? I mean, I'm not surprised, it's just . . . you've never mentioned it."

Amina sighs, her shoulders slumping. "That's because I don't."

"Don't want to be a doctor?"

"Precisely."

"Why not? You're like, the smartest person on the planet."

Another sigh. "I know I'm smart enough, and I'd probably be great at it, but there is no part of me that wants to be a doctor. That's just *not* what I want to do for the rest of my life."

"What *do* you wanna do?"

"Well," she says, lowering her voice, "I'm doing all of the prerequisites for medicine—because Papah said it was non-negotiable—but honestly, all I've ever wanted is to be a teacher."

"Oh my god, are you serious?" I reply. "Amina, you'd be an amazing teacher. A million times better than Mr. Jones, that's for sure."

Her cheeks flush. "Thank you."

"My dad's a teacher. You know that, right? You should totally talk to him about it."

"That would be lovely," Amina says with a sad smile. "But if Papah found out, he would be so disappointed in me. He keeps telling me how much he wishes he was blessed with a brain like mine so he could have provided more for his family. He says I have a gift, and that it would be disrespectful if I didn't use it."

"Disrespectful to your papah?"

"Yes, but also to myself. To my family. To Allah."

"Oh," I say. "Right."

I'm not quite sure what to say, because the thing is, I don't believe in God. And I did a bunch of research the other day—when I realized I knew as much about Islam as Talia does, which is *so* not okay—and I'm pretty sure I don't believe in Allah, either. But then it's weird, because Dad always talks about "the Universe," and "putting things out there," and how some things are "meant to be," and I find that easy to get on board with. Maybe because it sounds . . . I dunno . . . *nice?* But then I'm like, is Dad just using different words to talk about the exact same thing?

Who knows. I really do want to believe in something. I'm just not sure what that *something* is yet.

Eventually, I say, "But wouldn't your family want you to be happy? Wouldn't Allah want you to be happy? Wouldn't everyone want you to do whatever it is in life that *you* want to do?"

"Not according to Papah," Amina replies.

"Okay, so your only option is to spend ten years studying medicine, rack up a million-dollar HECS debt, and slave away in a career you never even wanted for the rest of your entire life?"

Amina sighs again, nodding slowly. "Yes, I'd say that's fairly accurate."

"Right," I say, and she turns back to the TV.

I let myself sink into the couch, weighed down by my thoughts. Because the whole thing just doesn't seem fair. I mean, *my* dream was ripped away from me because of a freak accident, and at the same time, Amina's papah expects her to just throw hers away as if it counts for nothing?

I dunno. I might be missing something, but it just doesn't make sense.

Nineteen

MY FIRST DAY BACK at North is predictably normal. I'm obviously *dying* to see Jordan—I know I said it was a good idea if I didn't see him for two weeks, but it was literally torture—but the only time I get to see him is during senior school assembly in the morning. And by "see him" I mean he gives a speech about what's coming up on the sporting calendar this term, and I bat my eyelids among the sea of students freezing their asses off in the gym.

After school, I get the bus to the OT for my usual Tuesday session with Sami, expecting to see Jordan waiting for me in our usual seats when I arrive, but he's not there. My stomach drops. And now I just feel sick, because I know what I'm going to have to do in that treatment room with Sami and I do *not* want to do it.

"Luca!" she calls out from her door. She's wearing her little rainbow earrings and smiling so wide that I suddenly forget what I was scared about. "It's so good to see—" she starts, but her expression drops when I grab my crutches and stand up.

"What are you . . .?" She knits her brow as I make my way over to the treatment room. She lets me pass without saying a word, but then shuts the door and folds her arms across her chest.

I sit down and stare up at her.

"Well?" she says.

"Well what?"

She raises her eyebrows, and this is not the face of someone you want to mess with. "*Well*, why on earth are you still on crutches? Didn't you get your cast off on the eleventh?"

I shrink down into my seat. "Yeah."

"Luca, that's almost *two weeks* ago. You need to use your foot again or—"

"The muscles will atrophy and the scar tissue will harden. I *know*."

"Then please tell me there's some kind of medical explanation for this?"

I swallow hard.

"Luca," Sami says, gentler now, "what's holding you back?"

"I'm scared."

"Of course you are, but—"

"No, Sami. Like, *really* scared. So scared that I can't actually make myself put weight on my foot, no matter how hard I try."

She walks to her desk and sits down, resting her hands on my leg. "Luca, your foot has healed. The bones would have been fully repaired weeks ago. You've got a titanium plate stabilizing your arch and screws holding everything in place. You wouldn't be able to damage your foot now if you tried."

"I know, but . . ." I look down at my moon boot.

"But what?"

"I don't know."

Sami slaps herself on the thighs and jumps out of her chair. "Come on. Stand up."

I go to grab my crutches, but she picks them up and moves them out of reach. "No crutches."

I groan in reply.

"Come *on*, Luca. You trust me, don't you?"

I roll my eyes and carefully push myself up out of my chair, balancing on my right foot. Sami grabs me by the hands and smiles encouragingly.

"Now," she says, "slowly put your left foot on the floor. Just lightly touch it down. Don't even put any weight on it."

I do what she says, lowering my moon boot to the carpet.

"Good, Luca! Good! Now, transfer your weight to the center. Let it settle evenly between both feet. Slowly."

I rock slightly to the side and let my left foot take half my weight. The hard plastic of the boot keeps my ankle in place, but the pressure increases on the sole of my foot. It feels totally weird. Kind of like the joints need to crack, but they can't because they're screwed in place.

Sami's face lights up. "Yes! Wonderful! Now lift your right foot off the floor."

"What?"

"It's okay," she says. "You got this. One leg. Let's go."

My heart is suddenly pounding in my chest, as if I'm about to step onto the stage in front of two thousand people. I take a deep breath and slowly lift my right foot away from the carpet, expecting my leg to collapse underneath the full weight of my body.

But it doesn't. And suddenly, I'm balancing on my left leg. And my foot doesn't shatter into a million pieces.

"Yay!" Sami claps her hands once. "Let's go for a walk."

"What?"

She chuckles. "In here, I mean. Not around the lake."

I hum an *I don't think so* in reply.

"You'll be fine, Luca, don't stress. Just walk from here to the wall and back. And try to walk normally, don't be too cautious. Let the boot do its job."

I want to say, *You'd be cautious too if you'd been through what I've been through,* but Sami is a goddess and I could never sass her like that.

"You got this," she says again.

"I got this."

I bite my lip and take a step on my good foot.

"And . . ." Sami nods gently, her little rainbows dancing.

And I take another step on my left. And another on my right. I walk all the way to the wall, slowly turn myself around, and walk back to the chair.

Sami smiles her Colgate smile and claps her hands. Like, she actually applauds me. "Yay, Luca! You did it! That was so *good.*"

Memories of Miss Gwen suddenly fill my mind. Sitting there in her white plastic chair down the front of the ballet studio, barking corrections at us. *"Better,"* she'd say. Never "good." I worked so hard, day in, day out, year after year, to get her to tell me I was good, to give me *one* compliment, and she never, ever did. I was brilliant. I could do things that literally no one else my age could do. Jumps, turns, lifts, beats, *everything.* But it was never "good." And now all I have to do is walk across the room and I get applauded. Like it's some kind of achievement. I just . . .

And I burst into tears. *Ugly* tears. I mean, I'm full-on sobbing out loud.

"Oh my goodness," Sami says, putting a warm hand on my shoulder. "Luca, what's wrong?"

But I have to get out of here. Without even thinking, I leave my crutches on the treatment room floor and walk out into the waiting room. I have a little limp because of the way the boot doesn't let my ankle bend, but I can actually walk pretty fast. And of *course* Jordan is there now, sitting in his usual seat. He frowns up at me as I walk past, but I keep going. I need air. Now. I head over to the metal railing at the edge of the ramp and lean against it for support. The cold air feels good as it fills my lungs.

"Luca," Jordan calls out from behind me.

It seems history has decided to repeat itself in reverse. And I feel like a total hypocrite, because after telling Jordan he was allowed to cry in this exact spot, I desperately want to disappear into thin air right now.

But before I know it, he's standing right behind me. He puts his hand on my shoulder, and it sends a chill down my spine. I let my head drop to my chest and cry even harder.

"Hey, it's okay, mate," he says gently.

I slowly turn around and notice Sami standing at the door. But as soon as I see her, she heads back inside the building.

My eyes flick up to meet Jordan's. He stares back at me, his face filled with warmth and concern, like he actually cares that I'm upset. Fresh sobs burst out from somewhere deep inside me and my body crumples in half.

"It's okay," he says again, catching me by the arms and holding me up. "It's okay."

I didn't realize I'd been bottling up so much emotion until right this second. It wasn't like I was forcing myself not to feel. I honestly thought I'd already cried enough. I thought I was done grieving the part of me that I lost forever.

Apparently I was wrong.

"Luca?" someone else calls out, and I look up to see Dad jogging across the car park toward us.

Jordan lets go straightaway, running a hand through his hair, looking down at his feet.

I wipe my cheeks and blink the tears from my eyes.

"Lu, are you okay?" Dad asks when he gets to the ramp, looking worried. "Did you hurt yourself?"

"No," I say. "I'm fine. I just . . . I'm okay, Dad."

Dad glares at Jordan like it's his fault I'm crying.

"Dad, this is Jordan," I say. "He's in Year Twelve at North. We're . . . OT buddies."

"Nice to meet you, Mr. Mason," Jordan says, holding out his hand.

Dad shakes it, looking him up and down. "Robert is fine," he says. "Only my students call me Mr. Mason."

"Cool," Jordan replies. "Nice to meet you, Robert."

"Let's go, Lu," Dad says, already heading off toward the car.

"Sorry," I say to Jordan, "I'll see you at school."

"Are you okay, though?"

"I'll be fine."

"Do you want me to come with you?"

I stare back at Jordan, waiting for him to crack up laughing and tell me he's kidding. But he kind of just stands there, and I swear he blushes a little bit.

"Wait, are you serious?" I ask.

"It's cool if you want to be alone," he replies. "I just thought you might need a mate right now."

And there's that word again. "Mate." Having never *had* a mate, I have no concept of what mates do for each other when they're upset—and to be completely honest, whenever I imagine it, it's basically pornographic—but it's Jordan, so it's not like I'm going to say no.

"Sure," I reply, and we walk over to Dad's car together. I jump in the front, which is so much easier without my crutches. Now that I think about it, I probably should go back to get them from Sami's office and apologize for running out like that, but it's too late now. Jordan's already in the car.

"Jordan's going to come back to our place for a bit," I say to Dad, trying to tell him with my eyes that he is not to say a single word about me finally bringing a boy home.

"No worries," Dad replies with a smirk as he starts the car. I roll my eyes and look out the passenger window.

And suddenly I'm driving home with Jordan Tanaka-Jones sitting in the back seat making small talk with Dad. Which is literally the last thing I ever thought would happen. Like, *ever*.

Twenty

DO YOU KNOW WHAT'S really weird? Sitting on the couch with Jordan Tanaka-Jones. In *my* lounge room. In *my* house. Drinking juice from *my* fridge out of *my* glasses. Having him in my space feels weirdly intimate. It feels like we're proper friends, which, I dunno, maybe we are. We've both cried in front of each other now, so I guess that counts for something.

"You wanna talk about it?" he asks, leaning forward to put his glass on the coffee table. "Sorry, where are your coasters?"

"What?"

"For this." He holds up his orange juice.

"Oh," I reply, "no, it's cool. We don't have any coasters."

"Lucky you. My parents would *kill* me if I didn't use a coaster."

"Really?"

"Hundred percent," he laughs. "It's not like we have expensive stuff or antique furniture or anything, they're just weirdly full-on about coasters."

I smile. "Are you just making stuff up to make me feel better?"

"No, I'm serious." His eyes are wide. "They've been known to ground me for *days* for not using a coaster."

"Wow."

"This house is like a fantasy land to me. No coasters. Holy shit."

I laugh, and he laughs, and then we're laughing together. This is *everything*.

"So . . ." Jordan says, drawing out the *oh* sound. "*Do* you need to talk about it?"

"Why do you care?" I ask, before I realize how rude I sound. "I mean," I add quickly, "why do you want to help me?"

"I said I wanted to repay the favor, didn't I?"

"People say stuff like that all the time, but they don't actually mean it."

"I meant it," Jordan says, his eyes locked on mine.

We're silent for a second that feels like a literal decade, and I can feel blood rushing to my face and my crotch. I have a mortifying flashback to when I first met Jordan at the OT, when I couldn't string a sentence together if my life depended on it.

"Only if you want to," he says, suddenly breaking the silence. His voice shocks me so much that I flinch, because I'm the most awkward human on the planet.

I look down at my feet, one in a black school shoe and the other in my chunky black moon boot. "Okay. But it won't really make sense, because you only met me *after* I broke my foot."

"What do you mean? What happened *before* you broke your foot?"

I glance up at the TV and an idea pops into my head. "Hang on . . ."

I get up and walk—it still feels so weird to be able to do that without crutches—out the side door into the garage. I grab the old cardboard box and bring it back into the lounge, plonking it down beside the TV cabinet. I pull out the USB, grab my laptop from the coffee table and sit back down next to Jordan.

"What's this?" he asks.

"You'll see."

I plug in the USB and open the video from last year's recital. It loads exactly where I stopped watching it last time, right in the middle of my solo.

I click play. And there I am, soaring around the stage in my white tights and brocade jacket.

I just sit there, waiting for Jordan to react. After a long moment, he leans in closer, squinting.

"Wait . . . is that—" he looks up at me, back down to the screen, and up at me again "—is that *you?*"

I nod, pressing my lips into a thin line.

"Holy shit."

"I know, right?"

"Mate," he breathes, turning back to watch the video, "you are . . . incredible."

"*Was.*" I hit pause and shut my laptop.

"What?"

"I'm never going to do that again."

Jordan turns on the couch to face me. "Because of your injury?"

I nod again.

"You're not gonna recover?"

"Not enough to do that."

"Did you just find that out today? Is that why you're upset?"

"No," I say with a dry laugh. "I found out before I had surgery, like, two months ago."

"I'm so sorry, mate."

I just shrug.

"So then, what was today about?"

I think back to when I watched Doctor Khatri saw my cast off. The way my leg looked. The weird musty smell. The wrongness of rolling my ankle and trying to point my foot.

"I think there was this tiny part of me that was still hoping for a miracle," I say. "As if the doctor was going to take off my cast and my foot would be perfectly healed and my leg would be strong and everything would just go back to normal. Like a butterfly coming out of a cocoon or something."

Jordan nods slowly.

"But when she took my cast off and I saw how much my leg and foot had wasted away, I realized—once and for all—that I really am done with dancing. It's over. I felt like I'd been punched in the stomach."

"Shit."

"But I guess I just, like, pushed all the emotion back down, because I'm sick of feeling so angry and pathetic all the time. It's *so* not who I am. But then when I saw Sami today, and she literally applauded me for being able to walk across the room, I just lost it. I mean, I'm used to being applauded for doing *that*." I point down at my laptop. "It just made me feel . . ." I look up at the ceiling, studying the grain in the wooden beams. "I dunno. It finally hit me that I'm a completely different person now."

Jordan reaches up and wraps one hand around the back of

his neck, kind of shaking his head and staring across the room. "Dude. I don't even know what to say. I'm so sorry."

"Thanks."

He smiles kind of sadly, his hazel eyes twinkling, and then glances down at his watch. "Sorry, man, but I probably should get home."

"I'll get Dad to take you," I say, wishing I'd already invited Jordan to stay for dinner.

He stands up. "Nah, it's all good, I'll just get the bus. I don't want to be a hassle."

"Oh, okay." I stand too, but I don't know if I should like, shake his hand or go in for a hug or do nothing at all.

But then he pulls his phone out of his pocket. "Here," he says, handing it to me. "Put your number in here, and I'll message you, so you've got mine. Just in case you ever need to chat or whatever."

My stomach swoops and my heart starts to punch the inside of my ribs, but I have to pretend to be one hundred percent *not* dying while Jordan is still standing in my lounge room.

"Sure," I say, as I type in my name and number. I hand the phone back to him and he taps the screen a couple of times, then shoves it in his pocket. "Thanks for this afternoon," I add. "It . . . it really helped."

"Anytime, man." He smiles, then leans in to hug me. And not a pat-on-the-back "bro hug" like the first time, I mean an actual hug. He doesn't even do that thing straight guys do when they're forced to hug you, where they keep their hips way back, so their junk doesn't come anywhere near yours. It's a real hug.

I breathe in, trying not to notice that he smells like shampoo and deodorant and *boy*. Then I realize I'm practically *sniffing* him and pull away.

"I'll text you so you've got my number," he says, heading for the door. "See you at school."

And then he's gone.

Two minutes later, my phone pings and I open the message from an unknown number.

Hey man. Jordan here. Have a good night.

I start typing a reply, but then three little dots appear beneath his message, so I backspace and wait . . .

I don't know how long I'm standing there waiting, staring at those three little dots. But then another message finally pops up and I honestly almost pass out.

You look good in tights btw.

Twenty-One

WHEN THE MAGPIES WAKE me up on cue at 6:00 a.m., I am one hundred percent certain the whole thing was a dream. There is no way the sexy, *straight*, perfect-in-every-way school captain of Ballarat North Secondary College sent me a flirty message last night.

There's just no way.

But when I roll over and grab my phone, there it is, staring straight back at me:

You look good in tights btw.

My stomach clenches, my heart flutters, and something stirs in my boxers, all at once. I stare down at Jordan's message for a full minute, then rub the sleep out of my eyes, still expecting the text to just disappear. But when it doesn't, I climb out of bed, head down the hall to the bathroom and jump in the shower.

By the time I make it downstairs for breakfast—after spending a possibly suspicious amount of time in the bathroom—Dad's already at the table. "That Jordan seems like a nice boy," he says through a mouthful of cereal, eyes flicking up from his newspaper.

I sit opposite him and fill a bowl with Just Right. "Yeah. He's cool."

Dad raises his eyebrows in the most annoying Dad way possible.

"What?" I ask, knowing exactly what he is implying. "Dad. No. Jordan is *straight*. He's the captain of the North rowing squad *and* football team."

"So?" he shrugs. "Rowers and footy players can be gay too."

"Yes, I'm aware of that, thank you, Mr. Gay Rights Activist of the Year. But Jordan is not. He's straight."

"And you two aren't . . .?"

"No."

"And you don't think—"

"*No.*"

But really, I have no idea what to think. I have no idea what Jordan and I are, or if we actually *are* anything at all.

"Well, when you do find yourself a nice boy who's into boys, he'll be more than welcome to come over whenever he likes." Dad pauses, then adds, "There are some condoms in the bath—"

"*Dad.* Oh my god."

"I'm just letting you know. Just in case."

"We're eating, can you not?"

Dad laughs. "Oh, come on, don't be such a prude, Lu."

"This conversation is *so* over, Dad."

"Fine," he says, still chuckling. "Hurry up and finish your cereal. We're gonna be late for school."

The prehistoric projector hums loudly beside me up the back of the class. While *Cabaret* plays on the whiteboard, I stare down at my phone under the table. I don't need to hide it, since my English teacher, Mrs. Moore, couldn't care less if we're on our phones during class—I'm pretty sure she's completely given up on our entire generation—but I don't want to risk anyone seeing Jordan's message.

As soon as I open our chat, I feel like everyone in the classroom is staring at me. My ears burn and I look up to see them all either asleep, on their phones, or doodling mindlessly in their exercise books. Just to be safe, I click into Jordan's contact and change his name to The Boy in the Waiting Room. The last thing I want is someone nicking my phone, seeing Jordan's messages, and getting all up in our business. New relationships are fragile. Not that it's a relationship. And not that I have a clue what I'm talking about.

I open up the messages from The Boy in the Waiting Room.

Hey man. Jordan here. Have a good night.

You look good in tights btw.

I delete the first message to erase all traces of his identity—just in case—and stare down at the second. It's only six words—if you count "btw" as a word, which surely the dictionary does by now—but I can't explain how those six words make me feel. For one, horny, but that's become my default setting ever since I met Jordan, so that doesn't count. Secondly, kind of ill. The message makes me feel stressed and excited and ecstatic and anxious and worried and proud and insecure and too many things to process all at once. I've had butterflies in my stomach before, and that's kind of a cute feeling, but this is not that. This is more like a swarm of giant blood-sucking bats flapping around in my guts.

Let's face it, my crush on Jordan has always been pretty overwhelming. From the second he walked into that waiting room at the OT in his sexy black exercise gear, I've been obsessed. But back then, being with him was not an actual possibility, so my feelings didn't really matter. I've had that kind of crush before. And it hurts a bit when you realize someone will never like you back, but this is so much worse than that. Because what if Jordan actually *does* like me back, and it doesn't work out? I have a very high pain threshold—all dancers do—but I'm not sure if I could recover from that. A shattered foot is one thing, but a broken heart? No, thanks, Universe.

But the most frustrating thing (and I think the main cause of the flapping, blood-sucking bats), is that I don't know for sure if Jordan likes me. You know, *likes* me, likes me.

What if his message was just another joke between mates? Like when he wrote on my cast? I honestly don't know what the rules are. Is flirting with your mates a thing? In a joking way? I don't have a clue.

Every time I go to reply to Jordan's message, my palms start sweating and I feel like I'm going to vomit. Because what if I write something cute back and then he tells me to piss off, he's not gay, that I'm disgusting, and how dare I hit on him? And I can't blow the message off as a joke in case he really *does* like me, because that will break his heart and he'll never speak to me again and there goes my one chance of being with the most perfect guy I'll probably ever meet.

Luckily, I haven't seen Jordan at school this morning—I don't usually see him anywhere until lunchtime—but what am I supposed to say when I do? "Hi, Jordan. Let me just ask, do you think I look good in tights in a friendly 'I wear tights to football training and you wear tights to ballet, so let's bond over the fact that we both wear tights' way, or is it more of a 'Damn, you look good in tights, please come over to my place so we can get naked in my bedroom while my parents are watching *The Block*' kind of thing?"

Because those two things are *very* different.

You look good in tights btw.

Six words.

But you can see why I feel like I'm going to throw up, right?

"I'm so stressed," Amina says as soon as we make it to our bench at the edge of the quad.

It's a lovely day today. Still freezing, obviously—because Ballarat—but the sun is out, and the sky is the exact same blue as Amina's hijab. It wouldn't surprise me if she wore it on purpose. The girl loves to color coordinate.

"And *why* are you so stressed?" I ask, sitting and unwrapping my boring ham sandwich, wanting desperately to pull my phone out of my pocket and show Amina Jordan's message.

She stares back at me like she's waiting for me to catch on to something incredibly obvious. When I don't reply, she scoffs and says, "Our mid-year exams are only *eight weeks away*." She says it like there's going to be a zombie invasion while we're sitting our exams in the gym. "Eight. *Weeks*," she adds for emphasis.

"Do Year Eleven mid-year exams even count toward anything?" I ask.

Amina glares at me harder than should be humanly possible. "Everything *counts*, Luca."

"Really? How? The marks don't actually count for anything."

"I have two Year Twelve exams, which *definitely* count for something." Her eyes are wide and her voice is weirdly high pitched. "But that's beside the point. We need to know what we've *learned*."

"You're kind of scaring me," I say, edging back on the bench.

"Shut up." She slaps me on the leg. "This is *important*."

"Look—out of everyone in the year, you of all people have literally nothing to worry about. You'd memorized the textbooks before we even started school."

"Be that as it may," Amina says, eyes popping out of her cute round face, "I have some stiff competition. Bree and Alicia are incredibly hard workers, and I need to ace the mid-years to put me at the front of the pack for Dux of Year Eleven."

"What does that even mean?"

Amina groans. "How do you not know this? The Year Eleven with the highest marks is awarded the title of Dux and a cash prize, donated by the Parents Committee."

"Ooh, how much?"

"Not a lot," Amina says, "but much more importantly, the Dux of Year Eleven gets to make a speech at the Year Twelve farewell assembly at the end of the year."

I wrinkle my nose. "Who'd want to make a speech at assembly?"

It's very clear from the way Amina's eyes go kind of shiny that *she* wants to make a speech at assembly. Desperately.

"That speech is an opportunity to speak your mind in front of the whole school," she says. "Not only to congratulate the Year Twelves and wish them well for their futures, but to inspire the rest of the school to do their best in the coming year."

I know I shouldn't, but I can't help but laugh.

"What?" Amina snaps, putting down her Tupperware container and folding her arms.

"Sorry," I say, "but you know we don't go to like, Harvard, right? This is *North*. You think any of these dickheads are going to be inspired by a *speech*? You think they actually *care* about school?'

"They're not all di—" Amina cuts herself off "—bad kids. A great deal of them are lovely people who are here to learn. Don't be such a St. Tom's snob. Just because North doesn't have a science wing that looks like NASA Mission Control doesn't mean the students can't achieve great things."

And suddenly I feel awful. "Sorry. That was . . . Sorry.

"I'll never forget sitting in the gym for my first Year Twelve farewell assembly," she says. "I was so inspired by what Sarah Peters said."

"How do you remember her *full name*?"

"I know it sounds silly," Amina goes on, "but her speech set me up for my time here at North. I think about what she said almost every day."

"Must have been a hell of a speech."

"And do you know what else?" she says. "I would be the first Muslim Dux of Year Eleven in North history. Do you have any idea what that means? How important that is to me? How proud my parents would be? I'd give *anything* to make that speech. I already know exactly what I would say. I've been planning it since Year Seven."

"You're—"

"Don't tell me I'm a nerd," Amina says, looking down at her lap. "I *know* I'm a nerd."

I smile. "I wasn't going to call you a nerd. You're . . . kind of awesome."

She looks up.

"And hey," I go on, "maybe if someone like you had given a killer speech at an assembly when *I* was in Year Seven, my life at school would have been very different."

Amina opens her mouth to speak, but no words come out. She doesn't deal well with compliments.

"*Anyway,*" I say, saving her from her own awkwardness, "you have nothing to stress about. I know you could take Alicia and Bree in a fight if you had to."

"It's not a fight. But thank you."

"I got your back, don't worry. My foot is made of metal now. Imagine a kick in the shin with that."

Amina's eyes flick up to the side, and I turn to see what's caught her attention.

I shiver runs up my spine. Jordan is about to walk past on his way to the quad. I breathe deeply, trying to think of something to say. Something casual. Something cool. Something flirty but not obvious. Something—

"Hey," he says, with a slight upward nod.

"Hi," I reply, trying not to pass out.

And he keeps on walking, all the way down the path to the middle of the quad.

My stomach sinks and I feel like the world is closing in on me. He just showed literally no sign of having sent me that message last night. No awkwardness, no smile, no stopping to chat, no fumbling his words. None of the usual signs of having a crush on someone. Nothing at all.

I desperately want to pull out my phone to triple-check that his message is still there, but I don't want Amina to get suspicious. She's way too smart for her own good.

"I gotta go pee," I say, jumping up from the bench.

Before she can reply, I'm already halfway down the path leading away from the quad, racing past the Year Seven lockers to the bathrooms near the tech wing. I shut myself in a cubicle, flip the toilet lid down, sit, and open my messages. And there it is, from The Boy in the Waiting Room:

You look good in tights btw.

I let out a long breath.

I didn't make it up.

Then it dawns on me: I never wrote back. Jordan sent me that message like, eighteen hours ago and I *still* haven't replied. Which is obviously why he just acted like the whole thing never happened. Here's me, trying to find the hidden meaning in a six-word text message, *meanwhile*, Jordan's probably thinking he made a huge mistake sending the message in the first place. He probably thinks I was so freaked out by it that I don't want anything to do with him anymore.

I need to reply. ASAP. I hold my thumbs over the keypad, trying to think of something to write. Whatever it is, it needs to make it clear that I'm interested, but not desperate.

I write: **Are boys in tights your thing?** and backspace immediately.

You should see me OUT of them. Ugh, no. Backspace.

You look good in everything. I cannot backspace that one hard enough.

And before I get a chance to write anything even more pathetic, three dots appear on the left. Jordan is typing.

Shit.

Jordan: **Was it just me or did you blush when I walked past?**

Shit, shit, shit.

What do I write?

Eventually, the only thing I can come up with is: **Am I that obvious?**

Don't worry, he replies. **Pretty sure I was blushing too. I'm glad we have that effect on each other.** Smirking emoji.

Oh my god. He's *glad*. And I'm glad he's glad. Really glad. But I can't say that. What the hell do I write back?

HELP ME, SOMEBODY! PLEASE!

But then, another message from Jordan: **Hey, I'm sure it's obvious, but keep this totally between us, yeah?**

Keep what between us? I write. Shrugging emoji. Smirking emoji.

Haha. Nice one. Have a good day.

You too.

Sitting there in the cubicle, surrounded by swear words written on the walls in permanent marker, a bubble of happiness fills my chest. I feel like I might float straight up to the roof and out the door.

Jordan is glad that I like him.

Glad.

And I know I usually read into things way too much, and I really don't want to jinx this, but I'm pretty sure that can only mean one thing:

He likes me back.

Twenty-Two

SCHOOL SUDDENLY BECOMES MORE bearable than ever—like, almost enjoyable. The weeks start flying by in a way time has *never* moved for me at school. I put this down to three reasons:

Reason #1: Amina and her endless cuteness (which is nothing new, but still needs to be pointed out).

Reason #2: Thanks to Reason #1, I kind of know what I'm doing in most of my classes now. Which is awesome, because it's nice not to feel so confused all the time.

Reason #3: Jordan likes me.

Obviously, having friends and doing well in class are both incredibly important, but Reason #3 takes the cake, I have to say. And it makes me think that maybe this was all meant to be, in some completely messed-up way. Because here's the thing: I would never have met Jordan if I didn't get kicked out of St. Tom's. And I would never have gotten kicked out of St. Tom's if I hadn't broken my foot. I mean, Dad always says everything happens for a reason, so in this completely ridiculous case . . . would it be insane for me to think that maybe—just *maybe*—Jordan is the reason?

Sometimes, if the timing works out, he'll visit me and Amina at lunch. He doesn't like, *sit* with us or anything, but he'll stop at our benches for a cute chat when him and his mates pass by on their way to the quad. The boys always seem super confused by it—which is probably why he never stays too long—but I'm sure everyone just thinks he's doing his school captain-ly duties or something. No one knows about his messages . . .

Most of Jordan's texts are just small talk. Things like **How was your weekend?** or **What's for lunch today? (Leftover pasta for me. AGAIN).**

But sometimes it's a little bit . . . more.

Like a couple of nights ago: **At the gym, picturing you in those tights.**

I had to hide my phone under the table at dinner so I could reply: **Oh? And** . . . Smirking emoji.

Good thing I wasn't wearing tights myself. Monkey covering its eyes emoji.

You don't have to be a genius to know that *that* is flirting. I mean, that's practically *sexting*. Not that I've ever sexted anyone before, but I'm pretty sure it starts like that.

But then sometimes I'll message *him*, and he won't reply. Then twenty-four hours will pass by with zero contact, and then he'll send me a flirty text as if he didn't just ignore me for a whole day. And I'm like, *How am I supposed to interpret that?*

Luckily, Amina doesn't seem to notice that I've started spending a *lot* more time on my phone. She's so hell-bent on nailing her mid-year exams that she's swapped eating for studying. I sit there with her at lunchtime, staring down at the quad to catch a few glimpses of Jordan mucking around with the boys while Amina buries her nose in her textbooks and marks her own practice exams.

After a whole week of this, I say to her, "Firstly, I just want to check that you know I still exist. Because I do. Exist. And I'm bored."

She looks up from her exercise book, her brow creased, a pencil in her mouth, and a red pen in her hand.

"And secondly," I say, before she can answer, "aren't you starving? You haven't eaten lunch all week."

"Iss yamanan," she says through the pencil.

"What?"

She takes it out and says, "It's Ramadan."

I pause for a long moment, trying to remember what I read online about Ramadan. Eventually—when all I can remember is that it's definitely something I *should* remember—I say, "And . . . remind me what that is, exactly?"

Amina shuts her book and sits up a little straighter. "Ramadan. Our holy month on the Islamic calendar."

"Oh, of *course*," I reply, internally face-palming myself. "And it's kind of like Lent, right?"

I've never done Lent, but Grace always used to stop eating meat for a month, and Talia pretended to stop eating chocolate.

"Well, *kind* of," Amina says, "but not really. We fast from sunrise to sunset every day, but we—'

"Every *day*? For a month?"

"Yes, but it's not just that. Ramadan is a lot of things. It's about prayer and family and charity and togetherness. It's my favorite time of year by far."

"Even though you only get to eat at night? I don't think I could do it. I think I'd faint."

"You'd be fine," Amina says, and even though she's smiling, she doesn't exactly sound happy.

"Sorry," I say, in case I've offended her.

She shakes her head. "It's okay. It's just that whenever I talk to anyone about Ramadan, all they can see is the fasting. It's the most important time of year for almost two *billion* Muslims all around the world, and the only question people ever have is whether or not we get hungry." She lets out a sigh. "I'm sorry, it's just frustrating. My faith means more to me than a few skipped meals, you know?"

"I'm sorry," I say. "I didn't mean—"

"I know."

"What's your favorite part?" I ask, to try to make up for being such an ignorant jerk. "Of Ramadan?"

"Well . . ." She smiles, and I can feel one of her mono-logues coming on. "At the end of the month we have our Eid feast, which is my parents' favorite thing in the world. Mamah decorates every inch of the house, and Papah cooks so much food that you'd think he's feeding the whole Muslim population of Australia." She laughs, her eyes twinkling. She adores her parents. "My cousins and aunties and uncles come up from Melbourne and Adelaide and cram into our little house for two days. It's wild and loud and overwhelming, but it's just so, so wonderful."

I gaze off into the distance past the portable beside us. I never see my relatives. My dad's side all live in Brisbane, and they talk about Ballarat like it's Antarctica, so they never visit, and we haven't been able to afford a big holiday to Queensland for a long time. Mum's side live in Melbourne, but they haven't really been around since Mum died. Maybe it makes them too sad to see me.

It's kind of always just been me and Dad. And the Bunheads. Which was always more than enough. And I may not have the Bunheads anymore, but I guess I have Amina now. And Jordan.

But then, *do* I have Jordan? I mean, maybe? How am I ever supposed to figure out if that's actually a thing or not? Like, I want to be positive about it. I want to believe that I'll finally have a boyfriend in the kind-of-near future. But I also don't want to get my hopes up, because I don't want to set myself up for heartbreak (which sounds exactly like the sort of thing I would do).

But, honestly, who the hell am I kidding? My hopes are already up so high I'd need to hijack a hot air balloon to bring them back down to earth.

"You're moving really well," Sami says to me.

It's my fourth session since I had my cast off. I'm only seeing her once a fortnight now, and Jordan has stopped seeing his OT completely. Apparently, his shoulder is feeling great at the moment. Which would have been devastating before—for me, I mean—because it would have meant I'd never get to talk to him. But now I have his phone number . . .

"I've been walking from my bedroom to the bathroom and back without the boot," I tell Sami. "It feels great."

"Great" *obviously* *means* *"reasonably* *normal,"* *not* *"I could do a variation from* The Nutcracker.*"*

"Awesome," she replies with a smile and a little nod. She turns to type some notes on her computer. "And when did the doctor say you can ditch the moon boot?"

"Umm—" I get my phone out of my pocket and flick through the calendar "—in like, three weeks."

"Okay, great." More typing. "Keep wearing it until then, even if you feel like you don't need it. Better to be safe than sorry."

"Got it." I glance over at the photo on Sami's desk. The one of her and her girlfriend with their faces squished together in the frame, their smiles big and bright and ridiculous. "Hey, Sami, can I ask you something?"

"Of course."

"How did you know that Julia liked you? At the start. How did you know it was . . . I dunno . . . real?"

Sami's eyes go wide. "Luca, I'm not sure if my Occupational Therapy degree qualifies me to give relationship advice to teenage boys."

I bite my lip, pleading with my eyes.

"But," she goes on eventually, "off the record—"

"I mean, we're not in court."

"—I can tell you that it was instant. I met Julia at a friend's birthday party in Melbourne, and as soon as I laid eyes on her, I knew she was going to be an important person in my life. I didn't know a single thing about her—not even if she was gay— and I don't think I knew in that instant that she was going to be my girlfriend, necessarily, but I just knew she was going to be in my life forever."

"But how?" I ask, thinking back to when I first met Jordan, just outside this room. "*How* did you know?"

Sami shrugs. "I just had a feeling. A gut-instinct, I guess. We . . . connected."

I want to ask, *But did you ever have any doubts?* and *Did she ever hurt you?* and *Did she ever send you completely confusing text messages?* but I don't.

"Does that help?" Sami asks. "I warned you I wasn't qualified."

"No, no," I say, still picturing Jordan and me in the waiting room, "that definitely helps."

Sami smiles, narrowing her eyes at me. "I get the feeling you already knew the answer to that question."

And who knows? Maybe I did. *I* certainly felt something when I first met Jordan. I've felt the same *something* every time I've ever seen him. But what I still don't know for sure—and what I'll never be able to figure out from a bunch of inconsistent text messages—is if Jordan feels that *something* too.

Twenty-Three

AS IF THE UNIVERSE is trying to tell me something, Jordan sits with me and Amina at lunch the next day. And it's not just a five-minute visit, this time. He actually *sits* with us. For the whole hour.

I mean, that *has* to be a sign.

"Ramadan must be almost over, right?" he asks Amina, who is sitting there in a kind of stunned silence.

I wonder why *she* thinks Jordan is sitting with us? She's been so distracted by her plans for world domination (aka becoming Dux of Year Eleven) that she hasn't been paying much attention to anything that's not inside her textbooks. And there's no way she could know about me and Jordan, because I haven't told a soul (not even Dad), and I know Jordan definitely wouldn't have told anyone either.

"Today's the last day," I reply for her. "And then Eid."

Amina nods silently.

"My mum always makes us a huge feast for Bon," Jordan replies. "Well, our Tanaka-Jones version of Bon, anyway."

"What's Bon?" I ask. Out of the corner of my eye, I can see Amina trying to form words. I'm sure she knows what it is. She knows everything.

"A Japanese festival," Jordan replies. "It's mainly about honoring our ancestors. My whole family visits my grandpa's grave, and then we eat *all* of the food. It's awesome."

"We visit my mum's grave every year on her birthday," I say, surprised at my own words. I never talk about Mum. "No feast though."

Jordan smiles and locks eyes with me. If we were alone, I feel like this would be some kind of moment. But sitting here on the benches between the portables with Amina right beside us doesn't quite feel like the right time for a D&M.

"Have you been to Bon in Japan?" Amina chokes out, breaking the silence. "I'd love to see the dances. The costumes are so beautiful."

Jordan clears his throat. "No, I've never been."

"To Japan?" I ask.

"Yeah. But funny you should mention it. Mum and Dad and all my aunties and grandparents chipped in and bought me flights for my eighteenth. They'd been saving for ages."

"That's amazing," Amina says. She seems to have finally pulled herself together. "I've always wanted to go to Japan."

"Same," I say, though I don't know much about Japan, except for the fact that my favorite principal dancer from the Los Angeles Ballet Company is Japanese.

"I can't wait," Jordan says. "The food, the culture . . . *Disneyland*."

I laugh. "Didn't pick you for a Disney boy."

"Oh," he says seriously, "*The Little Mermaid* is my favorite movie of all time."

"No way. Ariel's so whingey and annoying. I'm all about Moana. She's a boss."

Jordan sighs. "You just don't appreciate the classics."

I smile, and Jordan smiles back at me.

Oh my god, we're flirting out loud. I can practically feel myself turning into the monkey-covering-its-mouth emoji.

"TJ!" someone shouts from behind me. I turn on the bench to see Gibbo walking up the path from the quad.

"Hey, man," Jordan says, with one of those upward nods he gives everyone.

"Where've you been?" Gibbo asks, standing right in front of us now. "Me and the boys were looking for you."

"What's up?"

"I'm not gonna say it in front of these fuckwits," Gibbo replies, his eyes cutting to me and Amina.

"Excuse me?" Jordan says.

I glance at Amina, who is shooting Gibbo some serious daggers.

"Come on, mate," Gibbo says. "It's not a good look."

Jordan stands up. "What's not a good look?"

"You, sitting here with the fag and the towel-head."

Anger flares in my chest. I don't care if Gibbo wants to call me a fag, but I will *not* let him insult Amina. But before I get a chance to speak, Amina stands and says, "Leave us alone, Gibbo. We don't need your vile language over here, thank you very much."

"What?" he shrugs. "You can't tell me he's not a fag and

you're not a towel-head."

"Just fuck off, Gibbo," I say. "Why don't you run back to your mates and compare dick sizes for the hundredth time. Newsflash: they're all tiny."

"What'd you say to me?" He presses forward like he's going to hit me, but Jordan steps in front of him.

"Back off, Gibbo," he warns.

"What the fuck, TJ? What's your problem?"

"I don't have a problem."

"You *clearly* do."

Jordan looks to me and then Amina, as if he's making sure we're okay. I glance over at Amina, expecting her to be upset, but her expression is still weirdly calm. And kind of fierce, actually.

"Just piss off," I snap at Gibbo. "What do you care who Jordan sits with?"

"'Jordan'?" Gibbo laughs. "What are you, in love with him or something?"

My cheeks burn. My whole face burns. Everything burns.

Gibbo laughs again. Much louder this time. "Holy shit, you *are* in love with him." He looks at Jordan. "Watch out, mate, or these two are gonna try to tag-team you in your sleep."

"Shut *up!*" Amina yells, and the three of us turn to her. "How *dare* you come over here just to insult us. This is our school too. You have no right to—"

"No *right?*" Gibbo cuts her off. "What about how you've got no right to tell me how to act in my own country?"

"That's enough," Jordan interrupts, his voice low and dark. "You need to leave *right now*, Gibbo."

"It's okay, Jordan," Amina says, and I've never seen her look so feisty. "Let him finish. I want to know *exactly* what Gibbo has to say to me."

Gibbo scoffs. "What? Apart from the fact that you're a total fucking loser with a—"

But before he can finish, Jordan shoves him hard in the middle of the chest. Gibbo stumbles backward, looking kind of confused for a second, then launches straight at Jordan, fist aimed right at his best mate's face. Jordan somehow dodges the punch and tackles Gibbo around the waist, dropping him onto the path like a sack of potatoes. Gibbo rolls onto his back, ready to fight, but Jordan towers over him, legs either side of his body, breathing heavily.

"Don't you *ever* say shit like that to my friends again, you hear me?"

"What on *earth* is going on?" someone screeches as a pair of high heels click rapidly down the path toward us. It's Ms. Miles, one of the science teachers.

"Nothing, miss," Jordan says, reaching down to help Gibbo up.

"Well, whatever is *not* happening," she says, "it ends right now."

"Yes, miss," Gibbo replies. "I was just leaving." He dusts off his shorts and stalks off toward the lockers, rubbing his jaw the whole way.

"Sorry, miss," Jordan says. "It was just a misunderstanding."

"Yes, I'm sure." Ms. Miles rolls her eyes before turning to Amina and me. "Don't encourage them, please. Teenage boys and their testosterone. *Honestly.*" And without another word, she *clip-clop*s off down the path.

"You okay, Amina?" Jordan asks, placing a gentle hand on her shoulder.

"I'm fine," she says, looking kind of shocked, but not upset at all.

"Luca?" he asks.

"Fine. It's nothing I haven't heard before."

Jordan massages his shoulder. "I'm gonna go find the boys. Defuse this situation before it gets out of hand."

"Okay," Amina and I say together, a little stunned.

And then he's gone.

After a moment, I say to Amina, "*Are* you okay?"

"I'm fine," she says. "Honestly." She's staring after Jordan with this weird kind of not-quite-there look on her face, and even though she doesn't say anything, I know exactly what's happening here.

How did I not see this coming? I mean, the Bunheads did this on a weekly basis. A boy did one nice thing—because he's a *nice person*—and the girls had already planned their entire wedding down to the hot and cold canapés. And yes, I know, I'm hardly one to talk, after falling in love with Jordan in three seconds flat even though I thought he was straight and there was no chance of us ever getting together. But that is *so* not the point.

The point is—and this is not good news for any of us—I think Amina has a crush . . .

After a busy night of Netflix and trying to figure out if I somehow accidentally encouraged Amina to fall in love with Jordan, I say goodnight to Dad and head to bed. As I climb under the covers, I do a quick scroll through Instagram, then open my messages from The Boy in the Waiting Room. Jordan's last text was from this morning at 7:17 a.m.

Had a dream about you last night. It was . . . good. Smirking emoji.

And let's be honest, no matter what mood I'm in, reading flirty texts from Jordan in bed could only lead to one thing. But just as I slip my hand down into my boxers, my phone starts ringing. I yank my hand out from under the doona and flick my phone to silent, so Dad doesn't hear. My pulse is suddenly racing. Because this has never happened before . . .

Jordan is calling me.

I clear my throat, sit up in bed, and run a hand through my hair. And then I remember that Jordan won't actually be able to see me, so I could be wearing a baboon suit right now and it wouldn't matter. Unless he tries to FaceTime me halfway through the call, in which case I will die, because my room is an absolute shambles and I'm currently using a My Little Pony pillowcase because Dad washed all the good linen the other day, and it was either ponies in tutus or clowns having a picnic and I'm terrified of clowns. And then I realize I need to *answer* the phone if I actually want to talk to Jordan.

"Hello?"

"Hey," he replies, and my whole body turns to jelly. His deep voice sounds even more adorable through the slightly muffled phone line. "Were you asleep?"

"Not yet." I flop back onto my bed. "You?"

"What?" he chuckles, because he clearly wasn't asleep, since *he* was the one who called *me*.

"I mean . . . What are you up to?"

"Just got into bed."

Suddenly, there is one particular part of my body that is the complete opposite of jelly.

"Is it okay that I called?" Jordan asks. "I wasn't sure if . . ."

"It's fine," I say, when what I really mean is, *It's literally the best thing that's ever happened.*

"I just wanted to apologize again for what happened with Gibbo at lunch today."

"You don't need to do that. It wasn't your fault."

"I know, but Gibbo's my mate, so I kinda feel responsible for him sometimes."

I honestly don't understand how someone as perfect as Jordan could be friends with a complete wanker like Gibbo. But then, I guess I was friends with Talia my whole life, and she's clearly not a glowing example of a good person either. I was always making excuses for her being horrible to people, but it never occurred to me that she might just be a horrible person. Maybe we can all be blind to who someone really is when we don't want to see it.

"Well," I say, "I think you made your stance on the whole thing pretty clear."

Jordan chuckles into the phone and I squeeze my eyes shut, hoping this phone call will never end.

"So . . ." he says.

"So . . ."

And I just lie there for a second, picturing Jordan lying on his bed—which would have to be at least a double, because he's way too tall for a single like mine—and my mind creates a crystal-clear image of his entire bedroom. Footy posters, rowing trophies, photos of his mates stuck on the walls. A pile of unread books on his bedside table, clothes all over the floor. A desk with an old PC and a stack of computer games. A half-eaten bowl of cereal. A typical *guy*'s room, you know?

And then there's me and my My Little Pony pillowcase . . .

"What's your favorite color?' I blurt out, and then silently shout the words *Oh my god* up to the ceiling, because I couldn't possibly have chosen a more pathetic question if I tried. I'm like a five-year-old who just made a new friend at a McDonald's birthday party.

But Jordan just says, "Blue," and I swear I can tell by his voice that he's smiling. "What's yours?"

"Um . . . purple?"

"You're not sure?"

"No, I'm sure."

"But you said it with a question mark."

"No, I didn't."

"Uhh, you definitely did."

"Fine," I say. "*Purple.* Exclamation mark. Thumbs up. Smiley face."

He laughs again.

"Do you have any siblings?" I ask, which is another pathetic attempt at conversation, but I know that if I don't keep things going, Jordan will probably get bored and go to bed and this will all be over.

"Nope," he replies. "Only child. You?"

"Same," I say. "Although I'm pretty sure that's only because

Mum died before Dad and her got around to having more kids."

"I'm so sorry about you mum," Jordan says, and I can practically feel him giving me a hug through the phone. "I didn't know that until today."

"It's okay." I roll onto my side, the phone pressed between my face and the pillow. "It was a long time ago. My dad misses her a lot."

"Do you miss her?"

I take in a slow breath. "I mean, I don't really remember her that well, so I don't know if I miss *her* or if I just miss having a mum. But, I dunno . . . We don't need to talk about this right now. Sorry. I didn't mean to be a downer."

"It's okay," Jordan replies, and we're quiet for a moment. Then he asks, "What does your dad do?"

"He's a teacher. Primary school."

"Ah, nice. Mine works in construction. He wanted to be an AFL player, which explains why I was playing footy before I could even walk. There's this photo of me from when I was really little, wearing this *tiny* Collingwood jersey and holding a full-size football, which is literally as big as me. I couldn't have even been a year old."

"Well," I say, "I obviously need to see this photo ASAP."

"I don't know if we're quite ready for embarrassing childhood photos."

"Oh, don't worry," I say, "you've got nothing on me, I promise. My dancing photos are an absolute treasure trove of humiliation."

"In that case, I can't wait." Jordan chuckles, and we fall silent again.

"Did your dad—" I go to say *audition* but that's definitely not the right word "—try out for the AFL?"

"Yeah, when he was my age. But he *just* missed out on the draft. Or so he says. He was pretty devastated when I told him I didn't want to play footy professionally, but I softened the blow by saying I want to go into business with him when I'm a big-time architect."

"An architect? You don't want to play in the AFL?"

"Nah," Jordan replies. "It's not for me, I don't think. Don't get me wrong, I love footy more than anything in the world, but I think I want a more normal life."

Normal? Like, "Wife and Kids and a House on the Lake" normal? Or "Two Guys with Adopted Twin Babies and a Cavoodle" normal?

"And besides that," he goes on, "I don't want to rely on my body for work. Footy players' careers can be over after one bad tackle. I just don't think I'm cut out for it. This shit with my shoulder has been so frustrating. It hasn't stopped me playing yet but . . ."

"But what?"

"Sorry, man," he says. "I'm such a dick. Here's me complaining about my shoulder and talking about footy players' careers ending, when you've got this whole thing with your foot going on."

"It's fine," I reply. I try to point my foot under the covers, and it catches at the same point as always. It doesn't hurt, it just won't go where it used to. "Like you said, I'm not the only person who's ever had to quit because of an injury. It happens all the time."

"I know, but still."

"Keep going," I say, because I'm not ready for this to end. Not on this note. "It's fine. Honestly."

"Well," Jordan replies, "I'm lucky that I haven't had to stop playing, but I tell you what, I'm in a shit-load of pain. Pretty much all the time."

"You never look like you're in pain."

"No," he says with a soft chuckle, "I'm pretty good at pretending."

I'm quiet on the other end of the line.

"Sorry," he says. "I don't know why I'm telling you all this. I never talk about this stuff."

"You mean your feelings?"

Now it's Jordan's turn to be quiet. I can hear him breathing on the other end of the line, and if I close my eyes, it almost feels like he's lying here beside me.

After a long moment, he says, "I really like talking to you."

"Yeah," I reply, my throat suddenly as dry as a cactus. "I like talking to you, too."

There's another pause, and then, "You, um . . . haven't told Amina about us, have you? Or anyone else?"

"No," I say, shaking my head even though Jordan can't see me. "No one."

"Okay, good." He yawns into the phone and says, "Dude, I'm sorry. I should probably get to bed."

No. Please stay.

"Yeah, same," I reply.

"See you at school?"

"Yep."

"Goodnight, Luca." The way he says my name feels like a kiss on the cheek.

"Night, Jordan."

He hangs up and my heart pretty much bursts inside my chest.

Twenty-Four

JORDAN AND GIBBO OBVIOUSLY sorted out their shit, because they were laughing and mucking around the next day as if one of them *hadn't* tried to punch the other one in the face.

Straight guys are so weird.

Jordan has been hanging out with me and Amina a lot more, though, which is awesome, but I also think it's fueling Amina's secret crush. Which I could be completely wrong about, but I'm pretty sure I've spent enough time with girls in my life to know when one of them has secret feelings for someone. Especially when they have secret feelings for the same person I have secret feelings for.

What's *really* not helping is that people have started talking. You see, the super-popular, super-sexy school captain sitting with a couple of so-called "losers" every lunchtime is not something that would go unnoticed at North. At any school, really. And that's *before* the super-sexy school captain decked his best mate.

But the question on everyone's lips is: *Why?*

One rumor is that Jordan and Amina are cousins, and that

he feels bad that everyone makes fun of her. Another whisper I heard in the quad is that Jordan's dad owes Amina's dad money for drugs, so Jordan has to be nice to Amina or her dad will break Jordan's dad's legs. And I mean, *really?* Obviously no one has met Amina's dad, because he's literally the least likely person to break anyone's legs in the history of the world.

The most dangerous rumor is that Jordan *likes* Amina. That he stood up for her because he's been secretly in love with her since primary school. I don't know if it started out as a joke or if someone actually *believes* that, but it's bad news either way. And I know Amina has heard this particular rumor, because she's started acting completely different around Jordan. No more stunned silences. No more constant fidgeting. She's a regular Chatty Kathy now. Asking him about his mum and her Japanese heritage. Telling him about all her favorite AFL players. She even tells him her most embarrassing Harry Styles stories. I think it's safe to say if she had a cardboard cut-out of Jordan, she'd marry *it*, too.

"Are you excited for your mid-year exams?" she asks him at lunch one day. It's absolutely *pouring*, so we're sitting inside the dirty, awful canteen with six hundred dirty, awful students. It's cramped and stinks like sausage rolls and BO.

"'Excited' might be the wrong word for it," Jordan replies, shoveling a giant forkful of pasta into his mouth. "But I'm keen to get it all over and done with, if that counts?"

"I'm sure you have nothing to worry about," Amina says, batting her eyelashes.

I can't with her today.

Jordan chuckles. "Physics is the only exam I'm worried

about, but I reckon I'll survive. I tell you what, it'd be a lot less stressful if my parents would just *relax* about the whole thing. Mum found this online exam score predictor, which is clearly a barrel of laughs for all involved."

Amina's eyes go wide, and I know it's because she's making a mental note to find that website as soon as she gets home. If anyone knows about parental pressure, it's Amina. I love her mamah and papah, but man do they stress her out. Ever since she told me she wants to be a teacher, it seems like all her parents do when I'm over is talk about how wonderful Amina's life is going to be when she's a doctor. I don't know if I just didn't notice it before, or if they've ramped it up because mid-year exams are around the corner, but they talk about it *constantly*. And it's so ridiculous, because all it takes is one look at Amina's face to see she literally couldn't think of anything worse.

"Well," she replies, "it's good to be prepared."

"True," Jordan says, nodding. "I just hope they're happy when this is all over."

Amina smiles. "The only thing that matters is that *you're* happy."

"I'm happy," he says, nudging my knee with his. "Very."

Heat flares in my face. I try to think of a way to change the subject so Amina doesn't notice, but then Jordan says, "So when's the moon boot coming off?"

I swallow. "Monday."

"Three sleeps!" Amina chimes in with a little clap.

"Jeez, that soon?" Jordan says.

I snort. "Soon? It's been like, eight weeks. I'm *dying* to get rid of this thing."

"We need to celebrate!"

"Celebrate? How?"

"Dunno," he shrugs. "What's something you can't do with a moon boot?"

"Ride a bike?' Amina says, smirking, and I shoot her a *don't you dare tell Jordan I can't ride I bike* glare.

"I'm sure we'll think of something," he says, standing up. "Leave it to me. I gotta get to physics. See you guys later."

"Bye!" Amina chirps, waving after him, her head tilting slightly to the side in a way that I know—and I mean, I *really* know—means she's checking out his ass.

"It's pretty damn perfect," I say, because I can't help myself.

"What is?" she replies vaguely.

"Jordan's ass."

She whips her head around and gasps. "Luca Mason! I was not—"

"Checking out his ass?"

"I was *not*." She pats her cheeks. "I don't—I would never objectify anyone like that."

"Relax," I say, laughing. "It's not like you can get a detention for thinking someone is hot."

"Luca. Can you stop?"

But for some reason, I can't stop. Maybe because there's a big part of me that wants Amina to admit she has a secret crush on Jordan. Because then I can deal with it. Like, I'm not exactly sure *how* I'll deal with it—because I clearly can't tell her about me and Jordan—but I'm hoping the answer will miraculously present itself to me at some point.

"Okay." I shrug an apology. "I take it back. You were

definitely *not* checking out Jordan's perfect ass."

"No, I definitely was not."

"But, I mean, if you *were*—"

"Which I *wasn't*."

"—it would be a totally natural reaction. Jordan is hot. Like, ridiculously hot. You're allowed to appreciate his hotness."

"There's more to someone than being *hot*, Luca," Amina snaps, and I get the impression that *maybe* I pushed this a little too far. "TJ is kind and smart. He's ambitious. He's a good leader. He's a *nice person*. And he knows what Ramadan is, which is more than I can say for anyone else at North. No offense."

"None taken," I say. "At all. And I'm sorry. I didn't mean—"

But Amina jumps up from her seat and says, "I need to get to chem. I'll talk to you after school," then marches off across the canteen and out the door. Which tells me pretty much everything I need to know. I was right.

Amina likes Jordan. But Jordan likes me. And I like Jordan back.

I stare up at the ceiling and let out a long sigh.

Maths has never been my thing, but in *that* equation, it doesn't take a genius to figure out which one of us is going to get hurt.

Twenty-Five

"THIS IS IT," **SAMI** says, kneeling in front of me on the treatment-room floor. She's wearing my favorite outfit of hers: the sunshine-yellow top tucked into black skinny jeans with cute black heels. Today's earrings are pink donuts with rainbow sprinkles. I mean, can someone give this woman a medal for being the most glorious person alive?

"This is it," I echo.

I can't believe I'm finally here. I'm finally done. Recovered. Well, as close to "recovered" as I'm gonna get, I guess. The ridiculous thing is, no matter how many times I tell myself that I've come to terms with not dancing—I mean, I've literally lost count of how many times I've told myself that—I still feel weird about it. I don't know if I'll ever *not* feel weird about it.

I stare down at my moon boot. It's not like I need Sami to unstrap it for me, I've been taking it off to shower for the last eight weeks, but I like the ceremonial vibe we're going for. This feels important. It's the end of an era, after all.

Sami tears open the Velcro strips, one by one, and carefully slips the boot off my foot, placing it on the chair beside her desk.

"Tada!" she sings, pushing herself up to her feet. "Luca Mason, you are now officially a free man." She grabs my hands and gives them a squeeze, smiling her brightest smile.

"Thank you," I say, wiping a tear from my cheek. "God, why do I always cry in this office?"

"It's only been once or twice."

I lift an eyebrow.

"Well," Sami says, "maybe a *few* times."

I snort. "Also, if you think I'm not signing an old ballet photo and sticking it up on the wall in the waiting room, you've got another thing coming."

"Oh, of course," Sami says with a camp little shrug. "What are you going to write?"

"Um . . . 'Dear Sami, your cuteness causes me physical pain, even more than your elbows in my quads. Thanks for the lols.'"

She laughs, her head tilted back to the ceiling, and my eyes fill with tears again. I can't believe our time together is over. I honestly don't know if I can picture my new life without Sami in it.

I shake my head and slide off the edge of the treatment table, landing on two feet. I stare down at them, one in a sneaker and the other in a pink and blue polka-dotted sock.

"Oh my god," I say, only just realizing what I've done. "I didn't bring my other shoe."

Sami starts laughing again.

"*Stop*, don't laugh. I can't walk out of here in one shoe. I'll look ridiculous!"

"I'm sorry," Sami says, crying with laugher now. "It's

just . . . we always imagine that these momentous occasions will work out perfectly, but they never go quite to plan, do they?"

I roll my eyes. "This is not the time for life lessons, Sami."

"Sorry," she replies, wiping under her eyes with her pinkies so she doesn't ruin her mascara.

After a moment, I say, "I'm really gonna miss this."

"Me too, Luca," she says, her dark brown eyes sparkling like diamonds. "Me too."

"You done with that?" Dad asks, nodding at my empty plate. We're on the couch watching *Love Island UK*. Another one of Dad's faves. He's a smart guy, but he sure loves his trash TV.

"Thanks," I reply, handing him my plate.

"You feeling good?" he asks, already halfway to the kitchen.

I lift up my legs and plonk my feet onto the coffee table. No cast, no moon boot, just my own two feet. "Yep."

"I'm proud of you, Lu," he calls out over the sound of plates and cutlery clanging into the dishwasher. "For coping with all this. It's been a hell of a few months."

I scoff. "I mean, I was *kind of* a jerk most the time."

"You were not." He shuffles back into the lounge and sits beside me. "It was a massive thing for a kid—"

I raise one eyebrow.

"—a *young man* to deal with," he carries on. "And I think you showed a lot of strength. I really am proud of you, Lu. You're growing up."

"Dad, you don't need to get all cute."

"It's my job to get all cute."

"Whatever. I just . . ." I let out a sigh. "I'm just so ready to forget that the last few months ever happened."

Dad purses his lips, his eyebrows meeting in the middle.

"What?" I ask.

"No, nothing," he replies.

"Say it."

"Well, I just thought . . . you know, now that your boot's off, maybe you'd want to—'

There's a loud *ding* from my pocket. "Wait—hold that thought."

I pull out my phone and see a notification from The Boy in the Waiting Room.

I decided how we're going to celebrate. But it's a surprise. Smirking emoji.

"Oh my god."

"What's up?"

I look up at Dad. Did I just say that out loud? "Nothing. Thanks for dinner!"

I jump off the couch and run upstairs to my room—yes, *run*, for the first time in five months. I don't even realize I'm doing it until I'm already perched on the edge of my bed. I smile down at my foot for a second, then click back into Jordan's message.

A surprise? I write back. **Tell me more** . . . Monkey-covering-its-eyes emoji.

Jordan: **Haha. All I can say is that I'll pick you up on Monday morning. And you'll need a change of clothes.** Thumbs-up emoji.

Holy shit.

PS, he writes, **don't say anything at school, ok? Even to Amina.**

Of course. Can't wait.

I go to click the winking emoji, but my thumb hits the kissing one instead and my other thumb presses send before I even know what's happening.

Shit.

We haven't used any kisses or anything remotely cutesy in our messages so far. What if Jordan hates it? What if he thinks it's too girly? Too gay? What if he changes his mind about the surprise altogether? Why do my thumbs want to ruin my life?

But then a love heart pops up on my screen from Jordan.

I kid you not, a literal *love heart.*

I lie back onto my bed and press my phone to my chest, feeling like I might float straight out the window.

Jordan sent me a love heart.

The rest of the week absolutely flies by. I spend most of Saturday lounging around, and I sleep my way through Sunday—which is awesome, because nothing makes time go faster than sleeping. Then, suddenly, it's Monday. The first day of the mid-year school holidays.

Yes, I've been awake since 5:00 a.m. And, *yes*, I packed and repacked my change of clothes literally eight times because I couldn't decide what to bring. (Is it a casual vibe? Do I need a collared shirt? Is it a hat kind of occasion?) In the end, I squeezed three spare outfits into my backpack. But Jordan doesn't need to know that.

At 8:24 a.m.—no, I'm not just sitting on my bed waiting for him to message me—my phone pings.

The Boy in the Waiting Room: **I'll pick you up in half an hour.**

Yay! See you soon!

Yay? I roll my eyes at myself. I swear I used to be chill once upon a time.

Dad and I are sitting at the kitchen table being awkward— I'm shitting myself with nerves, he's sitting there looking like there's something he wants to say—when I hear a car pull up out the front.

"That the boy?" he asks, dropping his newspaper, his eyes wide.

When I told Dad about Jordan's surprise last night, the conversation went something like this:

"Are you sure about this, Lu?"

"Why wouldn't I be?"

"You told me he was straight."

"Well, I *thought* he was. But he's obviously not, so . . . ."

"Have you . . .?"

"Oh my god, *no*."

"Then how do you know he's into guys? What if he's—"

"Dad, we are *so* not doing this."

Definitely not the "My Son Finally Met a Cute Boy" song and dance routine I was expecting.

"Promise me you'll act normal," I say to Dad now at the table, jumping up from my chair and running into the lounge.

Jordan knocks and I open the door straightaway, which I instantly realize makes it look like I was just standing there waiting for him, but it's too late now, so I smile and say, "Hi!"

"Good morning," he says with a grin, hands in his pockets.

My god this boy is beautiful. He's wearing tight black jeans, a crisp white T-shirt, a washed-out denim jacket, and white sneakers, looking like he strolled up to my front door straight out of *GQ* magazine.

I swallow my heart back down where it belongs and clear my throat. "Hi. You look . . . um . . ."

He chuckles. "You gonna invite me in?"

"Oh, yeah. Sorry. Come in."

Jordan walks straight into the kitchen and shakes Dad's hand.

"Morning, Mr. Mason."

"Robert," Dad replies, getting up from the table, still shaking Jordan's hand.

"Of course. Sorry. Robert. How've you been?"

"Very well, thank you," he replies. "And you? How's school? You're in Year Twelve, right? How's all your coursework going? Have you—"

"*Okay*," I say, giving Dad a meaningful look. "No need for the interrogation. And you can let go of his hand now."

Dad releases Jordan from his grip. "Jordan doesn't mind," he replies. "Do you?"

"No, I—"

"*I* mind," I interrupt. "There'll be plenty of time to play twenty questions another day."

Dad sighs in defeat. "Fine. Am I at least allowed to know where you're going? Or does that count as an interrogation too? When I was a kid, I wasn't allowed out the door without a signed letter from Her Majesty the Queen."

Jordan laughs.

"You don't have to do that," I say to him. "Dad knows he's not funny."

"Excuse *me*," Dad says, pretending to be offended.

"I borrowed Mum's car," Jordan says to Dad. "I'm going to drive Luca down to Ocean Grove. My nan owns a caravan there."

Dad raises his eyebrows. "Oh?"

"We'll be back tomorrow after dinner," Jordan says, as if me staying *overnight* at his nan's caravan in Ocean Grove is just like taking a stroll around the block. When Dad and I don't reply, he adds, "If that's okay?"

I try to look calm, even though my heart is absolutely racing at the thought of going on an *overnight* trip with Jordan (because overnight equals sleeping, and sleeping equals beds, and beds and boys is completely unknown territory for me). I'm waiting for Dad to either ask Jordan an insanely awkward question about his sexuality or hand over an enormous value pack of condoms from Costco, but he just does this weird little cough and looks at me.

"Dad?" I say slowly. "That's okay, right?"

"If it's not," Jordan jumps in, "we can totally change our plans. No stress at all, Mr. Mason. Robert. I should have asked before I showed up. If it's a problem, we can just do something in Ballarat for the day."

But Dad just stands there, scratching his head. He's been hinting—well, not so much hinting as blatantly *saying*—that he wants me to find a boyfriend for *years*. So I don't know why he'd suddenly go all weird about it when an actual boy—especially one as beautiful and polite and charming as Jordan—is standing in our kitchen, asking to do something really nice for me.

"My parents will be close by," Jordan goes on, filling the awkward silence. "They're staying at my aunty's beach house around the corner from the caravan park. I'm sorry, I definitely should have asked your permission earlier. I just thought—after everything that's happened this year—Luca deserved some time to chill and let his hair down." He grins, looking from Dad to me and back again. "In a responsible fashion, of course."

Dad's shoulders relax but he still looks kind of wary. "Of course, mate. That's . . . very sweet of you."

"Thank you!' I wrap my arms around Dad's shoulders and whisper "thank you" about a million more times in his ear.

"Just drive carefully," he says in his "dad voice," walking Jordan and me to the door. "And don't take the back roads. They're not very well maintained."

"No problem," Jordan replies.

"And message me as soon as you arrive so I know you're safe."

"Yes, well, bye!' I say, ushering Jordan back outside. He struts off toward his mum's car, and I turn back to Dad, who's standing just inside the front door.

"Luca," he says in a half whisper. "He's a nice boy, right?"

"What?"

"He's not, you know . . ." He opens his eyes as wide as they'll go, like he's trying to get me to guess something in a game of charades.

"No, I don't know," I say, "but can we talk about this— whatever *this* is—when I get back? I have to go."

"Fine," he sighs. "Go. Have fun. Just . . . be safe, okay?"

"Oh my god, Dad. Can you not?"

"That's not what I meant—well, also that—but I—"

"Yep. Okay. Got it. Bye!" I kiss him on the cheek and jog over to the car.

"Love you!" he calls out.

"Love you too!" I reply as I slide into the passenger seat.

Jordan turns to me and smiles his perfect smile. "We good?"

"Yep," I say, glancing back at Dad, who's waving half-heartedly from the front door. "Let's do this."

Jordan starts the car and pulls out onto the road. And holy shit. This is real. It's actually happening. And there's no turning back now.

Twenty-Six

I'M NOT GONNA LIE, being alone in the car with Jordan is kind of awkward. It shouldn't be, because I've been spending a lot of time with him at school, but that's all been with an Amina buffer, and she's great at filling awkward silences with personal questions and random facts.

I've also never been in such a confined space with Jordan. The air in the car is thick with tension—hopefully of the sexual kind and not the "Have I Made A Horrible Mistake Taking Luca On This Getaway" kind. Or maybe it's just hot in here. Who knows. Either way, my cheeks and ears are burning and I'm basically back to square one in terms of conversation skills.

"I hope I didn't make a shit impression on your dad," Jordan says, snapping me out of my thoughts as we pass the GOODBYE CITY OF BALLARAT sign on the highway. "He's pretty chill, right?"

"Totally," I reply. (Well, *usually*.) "And there's nothing to not like about you. He's been wanting me to have a boyfriend for—"

Oh, *shit*. I just dropped the B-word. No, no, no.

I slowly look over at Jordan. His eyes are still on the road, but I can tell he's trying not to smirk.

"Sorry," I say. "I meant that he's been wanting me to *hang out* with a boy for ages. I didn't mean—I'm not saying—"

Jordan laughs. "It's fine. I didn't take it that way."

"Okay. Cool." I sink down into the passenger seat, trying to think of a new topic that doesn't make it sound like I'm desperately trying to change the conversation.

"What's—" I start, but Jordan says, "Do you—" and we both chuckle half-heartedly.

"Sorry, you go," he says.

Please, please, *please* don't tell me that after all these months obsessing over Jordan and slowly getting to know him through nine million text messages, a few lunchtime hangs at school, and one adorable phone call, that we're going to be weird for possibly the only two full days we're ever going to get to spend together . . .

"I can't remember what I was going to say," I reply, running my fingernails along the inside seam of my jeans.

"Do you want to listen to some music?" he asks. "There's an aux cable. Just plug your phone in."

Oh god. This is my worst nightmare. Choosing music is such a weirdly personal thing. It feels like you're baring your soul to someone, saying, *This is who I am. And if you don't like it, we should clearly never speak again.*

The thing is, I listened to a lot of classical music growing up. I know that sounds super nerdy, but I wanted to get to know all the composers and their ballets. It started out as research, but I actually really enjoyed it. There's something so . . . *epic* about classical music. But I'm obviously not going to play a

Stravinsky concerto in the car for Jordan right now—because that is so not cool or remotely sexy—so I'm not sure what my other options are.

I want to ask what *Jordan* would like to listen to, but I don't want to sound pathetic either, like I can't make my own choices in life and have no personality of my own. I just know that whatever song I put on first could either make or break our hypothetical relationship.

Then I remember something Jordan said at school a few weeks ago, and I have to stop a huge grin from spreading across my face and giving me away.

Oh, this is *perfect*. This is sure to win me some Potential Boyfriend points.

I hit play on Spotify and turn the volume up. As soon as the steel drum intro to "Under the Sea" from *The Little Mermaid* blasts through the speakers, Jordan lets out a loud "No fucking way!" and starts bouncing up and down in the driver's seat.

I look over at him, unable to contain my beaming smile any longer. He glances at me for a second, his eyes literally twinkling, a massive grin on his face. Then he turns back to the road and starts to sing along.

Yep. Nailed it. Hypothetical relationship intact.

We sing the hits of *Frozen* and *Moana* and *The Lion King* for the full hour and ten minutes it takes us to get to Geelong. It's a boring drive in terms of scenery—just brown fields, some sheep, and a few eucalyptus trees—but inside the car, we may as well be on a Disney float at Mardi Gras.

I'm an awful singer, always have been, but Jordan actually has an okay voice. As we drive through the outskirts of Geelong, he smashes out a mean rendition of "Out There" from *The Hunchback of Notre Dame*. It's way too high for me, so I just listen, giving him a full round of applause at the end.

"Thank you, thank you," he says, placing a hand on his chest and bowing to an imaginary audience at the traffic lights.

"I mean, you're really more of a Prince Eric," I say with a smirk, "but that was very impressive."

He laughs as the lights turn green, turns the corner, and then gently places his hand on my thigh. And I freeze. Suddenly I'm dizzy. His hand is so warm, the heat going straight through my jeans, making my skin start to tingle. I feel movement in my jocks and take a long, deep breath. Not now. *Not now.*

I look out the window to distract myself, trying to focus on the tacky shopfronts whizzing past as we make our way through the city. But all I can see is Jordan, standing there in the middle of his nan's caravan, completely naked . . . And before I can stop myself, I'm wondering what might happen if *both* of us were standing there completely naked. Together. Naked. Looking at each other. *Naked.*

"You okay?" Jordan asks as we stop at another set of lights. He pulls his hand away from my leg to turn the music down.

"Me?" I say, as if there are ten other people in the car he might be talking to. "Yeah, I'm fine. I'm great."

He narrows his eyes. "You went quiet all of a sudden back there."

"Did I?" Yes, Jordan, because it takes a *lot* of willpower to make an erection go down when your hand is *on my leg* and I'm picturing us naked in a caravan. "Sorry, I'm a bit sleepy from the drive."

"You want to turn the music off for a bit?"

"No," I say, "it's fine. I like listening to you sing."

"First time anyone's ever said that to me," he chuckles. "The boys at footy give me so much shit for singing in the showers."

"How's the season going?" I ask. "I should . . . I'd love to see you play sometime."

Something in Jordan's expression hardens just a little as we pull away from the lights. "Yeah. Totally."

"Or . . . sorry, would that be weird?"

Jordan thinks for a second. Or maybe he's just paying attention to the traffic. "No, it's cool. Lots of people come to watch. Especially if we have a home game."

Lots of people come to watch. Doesn't that imply that I'm no more important than anyone else at North? Like I'm just another student? Another adoring fan? Is that really all I am to him?

"Oh, okay, cool," I reply. "Well . . . maybe let me know?"

"Sure."

I tell myself not to overreact. He wouldn't bring "lots of people" on a surprise getaway to his nan's caravan in Ocean Grove. He wouldn't message "lots of people" every morning when he gets up and every night before he goes to sleep. He wouldn't tackle Gibbo to the ground for insulting "lots of people."

I'm not "lots of people." I know that.

So then, why do I feel so weird?

Twenty-Seven

THE CARAVAN IS NOT what I imagined. For starters, I thought it would be an actual caravan. This is a house. A tiny house in the middle of a caravan park, but it definitely shows no signs of rolling down the road any time soon. It has a wooden deck that wraps all the way around it and a cute little garden out the front. There's a big antenna on the roof and a wooden sign beside the screen door with some Japanese letters painted on it.

Jordan must notice me squinting at the intricate shapes, because he says, "Okaeri. It means 'welcome home' in Japanese. I made it for Mum in Year Eight."

"That's incredibly adorable."

He laughs off the compliment. "Come on," he says, gently pressing his hand to my lower back in a way that makes me go weak at the knees, "I'll show you inside."

When he opens the door, I see that it really is a caravan, after all. The outside may have fooled me, but inside, it is one hundred percent an orange-walled, lino-floored, tiny-kitchened, bunk-bedded, I'm-gonna-say-from-the-1970s, good ol' fashioned caravan.

"Cuuuuuute." And I'm not even being sarcastic. It's the cutest thing I've ever seen. Cozy. Kitschy. Vintage. "I love this."

"Really?" Jordan asks, taking off his jacket and chucking it on the bottom bunk. "I'm sure it's a crap-heap compared to your St. Tom's friends' clifftop mansions."

"It's a million times cuter than any clifftop mansion I've ever been to," I reply. I desperately want to say *because you're here*, but that's probably a bit too much at this point, and I still feel a bit thrown by his "lots of people" comment in the car.

"Do your friends really have clifftop mansions?" he asks, opening a cupboard door beside the sink.

"No," I laugh.

"Beachfront?" He opens another cupboard.

"No. Well, kind of." Talia's dad owns a four-story beachfront house—and by "house" I mean *castle*—in Lorne, down on the Great Ocean Road. But I've only been there once. She doesn't see her dad much. "I'm not friends with those girls anymore, anyway."

"Why not?" Jordan is crouching down in front of an open drawer, hunting for something. His T-shirt is riding up, revealing a strip of perfect, tan skin and the white band of his Bonds undies. He has two little dimples on his lower back, just above the line of his jocks.

"What?" I ask, when I realize I've been staring instead of answering his question.

"Why aren't you—ah, here it is!" He stands up, looking triumphant, a purple plastic CD case in his hand.

"I literally can't remember the last time I played a CD."

Jordan laughs. "Right? I don't know how people survived without Spotify. We had tons of CDs when I was little, but they were all so scratched. You could only listen to half a song and then the rest would be the same word over and over until the end of time."

"Yeah, some of my ballet concert DVDs are like that. Which is a shame because they were beyond adorable."

"Oh, I bet."

"But CDs are a whole other level of old-school."

"This one is *incredible*," Jordan says, opening the case like it's made of precious crystal. "It's a mixed CD my older cousin made. See . . ." He holds it out to me, and I see the words ASHLEIGH'S AWESOME MIX scrawled on the disk in black permanent marker.

"Classic."

Jordan opens another cupboard and pulls out a prehistoric CD player. One of those boom-box ones, like from that old movie with the guy on the ride-on lawnmower.

When he presses play, I don't recognize the song at all.

Jordan starts clapping his hands to the old-school R&B beat and rapping in time with the guy on the track, like he's revving up an imaginary crowd.

"Excuse me?" I laugh.

"Come on, you've never heard this before?"

I shake my head. Jordan moves around me in a circle. A very tight circle, since there's not a whole lot of dancing room in here.

"This is my *jam*," he says.

I snort. "Please don't say 'my jam.'"

"You seriously don't know it? 'One Two Step'?"

I shrug.

"It's Ciara. Come on," he pleads, in front of me again. Now he's doing this weird little hip movement that I *think* he thinks is cool.

"Wait? As in, 'Level Up' Ciara?"

"Yesssssss."

"She was around back then? We were like, literal babies."

"Doesn't mean it can't be our jam." Jordan makes his eyebrows dance.

"Please stop saying that." I try not to smile but fail miserably. What is it about hot jocks being dorky that is literally impossible to resist?

"Aren't you going to join in?" he asks.

"Right now? Shouldn't we, like—"

"The song's already on."

"I can't dance to this."

And it's true. Ballet gave me perfect posture and feet that turn out like a duck's. Which is *great* for ballet, but not for anything that requires you to look remotely relaxed or cool. When I try, I look like a baby giraffe learning to walk.

"Hip-hop is not really my thing," I say.

"What, like it's mine?" Jordan scoffs. "There's no audience. It's just you and me. It's *fun*."

"Ha." It's so weird—and I never really thought about it before—but in all my years of dancing, I never did it for fun. Don't get me wrong, I loved ballet more than anything. I was completely devoted to it. I was passionate and dedicated. I was determined to make a career out of dancing. But it was never about having *fun*.

Jordan grabs my hips and sways them from side to side, my feet still planted firmly on the floor. I look up to the low ceiling and roll my eyes. "I can't . . ."

"Come on. Do it for me. Do it for Ciara."

I groan and give in. Because how can I say no to him?

I start rocking my hips and bending my knees, mimicking Jordan's ridiculous movements. I feel so awkward and self-conscious but, staring into his eyes, his smile lighting up the tiny caravan, I eventually let myself give in to the beat and enjoy it. And you know what? It *is* fun. I laugh when I catch my awkward, bouncing reflection in the window, but force myself to let loose and give in to the moment.

Just as I'm *really* getting into it, the song finishes.

"Noooo."

"Quality track," Jordan says, panting a little. He's standing so close to me that I can feel the heat coming off his body.

The next song comes on. It's old too, but this one I know. "Beautiful Disaster" by Kelly Clarkson. Laura Pearson from Miss Gwen's used to do a lyrical solo to it. It's about a beautiful boy who's probably going to end up being a huge disaster. And I mean, seriously, Universe? This song? At this moment?

"Do you know this one?" Jordan asks.

I nod, my voice suddenly nowhere to be found. While Kelly sings, we both just stand there. Looking at each other. But like, more than looking. *Seeing* each other.

Jordan places a gentle hand on my hip and pulls me in a little closer. My breath leaves my chest. He slips his other hand behind my back and presses his hips just slightly into mine.

My heart is racing. My hands are sweaty. But I don't take

my eyes off his. Those perfect hazel eyes.

He glances down at my lips, and I can't believe this is actually happening. I was not expecting this. Hoping, yes, but definitely not expecting.

But here he is, the boy of my dreams, leaning in toward me . . .

Closer and closer.

His arms around my waist.

His breath on my lips.

His crotch vibrating.

Wait—*what?*

Jordan pulls away, slides his phone out of his pocket and says, "Hey, Mum."

He presses pause on the CD player, and just like that, the moment is gone. Like it never even happened. I turn and adjust myself in my jocks so my hard-on isn't quite so painfully obvious and walk over to the window.

"Yeah," Jordan says, "it was easy. Barely any traffic." A pause. "Yep, we will." Another pause. "No, you don't have to do that." He laughs. "I can so! I'm perfectly capable."

Hearing him talk to his mum, I realize I forgot to text Dad when we arrived. I pull out my phone to send him a quick message and see two texts and a missed call sitting on my lock screen.

The call is from Grace, which obviously must have been an accident, since we haven't spoken a word to each other since that day outside the cafe.

The first message is from Dad: **You good, Lu? Make it ok?**

Yep, I reply. **Bit chilly down here! See you tomorrow.**

And then Amina: **Do you want to come with me to the city library? I need to pick up a book I've had on reserve since January. I'm SO EXCITED!** Starry-eyed emoji. **Or we could meet for coffee afterward?**

Can't today, I type quickly. **Sorry!**

Oh, okay, she replies instantly, and I can practically *hear* her disappointment through the screen. **Another time!**

"Yep, talk soon," Jordan says into his phone, and I shove mine back into my pocket. "Love you, Mum. Bye. Yes, I will. Okay. *Yes.* Love you, bye."

"All good?" I ask.

"She's so funny," he replies, shaking his head, looking down at his phone.

"What did she say?"

He doesn't look up from the message he's typing. "Nothing. Just checking up on me."

It's only now that I realize there's no way he would have told his parents who he was bringing down to the caravan.

"Oh," I reply. "Cool. Tell her I say hi."

His eyes flick up from his phone. "Relax. It's not like she's gonna rock up and surprise us."

I want to say, *I'm not the one who would care if she did*, but fake a chuckle instead.

"I just gotta go pee and then I'll take you into town," Jordan says. "Gimme one sec." He places his phone down on the kitchen bench and ducks through a narrow door beside the bunk beds. "There's this cafe that has these mind-blowing burgers," he calls out over the loud sound of his wee splashing into the bowl.

"Great," I reply. "I'm starving."

I glance over at his phone and freeze. I don't mean to see it. But I do. I would never snoop through someone's stuff, but his phone is just sitting there, unlocked on his messages . . .

Below the text he must have just sent his mum, is the one I sent him this morning. **Yay! See you soon!**

But it's not the message that makes my stomach twist into a thousand sickening knots. It's the name my number is saved under:

Lucy.

The bathroom door opens, and I jerk away from the bench, pretending to look for a glass.

"You good to go?" Jordan asks.

I swallow. "Sure."

"I need a burger ASAP."

"Same," I lie.

Because I'm suddenly not hungry anymore.

Twenty-Eight

LUCY.

Lucy?

I mean, I'd be less insulted if Jordan had saved my number in his phone as "Lots of People" than fucking *Lucy*. I bet that's who he told his mum he was bringing down here. Some pretty blonde girl from school who plays netball and puts out.

"You okay?" Jordan asks.

I'm staring out the car window, watching the sleepy little beach town blur past. It's nice and sunny today, but it's still pretty deserted out, even though it's school holidays. I guess it *is* the middle of winter. Not really beach vibes.

I clear my throat. "Yeah, just . . . I dunno. A bit tired, I think."

Jordan turns to smile at me, and even though I'm having a complete mental crisis, I can't help but smile back.

That *face*. I'm literally powerless here.

Maybe I'm overreacting—we all know it's what I do best. I don't need Jordan to proclaim his love for me in the middle of the quad. I don't need him to come to school wrapped in a gay pride flag. This is new to him. I get that. But saving my number under a *girl's* name? It feels so . . .

Let's put it this way: I changed Jordan's name in my phone to protect what was between us. To make sure none of the jerks at school ruined our hypothetical relationship before it even started. But Jordan saving my number under a *girl's* name? That's completely different. He's basically saying we have something to hide purely because we're both boys. Not because it's new and we don't really know what we are yet, but because two boys texting is something to be ashamed of.

And that feels like shit.

But then he looks at me and I feel like I'm floating.

And, honestly, I don't see any shame in his eyes. I don't see that he's scared or trying to hide his feelings or deny who he is. I see what I've always seen. The most beautiful boy in the world. Who *likes* me.

I mean, he actually *likes* me.

Maybe I just have to accept it all? The shit and the floating and the weirdness and the beauty. Is that what you do when you really like someone?

"Luca?"

I feel my mind snap back into my body. We're parked outside a cute cafe with a pale blue wooden bench out the front and an old oar above the door with the word ARCHIE's painted on it.

"I think you fell asleep," Jordan says, giving my leg a little shake.

"Oh, sorry," I reply, because it's way easier to pretend I was asleep than to tell Jordan I was trying to figure out exactly *how* doomed our relationship is. Not that we *have* a relationship yet.

Jesus. I need to *chill* . . .

Turns out the burgers at Archie's *are* mind-blowing, and I gradually relax into being alone with Jordan again. Our conversations are kind of random and forced at first ("Why do you think they're called 'burgers,' anyway?") but by the time we're strolling along the beach, our shoes in our hands, the chat is easy and comfortable. There's this buzz of tension between us, like we'll get an electric shock if we stand too close to each other.

After a while, my weak left calf muscle starts to burn. Walking on sand is hard at the best of times, and it's the first time I've walked anywhere near this far since I broke my foot.

"Can we stop for a sec?" I ask.

"Yeah, you okay?" Jordan asks. His concern is just too adorable.

"Totally," I lie. "I just feel like watching the waves for a bit."

So we sit. I pull my knees up to my chest and hug them in close. Jordan does the same, and slides right up next to me, so that our hips and knees touch.

A shiver shoots up my spine and I swallow nervously.

Jordan knocks my knee gently with his, and I knock his back. He knocks a little harder, and I give his shoulder a little nudge with mine. He nudges back and I almost fall sideways onto the sand. We both laugh and then there's silence.

So. Much. Silence.

The weird thing is, I can *feel* that he's thinking about kissing me, and I'm obviously thinking about kissing *him*. But how does it start? Who makes the move? And if it's me, *how* do I make it? Do I just grab his head and pull him in? I don't want to hurt his neck. And is this a good position for kissing? Will we be able to get the right angle? I refuse to let our first kiss be uncoordinated.

I just sit there, contemplating angles and the proper positioning of limbs until Jordan lets out a long sigh.

Oh my god, he hates me. He probably thinks I'm totally frigid.

I have to just do it. Right now.

I wet my lips and turn to face him . . .

"We should probably head back," he says suddenly, standing up. "The wind is getting pretty chilly."

Aaaaaand I fucked it. Why didn't I just *kiss him?*

He brushes some sand off the back of his jeans. "I wish we parked closer."

I push myself up off the sand. I can practically *see* the perfect moment flying straight past us. Again. Giving us both the finger.

I turn and bend down to grab my shoes. "Well," I say, "we'd better get mo—"

But then Jordan's hand is around my wrist and he's pulling me toward him and we're kissing.

His lips are warm and soft but there's this . . . *hardness* in the way he's kissing me. This roughness. Like he's hungry for it. Like he needs it. His tongue finds mine and something explodes in my chest. My eyes flicker open for a second, and I see that his eyebrows are scrunched up, like he's in pain. For a second, I think he must be hating it, that I must be a terrible kisser, but then a soft moan escapes his mouth. The sound tickles my lips and I close my eyes. He presses his hips into mine and I can feel how hard he is, which gives me this weird ache in my balls. He slides one hand up under my T-shirt and I shiver. I feel his lips tighten and I realize he's smiling, and then I'm smiling, and then we're laughing, our foreheads pressed together, our noses kind of squished in the middle.

"Well . . ." he whispers eventually.

"Well . . ."

"You've done that before, right?" he asks.

"Nope." My heart is *pounding*. Can he hear that? "You?"

"Not with a guy."

I take a slow breath, inhaling his scent. Shampoo and deodorant and *boy*. "It was . . ."

"Yeah," he laughs, his eyes locked on mine. "It really was."

One of the first things I ever noticed about Jordan was his lips, and I vividly remember thinking it should be illegal for them not to be kissing someone at all times. Never in my wildest dreams did I think *I'd* be the one kissing them. But now that I've finally, miraculously, *somehow* kissed Jordan Tanaka-Jones, I can't imagine ever doing anything else.

In the car ride back to the caravan park, we're quiet. But it's that comfortable kind of quiet I've only really ever had with Dad, and maybe Grace. Jordan has this relaxed half smile on his face, like he's smiling so much on the inside that it's showing on the outside too.

If I had to guess, I'd say he's replaying our kiss over and over in his mind like I am. That kiss was *everything*. I used to be so frustrated by the fact that I'd never kissed anyone. But if I'd wasted my first kiss on anyone less amazing than Jordan—anyone in the world *but* Jordan—I'd be so, so mad right now.

A lot of people talk about their first kiss being strange and awkward, but there was nothing strange or awkward about that. Well, the bit *before* the kiss was horrifically awkward, and I wanted to dig myself a hole in the sand and shrivel up and die, but the kiss itself was perfect. The one thing I will say is that tongues are way slipperier than I thought they would be. I'm not saying Jordan was slobbering all over me or anything, but it was, like . . . wet.

I run my tongue over the roof of my mouth. I guess it *is* pretty wet in here.

I accidentally laugh out loud.

"What?" Jordan asks.

"Nothing, just . . . Never mind."

We pull into the caravan park and make our way inside.

Jordan presses play on the CD player and skips a couple of songs, until he lands on a chilled guitar intro. "Vintage Maroon 5 okay?"

"Sure," I reply. I couldn't care less what we listen to, as long as Jordan kisses me again.

"Sit," he says, gesturing to the round little table squeezed down the front end of the caravan. It's got a shiny orange top and rusty metal legs, with two matching chairs.

I take a seat and watch as Jordan hunts through the kitchen cupboards.

"I know I left some here last time . . ." he says to himself. "Unless Mum found it and—*yes*, here we go."

He pulls an old shopping bag out of the cupboard under the sink. Sliding the bag off like it's a magic trick, he reveals a tall, half-full bottle of vodka.

"Tada!"

Here's the thing, I *have* had alcohol before. Talia's been sneaking gin from her mum's cupboard since she was about twelve. She made me try it once. It was awful. Tasted like Pine O Cleen. And I had a can of vodka raspberry at the Boat Race after-party last year. It took me literally hours to drink it, and I think everyone assumed it was more than one drink—not just the same warm can in my hand all night—which was great because it meant no one tried to give me more.

It's not that I'm against drinking, I've just always been so worried about my body and making sure I'm in peak ballet condition at all times. Plus, I never wanted to do anything that would put my goals at risk.

But *now* . . .

"Are we drinking it straight," I say, "or . . .?"

Jordan smiles, puts the vodka on the table and goes back to the cupboard. He pulls out a bottle of coke and says, "It's not cold, but if we're lucky . . ." He opens the freezer and sighs. "Nope. No ice. Sorry. I know vodka and warm coke isn't that appealing, but we *are* here to celebrate."

He grabs two glasses and pours our drinks, bending down to see if they have the same amount of vodka in them. He splashes a bit more into both. "What should we toast to?"

"I dunno." The fact that I'm in a caravan in Ocean Grove with Jordan Tanaka-Jones and we just kissed on the beach?

He hands me a glass and holds his up to the ceiling. "To freedom?"

"To freedom!" I cheers him and take a sip. "Shit," I say through a cough. "That is . . ."

"Strong," he finishes for me. "Sorry."

"You're so not sorry."

"No," he says, taking the other seat. "I am not."

By the time I finish my second glass, I feel kind of warm and floppy. My neck is like rubber and my feet are tingling. I need to slow down before I get too drunk. I don't want to pass out or vomit or embarrass myself. I've seen Abbey get wasted *many* times, and I refuse to humiliate myself in front of Jordan.

"I need to wee," I say. I stand up and the room sways. Or maybe I'm swaying. Yeah, probably that.

"You good?"

"So good," I reply, on my way to the tiny little bathroom.

When I come back out, Jordan has moved to the bottom bunk bed. I pause in the doorway, heat rising in my cheeks. He pats the mattress next to him and smiles up at me. "Come sit."

I sit on the bed, having to slouch so my head doesn't hit the bunk above. Jordan scooches over so that our legs are touching. He puts one hand on the mattress behind me and the other one on my thigh, turning to face me.

"You're beautiful, you know that?" he says softly. And for some reason, I'm sitting here wondering if that's what he said to Rhiannon before they had sex for the first time. Maybe they did it right here on this bunk bed.

Suddenly, I feel nervous and uncomfortable and weird.

He kisses my neck so gently I wonder if I imagined it.

"Are you all right?" he asks.

I nod.

He kisses my cheek, reaching up to turn my face toward his.

"Are you sure? You look . . . stressed."

And before I know it, it's out of my mouth. "I'm not ready to have sex."

Jordan flinches, then leans back, frowning.

"Sorry," I say. "I just . . . I'm guessing you're not a virgin, and you've probably had sex with Rhiannon right here in this caravan, but I'm only sixteen and this is new to me and I'm sorry but I'm just not ready yet."

A smile tugs at the corner of his mouth. "Luca, no one said we have to sleep together," he says. "I'm sorry if you felt pressured."

"No, I'm not saying . . ." But that's all I've got.

"Did you really think I was gonna go from kissing a boy for the first time to having full-on sex with him on a bunk bed in a matter of hours?"

I laugh, feeling the tension evaporate from the room. "Oh my god. I'm sorry."

"It's fine," he says, putting his hand back on my leg. "Don't be sorry. Thank you for being honest. I respect that."

I bite my bottom lip. "So . . . you're not a virgin?"

"No, I am not."

"Have you had sex with Rhiannon on this bunk bed?"

He laughs and shakes his head. "No, I have not."

"And . . . you're totally over her, right?"

"I am."

There's a pause, and then I ask (because I can't help myself), "Is it weird?"

"What?"

"Sex with a girl? I mean, vaginas are kind of strange."

"Is that really what you want to talk about right now?"

Jordan asks, leaning in a little closer. "Vaginas?"

"Sorry," I reply. "Are you mad at me for being dramatic?"

"No, Luca, I am not mad. I'm a lot of things right now—happy, relaxed, relieved, turned on—but I am not mad."

"Okay. Good."

"Besides," he says, smirking, "there are . . . *other* things we can do, right? Besides, you know, *sex*-sex. If you want?"

Instead of wasting a single second on the most obvious reply in history, I lean in and kiss him.

We start off nice and slow. Gentle. Like we're both testing the water, but then Jordan dives straight in, grabbing me by the shoulders and lowering me down onto the bed. He climbs on top of me, the weight of his body pressing down on mine, and kisses me like our lives depend on it.

Suddenly, the world fades away around us. We're floating in space, fire burning between our bodies. Jordan presses his hips into mine. I run my hand up his neck and into his hair. He kisses my neck. I gently bite his lip. He lifts himself up onto one arm. I stare into his eyes. He reaches down between us and slides his hand under the elastic of my jocks.

I gasp in a breath, a shiver rippling through my body.

"Is this okay?"

I nod.

"Are you sure?"

"Yes."

And it's more than okay. It's everything I've ever wanted.

It's Jordan's eyes. It's Jordan's lips. It's his hands and his skin. (Why has no one ever told me how amazing *skin* is?) It's his naked body against mine. It's curves and angles that fit perfectly together. It's hands everywhere and heat and hardness and breath and friction and closeness. It's . . .

It's over too soon.

It's kinda messy.

But it's pretty damn incredible. Because it's just me and Jordan Tanaka-Jones.

And nothing else matters.

Twenty-Nine

"BYE," JORDAN SAYS WITH a lazy grin, hanging half out the window of his mum's car.

It's almost unbearable to say goodbye to him, but it's already past 10:00 p.m., and he promised he'd have me home by now.

"You sure you don't want to come in?" I ask from my doorstep. "Tea? Tim Tam? Tim Tam Slam?"

He laughs. "As much as I love a Tim Tam Slam . . . another time. I promise."

"Okay," I sigh. "Well . . . bye. Thanks for like, the best time ever."

"Any time. I'll text you when I get home."

"Yes, please."

He smiles, winds up the window and pulls out of the drive. I take a few deep breaths to steady my pounding heart while I watch the car disappear down the street.

That actually happened. The last two days *actually happened.*

Today was perfect. We slept in till ten (I took the top bunk, Jordan took the bottom—because no matter how much I wanted to snuggle, there was no chance we'd fit two teenage boys in one tiny single bed) then went out for brunch, strolled around town, went down to the beach, had ice creams for lunch, went for coffee in this cute, hippie cafe, and talked the afternoon away.

Jordan had this "brilliant idea" to take some bikes from the caravan park and ride up to the Barwon Heads Bluff to watch the sunset, but I was so not ready to ruin everything by telling him I didn't know how to ride a bike. I managed to weasel my way out of it by saying I thought it would hurt my weak calf too much and I didn't want to get all the way to the top of the lookout and not be able to get back down. I think he bought the story, and he seemed happy enough to drive up instead. Driving meant more sing-alongs.

Then we ate about eight-hundred dollars' worth of fish and chips for dinner down on the main strip in Barwon Heads and jumped in the car to drive home to Ballarat.

Now that I'm back, the whole thing feels like a dream. Hazy and patchy and too perfect to be true. I close my eyes, trying to make sure I burn the memories into my brain. I want to wake up tomorrow and still be able to remember every single beautiful second of the last two days.

As soon as I open the front door, Dad is up and out of his chair, his eyes wide.

"Well," he says, practically running to the door. "How was it?"

I laugh. "Can you at least let me come inside before you start the interrogation?"

"Sorry," he says, stepping aside for me. I head into the lounge and dump my bag on the couch, collapsing onto the cushion next to it.

"Well?" he says again, perching himself on the edge of the coffee table. "How did it go?"

"It was . . ." I shrug, feeling awkward and shy all of a sudden, " . . . great."

"And?"

"And what?" I laugh. "I had a great time."

"You're not going to tell me anything about the trip?"

"If there's something you want to know, Dad, just ask." As soon as I say it, I realize there's only one question he wants to know the answer to. "We didn't have sex. Okay? Are we done?"

He stares back at me. "Lu, that's not what I was asking."

"You're not fooling anyone, Dad."

"I'm serious," he says. "Thank you for telling me—you know you can always tell me anything—but I just wanted to make sure you had a good time."

"Why wouldn't I have had a good time?"

"I'm not saying you wouldn't have, mate. I'm just . . . making sure."

"Making sure? Dad, you're being weird."

"How am I being weird?" he says, his shoulders so high they're practically touching his ears. "I'm not allowed to ask my son—my *underage* son—if he had a good time on a completely unsupervised overnight trip to Ocean Grove with an eighteen-year-old boy I barely know, who—last I heard—was *straight?* I'm not allowed to just check in?"

"This is ridiculous," I reply, rolling my eyes. "What do you want to know? Just spit it out."

Dad exhales loudly through his nostrils. "Nothing. It's just that Jordan is virtually a stranger to me, and—"

"Yeah, well, he's not a stranger to *me*," I cut in. "And you said it was fine. You could have said no if you didn't want me to go."

"I know that," he says quietly, clearly trying to calm me down. "But like I was trying to say to you yesterday, you've been through a hell of a lot this year, and—"

"So?"

"*So,*" he replies in his teacher voice, "I don't want you getting your heart broken on top of all that."

"Who says I'm going to get my heart broken?"

"No one is saying that," Dad says, running a hand over his bald head. "I'm happy that you've finally found a boy you're interested in—you have to know that—and Jordan is very handsome and sweet and I can see why you like hanging out with him. But, the reality is, he's probably dealing with a lot of his own stuff right now, and I don't want you drowning in the deep end while he's just testing the water."

"What does that even mean?"

"It means," he replies, "I don't want you getting caught up in someone else's drama when you're still in such a fragile state yourself."

"Dad, you don't even *know* Jordan. You have no idea what he's like."

"*Exactly,*" he says, as if we're suddenly on the same side, arguing the same point. It makes me want to scream.

"You know what," I say, pushing myself up from the couch. "This is ridiculous."

Dad stands too. "Lu, I'm just trying to do my job."

"Yeah, well, maybe I don't need dating advice from someone

who hasn't been on a date in the last fourteen years."

Dad lets out a long sigh, looking up at the ceiling. "Fine. Do whatever you want, Lu. You never listen to me anyway."

He retreats into the kitchen but I follow close behind. "What is *that* supposed to mean?"

He grabs the kettle and starts filling it at the sink. "It *means* that you don't seem to care too much for my advice anymore, so I may as well stop saying anything at all. Ever since you broke your foot, you—"

"Wait, what?" I say, completely lost all of a sudden. "What does this have to do with my *foot?*"

"Don't worry about it," Dad replies, flicking the switch on the kettle. "Let's just forget I said anything."

"No, what were you going to say?"

"Nothing." His face is slowly turning red. "I just don't want you getting hurt again, that's all."

"Okay, well, I'm not going to, so . . ."

"And I don't want you to forget about the other important things in your life."

"Like what?"

Dad folds his arms and purses his lips, like he's wrestling with something internally.

"What?" I press.

"When did you get your moon boot off?"

"I dunno." I still don't know what my foot has to do with any of this. "Like, a week ago?"

"A week ago," Dad replies, like it's the answer to some riddle we've both been trying to guess since the minute I walked in the door.

"Yeah. *And?*"

"And you haven't even tried."

"Tried to what?"

"Dance."

Oh my fucking god.

The kettle starts bubbling. I don't know what to say.

"I just wish," Dad says gently, after a moment, "that you were putting as much energy into your recovery as you are into hanging out with Jordan. That's all."

"You're not actually serious, are you?"

He takes a deep breath, pinching the bridge of his nose. "I wasn't going to say anything. I've been trying *not* to say anything all week." (Which at least explains why he's been acting so weird.) "I just thought," he goes on, "that your first priority when the boot finally came off would have been dancing. That you would have jumped on the phone to Miss Gwen and Miss Prue—"

"This isn't *about* Miss Gwen and Miss Prue."

"No," he says, "you're right. It's about *you* prioritizing some boy, who—"

"Some boy?" I reply, my blood boiling. "Dad, you're—you know what, we're not having this conversation."

"Lu, I'm sorry, I didn't—"

"Nope," I say, turning around and walking out of the kitchen. "We're done here."

"Lu, please," he says, but I'm already at the top of the stairs. "Come down. Let's talk this out properly."

But I'm already gone.

Thirty

DAD IS QUIET AND awkward for the rest of the holidays. I can tell there's still so much he desperately wants to say, but he just holds it all in. Which is very unlike him. And I should be happy about it—because I obviously don't want to talk about my foot or ballet or Miss Gwen or anything that happened so far this year ever again—but I start sleeping in super late so I don't have to sit through the painful silence at breakfast.

I spend a lot of time at Amina's place, even though all she wants to do is study. I thought she might relax a bit now that mid-year exams are over, but "stressed and studying" seems to be her only setting these days.

Jordan stays down at the beach with his family for the whole holidays, so I don't get to see him at all. I want to suggest that he should come up to Ballarat so we can hang out for a day, but I don't want to seem clingy and desperate. And we message constantly, so it's bearable. Almost.

"Who on *earth* are you texting all the time?" Amina asks me one afternoon while we're studying. Her parents are cooking, so the air is thick with oil and chili.

"People," I shrug.

"But I'm your only friend."

I laugh, even though, sadly, it's kind of true.

She narrows her eyes. "Are you talking to the girls from your old school again?" There's this hint of jealousy in her voice that I haven't heard before.

"No," I say. "As if."

"Family?"

Amina already knows I don't really talk to my family, except Dad, which either means she's trying to catch me out, or . . . I dunno. She really is too smart for her own good.

"It's my OT."

"Your OT messages you every day? Aren't you finished with your sessions now?"

"Not *all* the messages are from her."

She puts her pen down and folds her arms across her chest. "Luca, what's going on? Why are you being so secretive?"

"I'm not being secretive," I say, forcing a *don't be ridiculous* chuckle.

"Is it a boy?"

"Is what a boy?"

"The person you're messaging?"

"No."

She lifts her eyebrows. "Really?"

"Yes."

"Are you sure?"

"Oh my god, Amina, you're as bad as my dad. Can we just leave it?"

"Fine," she replies, flipping the page in her psych textbook so hard that she almost rips it out. Which makes it *very* clear there is something else going on here. And if I had to guess, I'd say it was something Jordan related.

"Are you okay?" I ask, turning my page too (in a way that *won't* injure my textbook).

"Of course," she shrugs, her voice just a little too cheerful. "Why wouldn't I be?"

"Okay, well, great."

"Great."

For the next ten minutes, we don't make a single sound, except for the scratching of our pens on paper. Then, completely out of nowhere—with her head still in her book—Amina says, "I wonder if TJ is having a good holiday."

There it is. And suddenly I'm nervous, because the way she said it didn't sound like a question. It sounded like a trap. But I mean, there's no way she could know about me and Jordan, is there?

"I dunno," I reply, swallowing the awkward lump in my throat. "I hope so."

"Did he ever decide how we're going to celebrate?"

"What?"

Amina puts her pen down again. "Jordan said he was going to think of a way for us to celebrate you getting your moon boot off. Remember?"

"Oh, yeah," I say slowly, trying to figure out what the hell I'm supposed to say next. I honestly forgot Amina was even there when he said that. And now she's going to think we went behind her back to celebrate without her. Which is totally not what happened, but how am I supposed to prove it was an honest mistake?

If I'd just told Amina the truth weeks ago—when I first realized she had a crush on Jordan—we wouldn't even be having this conversation. I'd be telling her about the world's most adorable beach trip, and she'd be gasping in all the right places, and I'd be laughing at her for covering her ears when I got up to the bit about the bottom bunk. And I *know* she'd be happy for us.

I should just tell her. I *need* to tell her. But . . .

Maybe I'm a bad person. Maybe I'm the world's most awful friend. Or maybe I've been waiting my whole life in this town to meet a boy who actually likes me, and now that I finally have, I'm not about to ruin everything by giving away secrets he specifically asked me to keep.

I can't do that to him. I won't.

So, I just shrug—as if lying to my best friend doesn't make me feel physically ill—and say, "I dunno. I guess he must have forgotten."

On the first day of Term Three, I can barely contain my excitement about finally seeing Jordan again. But I have to just bottle it all up. Mainly because I feel like a big dirty liar every time his name is mentioned, but also because the *last* thing I want to do is gush to Amina about how amazing he is and give her even more reasons to fall in love with him.

"I'm guessing you heard about Gibbo's party?" she asks on the way to our benches after second period. There's no rain this morning, but the sky is full of angry black clouds. It's one of those days where it feels like the world might end at any second.

"You mean the 'party of the century'?" I scoff, drawing quotes in the air. People were whispering about Gibbo's eighteenth birthday party all through maths and English. And as much as I'd love to say I couldn't care less about it, it's hard not to feel like a total loser when you're one of literally four people in your whole year level who isn't invited. (Ten points if you can guess the other three.) "I don't know why he's making such a big deal about it already," I add. "It's not till October."

Amina shrugs. Party planning is obviously not her specialty.

"And where does he think he's gonna fit three-hundred people, anyway?" I ask as we sit down.

"His parents own a potato farm just outside of Ballarat," Amina replies. "If anyone's got room, it's him."

"Oh my god, I couldn't think of anything worse than going to a party at some gross potato farm. Especially to celebrate *Gibbo* being born." I pretend to throw up in my mouth.

"Exactly," Amina says, rolling her eyes in a way I'm sure is meant to make it look like she doesn't care about the party, but actually makes her look super desperate to go. "We don't need to go to some high school piss-up—pardon my French. While everyone else is out losing brain cells, we'll be at home *gaining* them."

I force a smile. I know she's trying to make us both feel better, but if I had to choose between staying home to study with Amina or going to the biggest party of the year with Jordan, I think we all know I'd take the party—potatoes or no potatoes.

But then I spot Jordan walking toward our benches, looking

as effortlessly glorious as ever, and I forget that Gibbo and his potato farm party even exist. Memories of Ocean Grove come flooding back to me, and I can't seem to breathe properly.

Jordan gets closer.

I smile. He smiles.

I stand up, literally exploding with joy, my body aching to be near him. But then he gives me one of his upward nods and keeps on walking down to the quad.

My heart freezes in my chest.

Jordan just walked straight past me. Like it was nothing. Like I was no one. Like Ocean Grove never even happened. I stand there, staring after him, feeling kind of dizzy. What the hell just happened? Does Jordan regret what happened between us? Now that he's seen me again in real life, has he changed his mind about the whole thing? Is it . . . Are we over?

"That was weird," Amina says in a low voice.

"What?" I reply, blinking myself back to reality.

"Jordan didn't stop to say hello. That's weird, right?"

I slowly lower myself back onto the bench and turn to face her, my brain ticking overtime.

"I thought he'd be excited to see us," she says. "I was really looking forward to hearing about what he got up to on the holidays."

Staring at Amina—at the hurt painted across her face—it suddenly makes sense.

Jordan isn't avoiding me, he's avoiding *her*.

He's clearly decided to put some distance between him and Amina to squash all those ridiculous rumors about them, once and for all. People are *still* talking about it—how they have nothing better to talk about after two weeks off, I don't know, but that's North for you.

I *almost* told Jordan that she asked about our "celebration" (and that she was really weird about the whole thing, and that I'm ninety-nine percent sure she's secretly in love with him) but then decided that was an absolutely terrible idea. Because what would it have achieved, aside from making things super awkward for all three of us? Especially me, because I'm the one in the middle of the whole thing.

But that would be it, right? The rumors? I mean, Jordan messaged me *three hours* ago saying how much he couldn't wait to see me. There's no way he could have changed his mind in the span of two periods.

Right?

But Jordan doesn't visit us at lunchtime, either.

The second I get home, I send him a message: **How was your day? Bummed we didn't get to hang.**

Two hours later, he replies: **Good. You? Dw, we can hang tomorrow.**

But Jordan doesn't sit with us the next day. Or the day after. He smiles and says hey on the way past—and I swear I can see in his eyes how happy he is to see me—but he doesn't stop to talk. And it's not like I expected him to do a full song and dance routine about us finally being reunited, but I thought he'd at least stop to give me a bro hug. And the weird thing is, he still messages me every morning and every night, telling me how beautiful I am and how much he can't wait for us to be alone together again. Which is actually kind of infuriating. I want to write back, *Then why the hell are you being so weird at school?* but I don't need to ask. It's so obvious what's going on. And it's nothing to do with those rumors.

Ocean Grove was a perfect little gay oasis. We danced, we drank, we kissed, we . . . did other things. We were *alone*. But now that we're back in the real world . . .

On Friday after school, I decide to message him about it. It's already killing me, and it's only been a week. But just as I'm about to copy the essay I've constructed in my notes into a text message, my phone pings.

Jordan: **Come over?**

I stare down at my phone.

Hey. I write back, trying to process the fact that Jordan just invited me to his place. Where his parents will be.

Are you doing anything tonight? he replies. **You should come to mine.**

And I know I'm meant to be mad at him, and I know there are important things we need to talk about, but my fingers are already typing.

What's your address?

Thirty-One

I DON'T WANT TO ask Dad to drop me off at Jordan's, so I get the bus. It's only a couple of suburbs over, just around the corner from Amina's. It's a slightly nicer part of Ballarat than where I live, but it's still nothing like the Bunheads' places across town and around Lake Wendouree.

I knock on the door, feeling a little ill. I run my fingers through my hair and brush some lint off my shoulder. I'm wearing a carefully selected outfit that's sensible enough for meeting the parents but still cute enough for hanging out with Jordan.

After a few seconds, I'm greeted by his smiling face at the door. He's in grey trackies, Ugg boots, and a navy hoodie with the Disneyland castle on the front, which makes me feel *slightly* overdressed in my chinos and knitted sweater, but he's so adorable that I don't care.

"Come in," he says.

His house is small and like, super minimal. It's the complete opposite to Amina's, which is packed to the brim with *things*.

Here, the furniture is all wooden, the shelves have a couple of family photos on them and nothing more, and every surface is sparkling clean. Now I understand why his parents are so full-on about coasters.

"How are you?" he asks, walking down the hallway. Before I can answer, he adds, "We can chill in my room."

"Is that cool with your parents?"

He winks at me over his shoulder and says, "They're out all night," and keeps walking.

"Oh, I thought . . ." I stop, halfway down the hall. It hadn't occurred to me that his parents wouldn't be home. I thought he invited me over so I could meet them, but . . . he only invited me over because they're not here. Which means they still don't even know I exist.

Jordan sticks his head out of the door to his room. "You okay?"

I swallow the awkward lump in my throat and nod. "Yep, I just . . ." I trail off when Jordan smiles at me from the doorway down the hall, his eyes sparkling.

"Come," he says, and his head disappears inside the room.

His bedroom looks nothing like what I imagined. No sports posters, no rowing trophies, no clothes all over the floor. It's neat and white and clean. Kind of like the rest of the house, I guess. There's one framed photo of Jordan and his parents on the wall, and a beautiful bonsai tree sitting on the window ledge.

"It's cool, right?" he says, when he notices me staring at it. "We've had it since before I was born. My nan—Mum's mum— gave it to her and Dad as an anniversary present one year."

"And it's still alive?"

"Yep. They can live for ages if you look after them properly. Mum taught me how to take care of it when I was little. I love it. It's kinda nice having something to nurture."

I can't imagine Jordan talking like this in front of Gibbo and his mates.

He sits on his bed, moving to one side so there's room for both of us. "You wanna sit?"

But I don't want to sit. I feel weird.

"Are you sure you're okay?" he asks.

"Yeah, I just . . ."

"Tell me. You can say."

But I don't know how to start this conversation. I bite my lip.

"Luca, what's going on?"

"I thought . . ."

Jordan has this worried look on his face, like I'm about to tell him I'm moving halfway across the world or something. I don't understand how he doesn't already know what I'm about to say.

"I thought you liked—" I go to say *me* but chicken out "—you know, hanging out with me or whatever, but if I was wrong, just tell me so I can move on."

"What?" He starts to laugh but then stops himself. "Wait, are you serious?"

"Why won't you sit with me and Amina at school anymore?"

His grin fades and he reaches up to scratch the back of his head.

"I've been dying to see you since Ocean Grove," I go on, "but you won't even talk to us."

"Please just come and sit." Jordan pats the bed beside him.

"No." I shake my head. "Because when I'm near you I can't think straight."

He smiles.

"Don't smile, it makes it worse."

"Sorry. No smiles."

I fold my arms and stand there, waiting for him to say something.

"Fine," he says eventually. "You wanna know why? Because when I saw you at school on the first day of term, all I wanted to do was run over and kiss you. More than kiss you. Much more, if I'm honest. But I couldn't do any of that."

"Why not?"

"Because it's not that simple."

"What's not that simple?"

He tilts his head to the side. "You *know* what, Luca. I'm not . . . I know it's bullshit, but I'm not ready for this thing between us to be, you know . . .?"

"Right. Because . . .?"

"Because it's a lot."

Why do I suddenly feel like I'm being shoved back into the closet?

"Is it okay if we keep things between us for now?" He smiles again, his brow crinkling in the middle.

"I said no smiles."

He laughs. "Please, Luca. I really like hanging out with you."

"What are we meant to do at school, then? Are you just gonna walk straight past me every day? You're never gonna sit with us?"

"I don't know if I can."

"Why not?"

"Because I don't know how to pretend like I'm not completely obsessed with you," he replies, and my heart skips about six beats. "After . . . *being* with you in Ocean Grove, having this perfect time there with you, the thought of sitting on those benches with you and Amina, pretending like we're just *mates* feels . . . unbearable."

"But so does ignoring me though, right? Like, that's not a better solution, is it?"

He draws his lips into a line. "No, it's not. I'm just . . ." He lets his hands fall into his lap. He looks up at me with this look of like, *Help me out, here,* and I crumble.

"Look," I say, offering him a smile in truce, "I get it. Every gay guy goes through this."

"But that's the thing," he says, a little pained. "I . . . I don't know if I *am* gay."

Which kind of throws me. "What?"

"I'm obviously not straight," he says, "because I'm clearly attracted to you. Like, *really* attracted to you. But I'm still attracted to girls, too."

"Rhiannon?" I ask, feeling weirdly jealous all of a sudden.

"No," he replies, "just . . . girls in general."

"So . . . you're bi?"

He shrugs. "I dunno."

"Well, there's no other option, is there? If you like boys *and* girls, you're bi. Or pan? Right?"

"I honestly don't know. Maybe I don't like boys. Maybe I just like *you.*"

"But *I'm* a boy."

He laughs. "I *know*. This is why I'm so confused. I've never looked at a guy and felt any kind of . . . anything. I've seen literally all of my mates naked, but I've never batted an eyelid. It just never did anything for me. At all. But with you, it's different. It's always been different."

"Different *how?*"

He shrugs. "I don't know. I guess that's what I'm trying to figure out."

I sigh and glance over at the bonsai tree.

He pats the bed again. "Please come sit?"

As I stare at the tiny tree—this beautiful thing that Jordan has kept alive his entire life—I feel my frustration melt away. I let out a sigh and climb onto the bed beside him. He reaches around and places his hand on the side of my jaw, turning my face toward his.

"I just need you to bear with me while I sort my shit out," he says. "Is that okay?"

And I don't know. *Is* it okay?

"I like you, Luca," he says, leaning in so close that his nose brushes mine. "A lot."

I breathe in his words, those words I've been longing to hear since the first moment I saw him in the OT waiting room. It doesn't feel real, but it feels way too real at the same time, like I've pictured this moment so often that I can't tell if I'm watching it happen inside my head again or if it's actually happening right here in front of me.

"I like you too," I say. "A lot."

And then he kisses me.

Thirty-Two

SO . . . IT SEEMS I have a secret relationship. It's not practical. It's definitely not ideal. I'm not quite sure if it even *qualifies* as a relationship (we haven't used the B-word yet). But I won't lie, it's actually kind of fun.

Some nights after school I go to Jordan's place—only when he's home alone, obviously—and we fool around in his bedroom until his parents are due back, and then I chuck my clothes on and jump on the bus home. Sometimes, if I walk past him in the corridor at school when no one's around, he pulls me into an empty classroom, kisses me, whispers something in my ear like, "Your bum looks cute today," or "I couldn't *not* kiss you," and then disappears as if nothing ever happened. One time, we found ourselves in the boys' bathroom next to the gym together, totally by chance, and we locked ourselves in a cubicle and made out for like, half an hour. I was super late to drama, but my teacher was ranting about arts funding and something to do with lobster costumes, so I don't think she noticed.

The only place in the whole of Ballarat that we could be openly together would be my house, because Dad already knows we're hanging out, and he's clearly not going to ruin Jordan's secret. But the problem is, the vibes are still super awkward between me and Dad. And I don't want Jordan to know that Dad's not okay with me dating a boy who is "testing the water" (the gay water, that is) or that he thinks Jordan is about to break my heart at any second.

So, Jordan and I take whatever secret time we can get. It's not nearly as much as I'd like, but it's better than "hi" on the way past our benches and that's it.

"Luca," Amina says on our way out of biology on Friday morning, and I just *know* what's coming.

She has a brand-new lavender hijab on today, with this cute little gold-beaded hijab pin at the back. I also think she's wearing lip gloss for the first time in history, but I don't want to make a big deal about how pretty she looks because I know she'll just get embarrassed. And I have a feeling she's doing it to get Jordan's attention, which I don't want to encourage. For obvious reasons.

"Yes, Amina?"

"Why do you think TJ's not hanging out with us anymore?"

It's already been *weeks*. I'm surprised she hasn't already launched a full-scale investigation.

"I dunno," I lie.

"Do you think we did something wrong?" she asks, her voice almost shaking. "Do you think maybe we offended him somehow?"

"Amina, we're like, the least offensive people in the whole

school. Except maybe Bree and Alicia, but that's only because they don't talk."

"But he basically hasn't spoken to us since last term. I just thought . . . you know, there were all those rumors . . ."

"Everyone's forgotten about that." Another lie.

"Are you sure?" she asks, and I can tell by the look on her face that *she* certainly hasn't forgotten. "Do you think I should talk to him about it?"

"No." I shake my head. "Definitely not." I tighten my scarf around my neck and lean into the freezing wind.

"And you don't think . . ."

"What?"

"Nothing," she replies, looking down at our feet as we walk. "Don't worry about it."

"Maybe he . . ." I'm thinking on the spot here, because I can tell Amina feels like this is somehow her fault, and I hate that it's affecting her. Especially when it's one hundred percent because of me, and I'm still talking to Jordan all the time. "Maybe he's just swamped with school stuff at the moment. Shit is about to get very real for the Year Twelves."

Amina doesn't reply, but I can see the cogs turning in her brain all the way to our lockers. When we stop, she says, "We should go to the game tomorrow."

"What game?"

"The footy semi-final. North is playing St. Peter's."

Oh. *That* game. "Why?"

"*Because*," she stresses. "I don't know what we did wrong, but we need to show TJ how much we care."

"If he wanted us to come and watch him play, he would

have already invited us." (Which is obviously not going to happen.) "It'd be like rocking up to Gibbo's eighteenth without an invitation."

"It would be *nothing* like that."

"Well, no one's stopping you," I reply, pulling my English books out of my locker. "But *I* will be at home studying. I understood about four words in psych this morning."

"Luca, *please*," she whines, and I never thought I'd see the day she tried to convince someone *not* to study. "It's a school event. Lots of people go."

My heart drops into my stomach. *Lots of people.* I can still hear Jordan saying it.

"Then it won't matter that I'm not there, will it?" I snap, feeling flustered and annoyed all of a sudden.

"But don't you think TJ would be happy we came to show our support? North hasn't made the grand final for *years*. It'll mean the world to him. I know it will."

"Then we'll go and watch next week if they make it through, all right?" I don't actually mean it, but I need this conversation to be over.

"But what if they don't *make* the grand final?" Amina presses. "This is Jordan's last season at North. Tomorrow could literally be our last chance to see him play."

As soon as she says it, it hits me: Jordan is leaving. The boy I'm falling head-over-heels in love with will be leaving school and never coming back in *two-and-a-bit months*. And I'll be stuck here without him. How did I not see this coming? Jordan is a Year Twelve. I am a Year Eleven. I've known this since our very first conversation.

I slam my locker shut. "I can't go, okay? I need to study."

"Fine," Amina huffs. "But you better pray North wins tomorrow."

But it doesn't matter if they win or lose. Because Jordan will still be leaving. And there's nothing I can do about it.

When I wake up the next morning, Amina's words are still ringing in my mind.

We need to show TJ that we care . . .

It'll mean the world to him . . .

Our last chance . . .

I lie there in bed with the doona pulled right up around my ears, thinking in circles.

Does Jordan really not want me at the game? Or is he just afraid to ask me to come? If I go, will he be mad? If I don't go, will he be secretly disappointed?

If it was me, and I had a big ballet competition coming up, I would definitely want Jordan there in the audience. Especially if it was my last competition ever.

Amina's right. I *do* need to show him that I care. That I'm interested in what he does. And it's not like I'm going to ride in on a unicorn with a big, rainbow sign that says I'VE KISSED THE CAPTAIN OF THE FOOTBALL TEAM.

Jordan probably just thinks I wouldn't enjoy watching him play—I've made it pretty clear I have like, zero interest in sport. And maybe I took it the wrong way when he said, "lots of people come to watch." Maybe he meant I *should* come and watch. Maybe it *will* mean the world to him.

After breakfast, I rug up in my warmest jacket, a pair of jeans, and a navy-blue scarf—almost North colors—and head to the bus stop. While I wait, I take a cute selfie and send it to Jordan with the caption **Ready to watch you run around in short shorts!** Monkey-covering-its-mouth emoji.

He writes back almost instantly:

Jesus. Careful. Gibbo almost saw that.

Shit, sorry! I write. **I'm just SO excited!** Love-heart eyes emoji.

You're not actually coming to the game are you?

I squint down at my phone. How am I meant to know if he's excited or angry if he doesn't use any emojis?

Of course! I reply, trying to stay positive. **Thought it was time I showed some school spirit haha**

Three dots . . .

Luca . . . I thought we were clear on this stuff.

What stuff?

You coming to the game, he writes. **It's not a good idea.**

I drop my hands into my lap, feeling heat building behind my eyes.

Another message: **Sorry if you're on the bus already but I really don't think you should come. I gotta go. Have a good one.**

Have a good one?

My vision blurs with tears as I shove my phone back in my pocket and start walking home.

Thirty-Three

I SPEND THE REST of the morning feeling totally ill, thinking that I might have just ruined everything. I write Jordan about six apology messages in a row, but he doesn't reply. But then I get a message from him in the afternoon saying: **Meet me out the front of the OT at 5pm?**

I squint down at my phone, thinking I've read it wrong. **The OT? Are you okay?**

5pm, yeah? he writes. **Please come.**

Yeah. Of course.

I get the bus into the main part of town and walk the few blocks to the OT. By the time I get there, it's only 4:25 p.m., so I wait by the railing with this weird weight hanging in my chest, like something awful is about to happen. I remember feeling the same thing when our old dog, Allegro, ate some snail pellets and had to be taken to the vet to have his stomach pumped. I was like, five, and Dad made me wait at home with one of our neighbors, watching some tacky '90s family movie, until he eventually called to tell me Allegro had died.

After about ten minutes, the sliding doors of the OT *whoosh* open and Jordan walks out with a white sling on his arm. He gives me a sad little wave as he scuffs over to meet me.

"Holy shit," I say. "What happened?"

"My shoulder." He leans back against the railing beside me. "I went for a mark in the last quarter and it just clicked and then started hurting like hell."

"Fuck."

"Yeah," he says, rubbing his eyes with his free hand. He looks exhausted. "North hasn't made the grand final since before I started high school, and when we finally do, I'm *injured*. It's the shittiest timing ever."

"Wait, you made the grand final?"

Jordan nods. His eyes are red, like he's been crying. Suddenly, there's no way I could possibly be mad at him. All that matters is that he's okay.

"What did your OT say?' I ask. "Does he think you'll be able to recover by next week?"

"He's not sure. He said it could just be a little spasm or something, or that it could be my bursitis flaring up. Or maybe something more severe. He said we'll reassess in a couple of days."

"I'm so sorry, Jordan. This really sucks. Like, really, *really* sucks. But . . . maybe you'll be totally fine to play next week?"

He kicks a loose stone across the ramp and into the car park. "Yeah, but what if I'm not? I've been playing footy since Grade Three. This is my last high school premiership. I'm the captain of the bloody team. If they play without me, win or lose, it will *kill* me."

I let out a dry chuckle. "I know the feeling."

"Don't laugh at me," he says. "It's not funny."

"I'm not laughing *at* you." I turn to face him. "I'm sorry, I just . . . I know exactly what you're feeling right now."

"Oh, really?" he snaps. "How many football premierships have you played in? You wouldn't even be able to kick straight."

I don't *think* that's a gay joke, but I'm offended either way. But . . . this isn't about me.

"Look," I say, "I know you're upset, but if you—"

"What? You want me to cry again? You think that'll magically fix this, too?"

"No," I say firmly, trying to stay calm for Jordan's sake. "All I'm trying to say is that I understand what you're going through. When I broke my foot, I thought the world was going to end. I wanted to scream and cry and throw shit across the room, every minute of every day. But I got through it, and you will, too. And it's not like you want to be drafted, so it—"

"Oh, so just because I don't want to be a *professional* AFL player means it doesn't matter? This grand final is *everything* to me, Luca. You have no idea what you're talking about."

"That's not what I'm saying. You're putting words in my mouth."

Jordan pushes away from the railing and whips around to face me. "You *want* me to be injured, don't you?"

"What?"

"You *want* me to miss out on the match. You *want* me to have to give up footy like you did with dancing, so the two of us can just sit at home and be depressed together."

"That is *not* f—"

"Well, I'm not gonna give up like you did, Luca. I'm not that pathetic."

It's like a slap in the face. I stand there, stunned, while Jordan turns away and swears at the top of his lungs across the car park. Tears fill my eyes, but I quickly wipe them away before he turns back around to face me.

"You think I'm pathetic?" I ask.

"No," he groans, both hands on top of his head. "I'm sorry. I—"

"You know what's *pathetic?* Not having the balls to be who you are."

His face hardens. "Excuse me?"

"You heard me," I say, my voice trembling. I know he's just taking his frustration out on me, but that doesn't make it hurt any less. "I know *exactly* what's happening here."

"You want to explain it to me, then?"

"*Fine.* You don't want me to come to your footy games because you hate the thought of anyone knowing I care about you. You won't even *talk* to me at school because you don't want people to get suspicious about us—which, by the way, means I have to lie to my best friend every day, which obviously feels *wonderful.* You won't let me come over to your place when your parents are home because you don't want them to know I exist, because then you'll have to actually tell them you're gay or bi or whatever the hell you are and you're afraid they won't love you anymore. You say you need time to 'figure things out' but that's just a bullshit way of covering up the fact that you're ashamed of who you are. Oh, and '*Lucy*'? That is some messed-up shit."

Now it's Jordan's turn to be stunned. He just stands there,

mouth open, for a long moment, then says, "You went through my phone?"

"No, I didn't. You left it unlocked on your message screen when we were in the caravan and I—"

"I can't believe you'd go through my messages."

"I didn't 'go through' them," I reply, frustrated that the only thing he picked up on in that whole speech was that I saw his messages. "I could see it right there on the bench. And this is not about that. This is about you forcing me back in the closet."

"What?"

"I came out when I was *thirteen*, Jordan. Because I was already sick of pretending to be someone I wasn't. That shit is *exhausting*. And no, it wasn't always easy, because we live in a fucking country town and kids can be awful. But it was a hell of a lot better than living a lie."

"Is that what you think I'm doing?" Jordan's eyes are wild. "Living a lie?"

"Yes."

"You know what? Fuck you, Luca. I don't need this. Not now. I've got more important shit to deal with."

He turns and storms off down the ramp.

"Well, you'll be gone soon," I call after him, "so what does it matter, anyway?"

But he doesn't stop. He walks across the car park and disappears around the corner. Only then do I let myself cry.

Thirty-Four

IT'S BEEN THREE WEEKS since Jordan spoke to me. Or messaged me. Literally nothing for *three weeks*. The last thing he said to me was, "I've got more important shit to deal with," and apparently he wasn't joking. I mean, I know Year Twelve is *kind* of a big deal, and I know Jordan needs solid test scores to get into architecture, but he's basically disappeared off the face of the earth.

The shit thing—well, it's not shit for Jordan, it's *awesome* for Jordan, but it's certainly shit for me—is that his shoulder was totally fine. The Monday after our fight, I spotted him down the end of the science corridor and he'd already ditched his sling. I was relieved, obviously, and all I wanted to do was run up to him and hug him and tell him how happy I was that he was okay. Instead, I turned and walked straight to the boys' bathrooms beside the gym, locked myself in a cubicle, and cried for a whole period.

And he ended up playing in the footy grand final against St. Tom's as if nothing had ever happened. He got to live out his childhood dreams while I stayed at home and ate three whole packets of double-coat Tim Tams and watched seasons one *and* two of *Will & Grace* back to back—which is like, fifteen hours of television, so don't ever tell me I can't commit.

Amina took her parents to the game—I told her I had food poisoning—and reported back with a minute-by-minute description of the match. It was like Boat Race all over again. Except this time, North won. They actually *won*. They beat St. Tom's by twelve goals—Jordan scored ten of them, which sounds like a lot, even to me—winning the Ballarat and Central Highlands School Premiership for the first time in eight years.

I wanted to be happy for him, I really did, but I was still so mad. Even though I may have *slightly* overreacted that afternoon outside the OT, I did mean what I said. Sneaking around with Jordan might have been kind of fun and exciting at first, but that's not what I want. I want a real boyfriend. I want to be with someone who wants to hold my hand as we walk across the quad at school. Who'll kiss me goodbye at the bus stop. Who's proud to introduce me to his parents. Not someone who refuses to sit with me at lunch or acknowledge that I exist in public.

And definitely not someone who thinks I *gave up*.

But still, I can't begin to explain how awful I felt the night of the grand final, and not only because of the twenty-seven Tim Tams sloshing around in my stomach. Jordan playing in that match—and *winning*—meant that our fight was completely pointless. Our big, dramatic, friendship/secret-relationship-ruining fight was all for nothing.

I blink and Term Three is over. I blink again, and it's the first day of Term Four. It honestly feels like time is messing with me. I need it to slow the hell down so I can get my life together, but it just keeps flying by, faster and faster. Our Year Eleven end-of-year exams are coming up in a few weeks, and since I have nothing else going for me these days, I actually need to *try*. Amina says I'm going to ace the English exam—I'm not quite so sure—but she still has her doubts about biology and psych. I'm nowhere near as terrible as I used to be, that's for sure, but I'm clearly not doctor material like Amina.

"Please don't mention the word 'doctor,'" she says at the end of our first week back. We're tucked away in a quiet corner of the library, so we have to whisper. "Papah has started lecturing me about it every night."

Our usual lunchtime chats have been traded in for study sessions. And when I say, "study sessions," I mean Amina studies and I attempt to, but end up scrolling on Instagram instead, until she snaps at me for distracting her, *even though* I'm just sitting there in total silence.

The best thing—well, the one good thing—about the library is that it has the only properly working aircon in the whole school, saving us from the spring heatwave that has "struck the state." I mean, thirty-six degrees Celsius in October is just plain nuts. Amina keeps ranting about how our government is full of "climate change deniers," and I can't say I even know who the prime minister is right now but, as usual, I'm sure she's right.

"Your papah lectures you about what?" I ask, putting down my phone.

"About me getting into medicine," Amina replies. She closes

her exercise book and leans back in her seat. "I don't know what I can say to him that I haven't already said. I. Don't. Want. To do. Medicine. I don't want to be a doctor. I've told him a million times now. How can I possibly be clearer?"

"You still have ages to convince them," I say with a flick of my wrist. "We won't have to submit our uni preferences until like, this time next year."

The thought of having to go to uni instead of joining a ballet company like I'd planned since I was three years old is still so weird to me. Like, what the hell am *I* going to study at uni? I'm not interested in anything.

Except Jordan . . .

"That's the problem," she says. "If this is what they're like *now*, imagine what they're going to be like next year. Historically speaking, I instantly crumble under pressure where my parents are concerned. I'm worried I'm going to turn into a big mess of anxiety next year and fail all my exams and have to work at McDonalds for the rest of my life."

"Amina, you could pass those exams with both of your arms tied behind your back and a blindfold on."

"How would I write?"

"I dunno, telepathy?"

She knits her brow. "I think you mean telekinesis."

"Whatever. The *point is*, you have literally nothing to worry about. And I'm sure you'll find a way to convince your parents that you know what you're doing."

Amina sighs, twisting her lips to one side. "It's just that the more I think about it, the more I realize how much I desperately want to be a teacher. It would be the most wonderful career."

"And you will be amazing at it."

She blushes a little. "Thank you. I just don't understand why my parents can't see that."

"At least they're talking to you."

"Your dad's still giving you the silent treatment?"

"I mean, we still *talk*," I reply. "It's just . . . different."

"Different how?"

"Like last night," I say, crossing my legs on top of my chair, "he got really mad at me because I said something about the weekend, and he was like, 'Don't you forget it's your mum's birthday next Sunday.' And I was like, 'Dad, we've done the same thing on the twentieth of October every single year of my entire life. It's not like I'm gonna forget.' I mean, re*lax*."

Amina sighs, giving me the universal *I'm sorry your mum is dead* look.

"Look, whatever," I reply, throwing my hands in the air. "Parents are weird."

Amina lets out a half-hearted laugh. "Agreed."

A week later, we're in the exact same corner in the library. It's become our new "spot." Which is something Bree and Alicia don't seem too happy about and something I never thought I'd say about a *library*, that's for sure.

Amina is quizzing me on the differences between dominant and recessive phenotypes—let's be honest, phenotypes are not my strongest suit—when a tall Year Twelve girl with tan skin and a short, brown bob walks straight up to us.

"Amina Ahmad, right?" she says.

No one ever talks to us, so we both automatically inch back in our chairs. Neither of us replies.

"And you're Luca Mason, aren't you?"

I nod, hoping this isn't some kind of prank. Or a distraction, maybe, and someone's gonna jump out and scare the crap out of us, like on *Ellen*.

"Okay . . . well," Brown Bob says through a pout, "Gibbo wanted me to tell you that you're invited to his party."

"Sorry, what?" I ask. "*Whose* party?"

"Gibbo's party." She glances over her shoulder like her biggest concern in life is that someone is going to see her in the library. "Tomorrow night. Eight o'clock. Four-four-two Milliners Road."

"Umm . . ." I blink up at her.

"Okay . . . so," she says, "I'm gonna go now." And as she walks away I swear she calls us "freaks."

I can't help but laugh. "This has to be a mistake."

"How could it possibly be a mistake?" Amina replies, her eyes as wide as dinner plates. "She was looking *specifically* for us."

"I know, but . . ."

"Luca," she says, a smile slowly spreading across her face, "we're invited to Gibbo's party."

"But Gibbo hates us."

"Maybe he's turned over a new leaf?"

"He called me 'Poof the Magic Drag Queen' in maths this morning." (It was his best insult of the year—I'll give him that.)

"Maybe he *very recently* turned over a new leaf."

"Yeah, or his parents forced him to invite us out of pity."

"Luca," Amina says softly, "we're going to go, right?"

"I just . . . I dunno if it's a good idea," I reply, knowing that the only reason she wants to go is so she can be in the same room as Jordan Tanaka-Jones. Which is the exact reason I *don't* want to go. "What if it's part of some big prank? Like in that old movie where they tip blood all over that girl?"

"You mean *Carrie*? I don't think Gibbo cares about us enough to plan an elaborate stunt like that. And I'm sure there'll be parental supervision. We're going, right? We *have* to go."

But I'm not imagining someone pouring blood all over us. I'm picturing Jordan flirting with some girl from school. Leaning in to kiss her. Sliding his hands underneath her top . . . I honestly don't think I could handle that.

"I dunno, Amina," I say. "Gibbo's party? Really?"

"*Please*, Luca," she replies, fidgeting with the hem of her school dress. "I've . . ." But she stops.

"What?"

She looks down at her shoes. "I've never been invited to a party."

And no matter how much I desperately don't want to go, how the hell could I say no to that?

Thirty-Five

WHEN WE STEP OUT of the taxi, my jaw drops. I was expecting this to be big, but this is like walking onto the set of some crazy American frat movie.

"Whoa," Amina says from beside me.

"Um . . . *yeah.*"

Gibbo's family's property is huge. It's almost dark, but I can just make out the fence on the horizon. His long driveway ends with a roundabout-garden thing, and then a gravel path leads up to his house. It's a normal-sized brick house, but because it's sitting in the middle of an enormous potato farm, it looks kind of ridiculous, like a Lego house plonked down in the middle of a football oval.

Beside the house is a massive, corrugated iron shed, which is at least as big as our North gym. Kids from school are crammed inside, spilling out onto the lawn, and running around like dickheads in the paddock behind. Loud (awful) music fills the sticky night air, along with general shouting and squealing.

"Maybe this was a bad idea?" Amina says.

She lied to her parents for the first time in history tonight—
we're having a "movie night" at my place right now—then paid
for a taxi with money straight from her savings, so there's no way
I'm letting her bail.

"Come on," I say, grabbing her hand and pulling her across
the gravel. "We're doing this. It's happening. We're going to
have a good time. Do you hear me?"

Amina half laughs, half groans.

"See?" I say, turning to grin at her as we get closer to the
shed. "We're already having fun."

"Wait!" She tugs on my arm and stops me in my tracks.
"Can I ask you something?"

She looks nervous. No, terrified.

"What?"

"Do I . . . Do I look okay?" she asks, shrugging one shoulder.

She's wearing black jeans, black flats, a flowy blue top, and
a bright purple hijab that kind of doubles as a long shawl. She's
got the tiniest bit of mascara and eyeliner on and some cute pink
lip gloss. She certainly doesn't look like she's about to walk into a
high school piss-up in Gibbo's shed, but . . .

"You look cute," I say. "Super cute."

"But do you think . . . oh my gosh—" she covers her eyes
"—I can't believe I'm about to ask this question, but would you
say I look . . . *hot?*"

She lowers her hands and stares at me with wide eyes.

"You know I think you're beautiful," I reply. And I mean it.
She is.

"I know, but . . . beautiful isn't *hot.* They're different."

"So, you want to know if I think you look hot *specifically.*"

"Not you," she says, looking past me to the shed. "Other people. Boys."

"I am a boy."

"Boys who like *girls*," she says, flapping her hands in the air. "Luca, please. I'm serious."

"Okay . . . So, you want to know if I think boys who like girls—specifically—will think you look hot. Specifically."

"That's correct."

Oh. I see what's going on here. She's not asking if straight boys in *general* will think she looks hot. She's asking me if *Jordan* will think she looks hot. Which puts me in a highly awkward position, because a) I don't want to give her a single ounce of false hope, and b) footy boys only use the word "hot" for leggy, booby, popular girls, and Amina is none of those things. Then again, *I'm* none of those things—well, I'm kind of leggy, but I'm definitely not booby or popular or, you know, a *girl*—so maybe I'm wrong.

But the last thing I want is for Amina to walk into her first—and possibly *only*—high school party feeling anything less than amazing, so I smile and say, "Amina, you look incredibly, *specifically* hot."

She giggles self-consciously. "Are you sure? You're not just saying that?"

"Would I lie to you?" The words are out of my mouth before I even realize. My stomach does a sickening little swoop.

But then a huge smile lights up Amina's adorably round face. "Thank you," she says. "You look specifically hot too."

I'm in black jeans and a white T-shirt with a little rainbow printed on the pocket over my heart.

"Let's face it," I reply, "when have I *not* looked hot?"

She laughs and slaps me on the arm. "Let's do this. Let's go to a party."

I hold out my elbow and give her a gentlemanly nod. She threads her arm through mine, and we strut into Gibbo's shed like we own the place.

First mission: get a drink. If I have to be at the same party as Jordan, I'm gonna be here with vodka. We obviously couldn't bring alcohol like everyone else—not that Amina is drinking, of course—because I didn't want to ask Dad, and Amina's parents think we're sipping herbal tea and watching '90s rom-coms right now. If I was talking to Jordan, I could have asked him to buy me some drinks, but . . . you know. I'm not. So . . .

"This way," I say to Amina. The music is so loud in the shed that I have to yell.

It's pretty dark in here, except for the light coming from the giant disco ball hanging in the middle of the tin roof, way above our heads. It doesn't quite match the rest of the decor—old car parts and a few bales of hay—but it definitely makes it feel like a party. There are some dirty couches set up around the walls and a table tennis table up the back corner, which is currently being used as a podium by a couple of Year Twelve girls.

"Where are we going?" Amina asks.

"To find the booze."

She says something about that being a bad idea, but I pretend I don't hear her and lead her through the crowd in search of drinks. And I mean, it's literally a crowd. There are some people scattered around the edges of the shed, talking, but—much to my surprise—most of them are dancing. And by "dancing," I mean jumping up and down and nodding their heads. You know, what normal people *think* dancing is.

It smells like petrol and sweat and cheap perfume, and it's an effort and a half to push our way through the mash of people, but we eventually reach the other side. Lined up against the wall are five white fridges, a bunch of red coolers full of drinks, and an old tool bench in the corner.

"Why would they leave hammers out at a party?" Amina shouts in my ear, pointing at the bench. "There's even a chainsaw there!"

"And?"

"And it just seems like alcohol and chainsaws are a recipe for disaster, don't you think?"

"Amina, chill."

"It's just not very responsible, that's all."

"Parties are for being *irresponsible*. That's the whole point!"

"That seems ill-advised."

"Just relax," I laugh, as I bend down and pop the lid of a cooler. I fish around through the half-melted ice, and by the time I turn around with a can of someone else's vodka raspberry in my hand, Amina is smiling and bopping on the spot.

"There she is!" I say, holding the can up in an imaginary cheers. "Who's this party animal and what has she done with Amina?"

"I might never get invited to a party again," she says, glancing around the shed. "And, OH&S nightmare or not, this is pretty darn cool."

"Right?"

"And we're here to party," she goes on, looking like she's gearing up for a fight, "so let's bloody *do it*!"

I let out a long, loud "Yaaaaasssss" as Amina drags me by the hand onto the dance floor.

Within minutes, sweat is dripping down my forehead, and the armpits of my T-shirt are soaked. But my stolen drink is nice and cold, and soon I'm tipsy and feeling lighter than I've felt in weeks and weeks. Probably since . . .

And I kid you not, the *second* Jordan pops into my mind, I spot him over Amina's shoulder. He's right in the middle of the shed, leaning on a post, talking to a bunch of girls I vaguely recognize from school. They're all laughing and tossing their hair like he's the handsome Bachelor and they're the Bachelorettes who've just arrived at the mansion.

I don't know if he feels me looking at him, but he turns his head almost as soon as I see him.

Then he smiles. And everything stops.

"Why aren't you dancing?" Amina shouts over the thumping bass, bouncing up and down in front of me. I tear my eyes away from Jordan.

"Sorry," I say, not knowing how long I was staring. "I'll be back."

"What? You can't leave me here by—"

But I'm already shoving my way through the sea of drunk North kids toward Jordan. By the time I make it to the big wooden post, though, he's gone. I look left, I look right, I turn around on the spot, but I can't see him anywhere. The girls are all gone, too. Knowing my luck, he's probably taken one of them to a nice quiet spot to have some very not-quiet sex.

I slump against the pole and feel my body deflate. One minute ago, I was happy. One minute ago, I was dancing and laughing and having the best time with Amina. But seeing Jordan . . . Seeing him smile . . . Seeing him chatting up those girls . . .

I down the rest of my drink and let out a loud, fizzy burp.

"Gross," a girl says as she walks past with her friends.

And now I need to pee. I toss the empty can on the floor and head for the door.

"Where's the bathroom?" I ask a girl from my health class, who's drinking by herself out the front of the shed.

"Bathroom?" she laughs. "Just piss around the back like the rest of the boys, you prissy little shit."

People are so charming, aren't they?

I walk around the side of the shed and see about ten boys all lined up along the wall, peeing straight onto the corrugated iron. This is *not* my usual peeing style—I use the cubicles at school because standing next to other boys at the urinal either gives me stage fright and nothing comes out, or I get hard, which is a million times worse—so I walk down the very far end of the shed and find my own private patch of wall.

Just as I unzip my fly, a tall, shadowy figure cuts around the corner. I actually gasp—because I swear I've seen this in a horror movie—zip up my fly, and stagger backward.

"Shit, sorry," the guy says. But it's not just any guy.

It's Jordan.

"Oh," he says, quieter. "Hi."

"Hi," I reply, wishing the sight of him didn't make me feel

like bursting into tears.

"How's it going?"

"Fine." Everyone's favorite word, back with a vengeance. "What are you doing out here?"

"Needed some air."

Silence, except for the muffled bass beat from inside the shed.

"Look—" Jordan starts, but I cut in.

"Don't," I snap. "Just . . . don't bother."

"Can you just let me explain?"

I can't help but scoff. "Explain what? Why you're suddenly Mr. Straight School Captain again? I saw you with your little fan club inside."

"Oh, come off it," he replies, looking stung. "I'm not into any of those girls."

"Maybe not any of *those* girls, but—"

"Or anyone," Jordan says firmly. "Except . . ." He takes a step forward and I take a step back. "Luca, do you really think I would've made Gibbo invite you to his party if I wanted to hook up with a bunch of random girls from school?"

"Wait, what?"

"I asked Gibbo to invite you and Amina."

"Why?"

"Because I wanted to see you. Talk to you."

"Talk to me? *Really?* You've been ignoring me for weeks, and *now* you suddenly want to talk to me? Standing out the back of Gibbo's shed with half our school taking a piss right next to us? You couldn't have just *called?*"

He runs a hand through his hair, which, of course, is literally shining in the moonlight.

"Can we go just somewhere and talk? Please?"

"I need to wee," I say, hating that I sound like a toddler all of a sudden.

He turns and walks off around the corner. "Follow me."

Thirty-Six

"THE BATHROOM IS DOWN there." Jordan points to a wooden door down the end of the hallway.

We're in Gibbo's house, which obviously feels so weird. Mainly because it's a totally normal house, and Mrs. Gibson—who we met on the way in through the back door—is a totally normal mum. No sign anywhere of what turned Gibbo into such an asshole.

"Thanks," I say, squeezing past Jordan and heading to the bathroom.

When I come back out, he pushes a door open beside him and walks through it, so I follow, only realizing when he shuts it behind us that we're in Gibbo's room. It's dark and messy and smells like corn chips. Not the ideal place for a romantic chat, if that's what Jordan's going for. Which I'm sure he's not.

We both just stand there for a while, looking at each other but not saying anything, and then his phone starts pinging over and over again. He slides it out of his back pocket, switches it to silent, and sits it on the chest of drawers beside Gibbo's bed.

He plonks himself down on the mattress and stares up at me, like he wants me to sit, too. But there's no way I'm sitting on that bed. God knows what Gibbo's done to that doona . . .

"Well . . ." Jordan says.

"Well . . ." I echo, standing at the foot of the bed, hands on hips. "Did you want to talk, or are we just here to take in the atmosphere?"

"I want to talk," he replies. "I just don't know where to start."

"I reckon 'Sorry for ghosting you' is probably a good place to start, don't you?"

He drops his head into his hands. "I'm sorry," he says through his fingers.

"Yeah? And?"

He looks up, a pained expression on his face. "I really am. I'm so fucking sorry, Luca, you have no idea. I've been a complete wanker—"

"Well, yeah, you have."

"—and you don't deserve to be ignored. But . . . you kind of ghosted me, too, you know."

"I did not. I—" But he's right. I didn't message him. I didn't apologize for any of the horrible things I said that day out the front of the OT.

"I'm sorry," he says again. "I'm not here to blame you." He shakes his head and looks up to the ceiling, as if the words he needs might be stuck up there with Blu Tack. "I'm sorry if you felt like I was trying to force you back into the closet. I'm sorry you thought I wanted to hide you from my mates and my family. I'm sorry you think I'm ashamed of being with you.

Because none of that is true. I . . ." He blows out a slow breath. "I know you're totally comfortable being, you know, who you are. But this is harder for me. When I'm with you, it's fine. It's amazing. I just need some time to work it all out in my own head."

"You've had plenty of time to work it out."

"By whose standards?" he says. He turns and crosses his legs on the bed, facing me head-on. "You don't get to dictate how and when I deal with this. This is *my* experience, not yours."

"Yeah, but I'm a *part* of that experience. Aren't I?"

He lets out a sigh.

"I wasn't trying to rush you," I say. "After Ocean Grove . . . I honestly thought you'd be okay with it."

He shrugs. "I thought I would too. I really did. But certain things still got to me. Like the idea of you coming to watch me play footy? The only people who have ever come to watch me play—apart from my family—have been my *girlfriends*. So, saying you could come along kind of felt like I was committing to a full-blown relationship."

"That's . . . dramatic."

"I know," he says through a laugh. "And I just had it in my head that if I got into a relationship, it would be like choosing a side."

I blink back at him. "What do you mean?"

"As in, guys or girls."

"No one said you have to choose."

"I know," he replies. "But you know what people in this town are like."

I decide to take my chances with Gibbo's doona and take

a seat opposite Jordan, crossing my legs like him. "I'm sorry for what I said outside before. About those girls . . . I didn't mean—"

"It's all good." He gives me a half smile. "Actually, speaking of girls, I have a funny story for you."

"Oh god."

"No, no, nothing like that," he says with a chuckle. "And it's not so much *funny* as incredibly awkward . . . Gibbo saw our messages."

I gasp out loud. "What? Which ones?"

"The last ones. About meeting me at the OT."

"And . . ." I shift awkwardly on the bed. "What did he say?"

"He asked who Lucy was."

"And what did *you* say?"

"You're probably gonna hate me," Jordan replies, scrunching up his nose, "but I said she's my girlfriend. And that she's a ballerina from St. Tom's."

And I know I should be offended, but I can't help but laugh. "Did he believe you?"

"Yeah, but he wanted proof. Photos. I said I don't have any because her parents are super religious and the whole thing is strictly on the down low. I made him promise not to tell anyone."

"And did he?" I ask. "Tell anyone?"

"I don't think so," Jordan says. "I'm pretty sure the whole school would know by now if he did, right?"

"I mean, probably," I shrug. "Also . . . how did you convince him to invite me and Amina tonight? He literally *hates* us."

"I told him I wouldn't come unless he invited you guys."

I scoff. "And he didn't think that was like, a bit over the top?"

"Not really," Jordan laughs. "Gibbo knows I'm pretty

hardcore when it comes to my friends."

Silence falls between us again. After a long moment, Jordan reaches his hand out and places it palm-up in the gap between us. I stare down at it, wondering what it would mean if I placed my hand in his, what I'd be agreeing to.

"I'm sorry," he says, and I know he means it.

I reach out and rest my fingertips on his, not quite holding hands, but connected all the same. "I'm sorry, too."

He takes a deep breath, puffing out his chest. "I'm going to tell my parents soon," he says, nodding like he's still trying to convince himself he can do it.

"You don't have to do that. Not for me."

"I want to. For me. And for you. I've wanted to tell them for ages, I just wanted to have something concrete to tell them."

"What do you mean?"

"I mean, I wanted to wait until I could tell them I have a *boyfriend*."

My heart just about stops.

"Are you saying . . .?"

"Yes," he replies, his hazel eyes warm and twinkly. "I want you to be my boyfriend."

"But you're leaving." The words are out of my mouth before I even realize.

"What?" He slides his hand away from mine.

Shit. Why the hell is my brain trying to ruin this for me?

"I just mean, you're about to finish school. You'll be moving to Melbourne next year."

"It depends on what course I get into. It depends on a lot of things, actually."

"Yeah, but either way, you won't want to be dating some guy who's still in high school. You'll want to be out having sex all the time. A different person every night."

He snorts. "Is that what you think happens at uni?"

"Well, I dunno. Maybe. You're allowed, if that's what you want."

"Look," he says, "can we just worry about next year, like, *next year?* Right now, all I know is that I want to be with you. I want us to be together. Officially. I want to be your boyfriend, Luca."

My pulse is pounding in my ears. Or is that the music coming from the shed?

"Really?"

"Yes." He leans in and kisses me gently on the lips. "Just . . . I know how frustrating this is for you, but can we please keep it to ourselves for just a bit longer? You can tell your dad, but I want to tell my parents before we tell anyone else. I want to do this right. Is that okay?"

"Of course," I reply. "We can tell people when you're ready."

Jordan smiles his brightest smile and fireworks burst inside my heart.

Then he kisses me again.

"Can I tell you something?" he whispers, his forehead pressed against mine.

"Yes," I say, feeling like he's literally taken my breath away.

"I think I'm f—"

"TJ!" someone shouts from inside the house.

Jordan jumps up from the bed.

"Are you in here?" the boy's voice calls out.

"Shit," Jordan says, motioning for me to get up. "It's Gibbo. We need to get out of here."

Thirty-Seven

JORDAN OPENS THE DOOR, just enough so he can peek out into the hall. "All good, let's go."

As we walk back down the hall, I try to be chill, try to make it look like the guy walking two steps ahead of me is not my *boyfriend*.

Gibbo is standing in the middle of the lounge room, swaying on the spot, a can of beer in each hand.

"Where have you—" He stops when he sees me walk in behind Jordan. "What the fuck's *he* doing in here?"

"Needed the bathroom," Jordan replies. "And I wanted to say hi to your mum, so I said I'd show him where it was."

Gibbo squints at us. "Mum's in the shed."

"She was in here before."

"How long have you been in here?" Gibbo asks, glaring at me, even though he's talking to Jordan.

"Dunno," Jordan says. "Come on, let's go back to the shed." He grabs one of Gibbo's beers and downs it on his way out the back door.

When the three of us get closer to the shed, I see Amina

sitting just outside the door on a bale of hay. She smiles at Jordan as he walks past, then runs over to me, looking furious.

"Where on *earth* have you been?"

Jordan turns and winks at me before heading back into the party.

"Bathroom."

"You've been gone for an hour. I thought you were *dead.*"

"Sorry, I . . ."

I try to follow Jordan's path into the crowd but lose sight of him almost instantly behind a group of drunk Year Ten boys doing what looks like a cancan.

"Why didn't you tell me where you were going?' Amina says, her voice an octave higher than usual. "You just disappeared! I've been so worried, Luca. You left me all alone."

"I thought you'd be dancing?"

"Oh, sure, like I was going to dance by myself with a bunch of people who think I'm the biggest loser on the planet."

"Sorry," I say, holding up my hands in surrender. "I should have told you I was going to the bathroom."

"You can't have been in the bathroom that *whole* time."

"I wasn't . . . I was . . ."

"You were with TJ, weren't you?" she says, jealousy creeping into her voice. "You just walked back from the house with him and Gibbo. What were you doing in there?"

"Peeing?"

"All three of you?"

"I guess."

Amina huffs. "What do you mean, you *guess?*"

"Can you just chill, Amina? I'm here now."

But she's not convinced. She stares back at me, and I can see her mind ticking. She knows something went down in the house just now.

I force a grin. "Come on, let's go dance!"

"But—"

"Come *on*." I grab her hand and twirl her under my arm. "I'm sorry I disappeared, okay? But we're wasting time. When will we ever be at a party like this again?"

"Probably never."

"Exactly."

"Fine," she replies. "But only because we already missed one Harry Styles song, and I refuse to miss another."

This time I smile for real.

"Just don't desert me again," she says, pointing a finger at my face.

"I won't."

"Promise."

"Amina, I promise I will not desert you again."

She holds out her hand. "Shake on it."

"Really?" I laugh, but she stares me down until I realize she's definitely not joking.

I shake her hand and she finally smiles. "Thank you."

"All right," I say, turning back to the shed. "Let's do it."

"Wait!" she says, dragging me over to the bale of hay. "Before we go back in, we need to discuss the important business of the evening."

"What important business?"

She sits me down and says, in a weirdly official voice, "I have a confession to make."

Oh god. Please don't let this be what I think it's gonna be . . .

She takes a deep breath and looks me square in the eye. When she speaks, her voice is quiet, like she's afraid of her own words. "I think I'm in love with TJ."

"What?" And I mean, I've known this for months, but hearing her say it out loud still feels like a knife in the eyeball. "Since when?"

"Since forever!" she replies. "But this year . . . Spending all that time with him . . . It just made everything so clear. And . . ."

"And what?"

"I wasn't going to say anything," she goes on with a frown, "because I didn't want to jinx it, but . . . well . . . TJ kissed me."

"What?" My whole body clenches at the thought and my face starts to burn. *"When?"*

"After the football grand final. It was only on the cheek—" instant relief washes over me from head to toe "—but it felt like it really meant something. So . . . I've decided that tonight is the night. I'm finally going to tell him how I feel."

I almost choke. "I'm sorry, what?"

"This is my last opportunity! He'll be in exams soon and then he'll be gone from North forever, and I will regret not saying anything for the rest of my life."

"Amina, have you been drinking?"

"No!" she replies. "Why would you even ask that?"

"Sorry, I just . . ." I squeeze my eyes shut, trying to think of a way to stop her from doing what she's about to do. "Amina, Jordan has a girlfriend." Which is not a total lie. Just swap "girl" for "boy" and it's one hundred percent true.

"What? Since when?"

"It's . . . pretty recent."

"How do you know?" Amina asks.

"Because I just talked to him about it."

She edges back on the bale of hay. "So, you *did* talk to him?"

"Yes."

"What's her name?"

If I say *Lucy*, she'll figure the whole thing out, I know she will.

"I can't remember," I reply.

"But you *just* talked to him about it."

"I'm drunk, leave me alone."

"You seem fine to me."

"Oh my *god*, Amina," I say, a little too loud. "Just forget about it. You can't tell him how you feel. End of story."

But she folds her arms across her chest. "You're lying to me."

I don't reply.

"Why are you lying? What is going on here?"

I stand and turn away, trying to give myself time to think. I *cannot* tell Amina about me and Jordan. Not five minutes after he specifically asked me not to tell a soul. It will ruin *everything*. When we're finally in a good place again.

"Luca. What is going on? *Tell me*."

I turn, and Amina is standing now too, looking worried and angry and confused.

"Just . . . don't do this," I say. "Trust me."

"But you're lying to me. Why should I trust you?"

"Because you're my best friend! Because I'm looking out for you."

"*Looking out* for me? What is that supposed to mean?"

"You can't tell Jordan you're in love with him. Not here. Not in front of all these people."

"Why not?"

"Because it will end *very* badly, Amina."

"*Why?*" She's almost shouting now.

A group of girls snicker at us as they walk past. "Lover's quarrel?"

"Fuck off," I snap at them.

"Luca, what is your problem?" Amina says. "I thought you'd be happy for me. Why are you so against this?"

I groan. "I'm not *against* it."

"Then why are you trying to talk me out of it?"

"Look, I just know it's not going to work out, okay?"

"Why?" she asks, her eyes a little wild now. "Because I'm not good enough for him?"

"What? No, that's not it at all."

"You said I looked beautiful tonight. You said I was . . . hot."

"You *are* hot, but—"

"Not hot enough for TJ? Not pretty enough to go out with the captain of the football team?"

"No, Amina, that is *not* what I'm saying, just—"

"Then what *are* you saying? That I won't have a chance with him because I'm not skinny and ditzy like all the other girls he's gone out with? Like your vapid dancer friends from St. Tom's?"

"No, it's—"

"Is it because I'm Muslim?"

"*No.* Oh my god, Amina. Can you just let me talk? I'm trying to help you. You just . . . you don't understand."

"Then tell me, Luca. *What* do I not understand?"

My heart is pounding in my chest. How the hell did I let this get so out of hand? I should have told Amina everything, right from the start.

But it's too late now.

She shakes her head at me, mutters a "whatever," then whips around and storms inside the shed.

"Wait!" I call out. I run after her, following as close behind as I can manage as she weaves her way through the crowd, looking for Jordan. We end up on the other side of the dance floor, near the fridges, where Jordan is leaning against the tool bench with Gibbo, laughing and drinking.

"TJ," Amina calls out, but he doesn't hear her. *"TJ!"*

And he turns. He looks at Amina and then at me. When our eyes meet I try to communicate just how much he needs to get out of here *right now*, but instead, he walks up to Amina with an enormous grin on his face.

"Hey, Amina," he says over the music. "You having fun? I'm so glad you came."

Not helping, Jordan.

"Jordan," she starts. "I know we haven't seen a great deal of each other in the last few weeks, but there's something I need to tell you."

"Amina, don't," I say, but she ignores me.

"Ever since primary school," she says, "I have known how truly special you are."

Gibbo snickers from behind Jordan's shoulder.

She clears her throat and carries on. "Over the last few months, I've felt a real connection developing between us."

"What the actual . . . ?" Gibbo says.

Please, Universe, can the whole world just implode right this second?

"So, before you graduate and leave North forever . . ."

"Amina." I try to grab her hand but she yanks it away.

" . . . I need to let you know that I have very strong feelings for you."

Jordan is frozen on the spot, his face like stone.

"And whether or not those feelings are reciprocated," Amina continues, "I wanted to confess how I truly feel—how I've felt about you, all these years—before it's finally too late. Jordan Tanaka-Jones, I—"

"Stop," Jordan interrupts, holding one hand up in front of Amina's face. "Please don't say what I think you're about to say." He lowers his hand onto her shoulder. "I think you're awesome, Amina, and I like hanging out with you, but I . . . I don't have feelings for you. Those rumors were just rumors. None of that was true. I . . . I'm with someone else."

"Yeah," Gibbo says. "*Lucy*. She's a ballerina."

Jordan's eyes flick over to me and I feel like I'm going to throw up.

Amina turns around in slow-motion and looks me dead in the eye.

She knows.

And before I can say a word, she pushes past me and disappears into the crowd.

"Amina, wait!" I call out, but she's gone.

Gibbo bursts into hysterical laughter. "That. Was. Fucking. *Incredible*," he says, giving her a slow clap.

"Why did you let her do that?" Jordan asks, looking shocked and embarrassed.

"How was I supposed to stop her without . . ." But I can't say anything. Not here.

"I wish I got that on film," Gibbo laughs. "That shit would've gone *viral*."

"I need to go and find her," I say to Jordan. "I'm sorry."

I squeeze my way down the side of the shed, climbing over the clumps of people making out on the dirty couches along the wall. But by the time I make it outside, Amina is nowhere to be seen.

I pull out my phone and call her.

No answer.

I call The Boy in the Waiting Room.

"Come on, Jordan, pick up."

No answer.

"Shit."

I run across the gravel to Gibbo's house and knock on the back door. I'm greeted by Mrs. Gibson in a dressing-gown.

"You okay, love?"

"Have you seen Amina? Did she come in here?"

"Who's Amina?"

"Amina Ahmad? The girl in the purple hijab?"

"What's a hijab?"

I can't help but roll my eyes. "Don't worry."

I try calling Amina again, but it goes straight to voicemail. I try Jordan and it rings out.

Defeated, I trudge back to the shed. Horse, Jordan's ex-friend, is making out with a girl from my English class next to the door, pressing her up against the corrugated iron wall. I can tell how wasted they are by the fact that they can't seem to find each other's mouths.

"Gross," I can't help but say as I walk past them, back into the party.

I search for Jordan for like, half an hour, but I can't find him. We're probably both doing laps of the shed, looking for each other. Or maybe he's furious and he's not looking for me at all. Eventually, I give up and go sit outside on the bale of hay and down two more stolen drinks.

I message Amina. **Please answer your phone. I need to talk to you. I'm sorry.**

I message Jordan. **Where are you?? I've been looking for you everywhere. I'm sorry.**

Neither of them replies. Maybe if I stay put for a bit, one of them will turn up.

I check the time on my phone. 1:00 a.m.

I call them both one more time—no answer—and then call the only other person worth calling right now.

"Hey, Dad," I say, feeling my voice catch as tears build behind my eyes. "I'm sorry to call so late. Can you please come and pick me up?"

Thirty-Eight

I'VE NEVER HAD A hangover before. And I'm not exactly sure if I have one right now, because I didn't have *that* much to drink last night, but my head hurts and my eyes hurt and I feel like total and utter crap. Maybe it's less to do with the alcohol and more to do with the fact that last night turned into a total shitstorm of awkwardness.

Amina and Jordan still won't answer my calls. I've tried about nine hundred times since I woke up an hour ago, but no deal.

I roll over in bed and put my head under the pillow. Why won't my ears stop ringing?

Knock, knock, knock. "Lu?"

"Come in," I say, my voice muffled by the pillow.

"You okay, mate?" Dad asks through a crack in the door. "It's almost midday."

I take the pillow off my head and flop onto my back. The light spilling in from the hallway kind of hurts my face. "I'm fine."

"Did you drink last night?"

There's no point lying, is there? I've done my fair share of it lately, and it *clearly* hasn't worked out for me.

"Yes," I reply. "But not a lot."

Dad hums like he doesn't believe me. I must look as bad as I feel.

"I'll go grab you a Powerade from the shops," he says. "And some aspirin. Used to help me if I'd had a big night."

"Okay. Thanks."

"You should try to get up soon. Things to do today, remember?" He gives me a half smile, with this weird sadness in his blue eyes, and gently shuts the door.

As soon as he's gone, I grab my phone from my bedside table and call Jordan again. No answer. I know he's probably mad at me for putting him in such an incredibly awkward position, and for letting Amina embarrass herself like that, but I know he'll pick up eventually. He's my boyfriend. He has to pick up.

I try again. And just as I'm about to hang up, he answers.

"Lucy?" he says. His voice is all husky.

"Ha, ha," I reply, rubbing my eyes with my free hand, "very funny."

"Who's this?"

"Are you still drunk?"

"What?" he says. He sounds kind of different. "Sorry, who's this?"

"Don't be like that," I say. "I'm sorry about last night. I—"

"Wait, who *is* this?"

"It's Luca."

"Luca?"

"Yes," I laugh, "Luca. You know, your *boyfriend*."

He coughs loudly into the phone, and when he speaks again I realize something is horribly wrong.

"What the hell are you on about?" he says.

And holy fucking shit. It's not Jordan.

It's *Gibbo*.

"Um . . . uh . . ." Panic sets in. I feel like I'm gonna be sick. "Is Jordan there?"

"He's at home."

"Why do you have his phone?"

"Fuck should I know. He must have left it here."

I think back to last night when Jordan and I were talking in Gibbo's room. When Jordan took his phone out of his pocket, put it on silent and . . . put it on Gibbo's bedside table. *Shit.*

"I gotta go."

"Wait!" Gibbo says. "This is *your* number, isn't it? *You're* the one who's been messaging TJ all the time. *You're* Lucy."

I hang up and throw my phone down onto my doona like it's going to explode. I sit there on my bed, staring down at it, struggling to breathe.

This is bad. This is worse than bad. This is like, falling-down-a-flight-of-stairs-and-shattering-the-bones-in-your-foot kind of bad.

My stomach churns. I stumble to the bathroom and throw up into the toilet bowl, tears running down my cheeks. Spewing always makes me cry. Not that I don't already feel like crying right now.

Amina knows. Gibbo knows.

And I bet they're not the only ones.

I need to tell Jordan what just happened. But I can't *call* him because Gibbo has his phone. But that also means Gibbo can't call him. Unless Jordan has a home phone, but I'm pretty sure they only exist in museums now.

I wash my mouth out, splash some cold water on my face, and stare up at my reflection in the bathroom mirror.

What have I done?

I grab my laptop from the lounge and sit at the kitchen table, feeling like I could throw up again at any second.

I take a deep breath, open Facebook, and click into a new message to Jordan.

Hey

But what the hell comes next?

I just screwed up.

I just outed you to your best mate.

I just ruined everything once and for all.

No.

All true, obviously.

But no.

I need to talk to you, I write, **but I know you don't have your phone. I hope you see this soon. If you're reading it, come to my place ASAP. I am so sorry.**

Dad's been gone for half an hour, and Jordan still hasn't seen my message. I've given up trying to get through to Amina, because if she hasn't called me back after seeing the first eighty-seven missed calls, one more isn't going to change her mind. So, I'm just sitting in the kitchen, eyes glued to my laptop, waiting for that little blue tick below my message to turn into Jordan's tiny DP.

But nothing.

I know he doesn't have footy training anymore, so he should be home. Maybe he's still asleep? Maybe he has a massive hangover? Is it bad if I hope he's sick in bed right now?

All I know is that I need to find him and tell him what happened before he hears it from Gibbo. Otherwise . . . well, I don't want to think about the otherwise.

I run upstairs and throw on some semi-respectable clothes, grab my wallet and keys from the kitchen bench, and barrel out the door and down the road. When I turn the corner, there's an orange and white bus already letting off passengers at my stop.

"Wait!" I shout, sprinting toward the bus as an old lady climbs aboard and the doors swing shut with a loud squeak. I skid to a stop in front of the bus stop, slapping my hands on the glass door as the bus pulls out onto the road. The driver meets my eye and shakes her head. She looks like Rebel Wilson. I can't hear her voice over the growl of the engine, but I can tell by the exaggerated movement of her lips that she is saying, "Too late."

I slump down onto the bus stop bench, beads of sweat dripping into my eyelashes. Why does it have to be it so damn *hot* today?

I take a few deep breaths, trying to convince myself that everything is going to be okay. It's going to be fine. There'll be another bus. In *half an hour*.

My phone pings, and I fish it out of my pocket like my life depends on it.

Please, please, *please* let it be Jordan.

Dad: **You hiding? Got your Powerade.**

Sorry, I write back. **Home soon. Something important I have to do.**

I swipe out of the text and open Messenger. Jordan still hasn't seen my message. Which hopefully means he's still asleep.

When the next bus comes, I'm so busy staring at the ground, thinking of all the terrible things that might happen when Jordan finds out what I've done, that I almost miss it.

"Getting on?" the driver asks. He's a young white guy. Kind of cute. Much too young and cute to be driving a bus, if you ask me. But I get on anyway, because I don't have a second to waste.

We wind our way through the suburban streets toward Jordan's house in the least direct route possible. I can't keep still in my seat. My palms are sweating. Actually, my whole body is sweating. Is the aircon broken or am I having a panic attack?

When we finally arrive at Jordan's stop, I jump off the bus and sprint the three blocks to his house. As I step up onto the front veranda, I realize Jordan's parents probably still have no idea who I am. He said he needed more time, so there's no way he would have told them between the party and now. It's only been like, twelve hours. Unless he did tell them and it didn't go well, and that's why he's ignoring me . . .

And here's me, showing up unannounced, un-showered, panting, dripping with sweat, on the verge of tears, and probably stinking of alcohol and spew. Not the best first impression.

But who the hell cares. This is more important than me looking cute to meet the parents.

I knock three times and wait. After a painfully long moment, a beautiful Japanese woman opens the door. She has a streak of grey in the fringe of her jet-black hair, tan skin, and a kind smile. She also has Jordan's perfect cheekbones.

"Hello?" she says, with a faint accent, her head tilted slightly to one side.

"Uh, hi," I reply, still a little short of breath. "My name is Luca, I'm Jordan's . . . friend. From school."

"Hello, Luca."

"I'm sorry to just turn up on the weekend, but I, um, need to talk to Jordan. Is he home?"

"He's not, sorry," his mum says, and my stomach drops. "He left about five minutes ago."

"Did he say where he was going?" I ask.

"He said he needed to collect something from one of his friends. He took my car."

No, no, no, no, no.

He's gone to Gibbo's place to get his phone. Which means I'm too late. Too late to prepare him for Gibbo's reaction. Too late to tell him I'm sorry for giving away his secret. Too late to stop him from breaking up with me and never talking to me again.

That cranky Rebel Wilson bus driver was right.

I'm too damn late.

Thirty-Nine

I SAY GOODBYE TO Jordan's mum and trudge back to the bus stop. On the way, I google how to get to Gibbo's potato farm, but it's a complete public transport nightmare and would take me like, two and a half hours. And even if I went home and got Dad to drive me out there, there's still no way I'd arrive in time to stop Gibbo from telling Jordan what happened. There's just no point.

I can't be bothered waiting for a bus, so I decide to walk home. Maybe some fresh air will do me good. Even though it's six million degrees and I'm drenched with sweat. Google Maps says the walk will only take an hour, but if I go really slowly, I reckon I can stretch it to two.

Dad calls a bunch of times, but I'm not in the mood, so I put my phone on Do Not Disturb and keep walking. If I can't talk to Jordan right now, I don't want to talk to anyone. I need to be alone. Just me and my big, stupid mouth.

When I finally make it back, it's almost 3:45 p.m. and I still haven't heard from Jordan. He saw my Facebook message about an hour ago but didn't reply, which is obviously not a good sign. I wanted to get the bus straight back to his house so I could try to explain, but he clearly doesn't want to talk to me, and I don't want to make things worse than they already are.

"Dad," I call out as I open the front door. "You home?"

"In here," he replies, the top of his bald head poking up from the couch. I put my keys in the bowl next to the door and walk into the lounge. Dad stands up, switches off the TV and turns to face me, hands on hips.

"Is everything okay?" I ask.

"You tell me, Lu." His face is kind of flushed.

"What?"

"Where were you?"

"I had to go and see someone."

"Who? Jordan?"

"Yes."

"And you had to see him today? You had to see him *right now*."

"Yes," I reply. "It was very important."

"Oh, 'very important,' was it?" Dad huffs. "More important than our plans?"

"What plans?"

He shakes his head and mutters something under his breath, then says, "What day is it today, Lu?"

"Sunday?"

"Yeah, and what's the date?"

"Ummm . . . I dunno," I reply. "Why are you being so weird?"

"Just think, mate. What's today's date?"

Well . . . Gibbo's party was on the nineteenth, so unless I accidentally slept for three days . . . "It's the twentieth."

Dad crosses his arms and lifts his eyebrows, his eyes burning into mine.

Oh, *fuck*.

This is what Dad meant when he said we had things to do today. Why he had that weird sadness in his eyes when he woke me up this morning.

Today is the twentieth of October.

Mum's birthday.

"Dad, I—"

"No." He holds up one hand. "Just let me talk for a sec, okay?"

I bite my bottom lip and nod. My stomach sinks down into my feet. I can already feel tears building behind my eyes.

Dad looks down at the carpet and takes a deep breath. I know he hates this kind of conversation.

"When you said those things a few months ago—" he looks up, but he can't seem to look me directly in the eye "—about Mum . . . I didn't do my job. As a parent. I got angry and flustered by my own feelings and I walked out, which was the wrong thing to do. And I didn't do my job when I came back, either. Not properly, anyway. I got swept up in what you were saying about moving on, that it's wrong to dwell on the past and, you know what, you're probably right. I don't deny that. But there is a big difference—a *huge* difference, Luca—between moving on and *forgetting*. And what you did today . . ." He clears his throat and wipes a tear from his cheek. "Forgetting your mum's birthday, forgetting our family's only tradition, forgetting what this day means to me—to *us*—is inexcusable."

I feel like I've been thrown to the ground, like when Jordan tackled Gibbo at school.

"I know Mum has been gone for a long time," Dad goes on, barely keeping it together, "and you didn't know her like I did, but she will always be your mother. She's the only one you're ever going to get. She will always be a part of you, just like she will *always* be a part of me, and you don't get to cut her out of your life—and mine—because you feel like it. This isn't ballet. It's not something you can just quit."

"What does this have to do with ballet?"

"Dancing was *everything* to you," Dad presses, his face turning bright red. "You stood right here in this room on Boat Race night and told me that ballet wasn't just something you'd lost, that it was *you*. That it was *all* of you. What kind of father would I be if I let my son walk away from something like that?"

"Dad, that's—"

"And I tried to get through to you—god knows I tried—but you wouldn't listen. So, I just went along with whatever made you feel better at the time. Which was a mistake. Because to watch you give up ballet without a fight—without even *thinking* about putting up a fight—has been more painful than you'll ever know."

"Oh really?" I say, a bitter taste rising in my mouth. "More painful than shattering your whole fucking foot? More painful than actually *being* the one who's never going to dance again?"

"You just gave up, Lu!"

"I didn't have a choice!"

"You *always* have a choice. Always. At every step of the way, you have a choice to make. And you made the wrong one when you broke your foot. You *chose* to give up on the life you'd built."

"Dad, it's a *career-ending* injury, we've been through this a hundred times."

"Oh, don't give me that crap, Lu. Dance is more than just having a career with one bloody ballet company and you know it. You chose to cut off all ties you have with ballet. You chose to pretend like the last thirteen years never happened. You *chose* to abandon your teachers and your friends—friends you've had since you were three years old, for god's sake. You chose that. And you've obviously chosen at some point to forget about your own mother, too—"

"That is *not* fair, Dad."

"—or you wouldn't have gone gallivanting around with some boy—"

"I wasn't *gallivanting!*"

"—on the *one day* we set aside every year to spend time together, just me and you, to remember her."

"But I *don't* remember her!" I shout.

Dad freezes. The silence is painful. I can hear the clock ticking in the kitchen.

"I wish I did, Dad. Trust me, I do. But I don't remember her. I didn't get to spend twenty years of my life with her like you did. I got *two.*"

"And you think twenty years with the love of your life is enough, do you?" He's stopped bothering to wipe away his tears.

"That's not what I meant . . . I just . . ."

Dad looks up to the ceiling and shakes his head. "I'm sorry, Luca, but I'm not going to let you make excuses this time. Even if you don't remember her the way I do, today is *her* day. And you need to respect that. She was the most beautiful person I've ever laid eyes upon, and I curse the Universe every day for taking her away from us. She brought more light into this world than you will ever know, and it *kills* me that you will never get to see that."

Tears spill from my eyes. "Dad, I'm sorry . . ."

"She loved you *so much*, Lu. And she would be so disappointed in you today."

He turns and walks to the bottom of the stairs.

"Dad . . ."

He pauses and says, "There's spaghetti in the fridge if you're hungry," then walks straight upstairs.

I want to follow him. To explain. To argue my point. To beg for forgiveness. To apologize for being the most awful son in the history of the world. But I just stand there in the lounge, arms wrapped around my chest, tears streaming down my face. Hating myself for existing.

Forty

I STILL HAVE NIGHTMARES about falling down the stairs at Miss Gwen's. Sometimes the dreams start in the ballet studio. Sometimes they start on stage at a competition. Sometimes they start in my bedroom, with me using the windowsill to practice my barre work. But then, in that weird way where dreams can change location in a flash but it still seems real, I'm on that staircase again.

Falling.

Falling.

Falling.

And I can feel it too. In my dreams. I can actually *feel* it. And hear it. The bones snapping. My body thudding against each step. I don't think I'll ever be able to escape that feeling. It's like it's ingrained in my soul.

When Dad drops me off at school on Monday morning—in complete silence—I have the same feeling I had in the hospital after I broke my foot. That one where it's like it's all happening to someone else. That I'm watching someone *else's* life being ruined right before my eyes.

As I walk through the gates, I feel sick and exhausted and nervous and embarrassed and just plain fucking awful. And everyone I walk past gives me the *look*. The one the nurses gave me. Like I'm wounded. Broken. Useless.

I've been dreading this morning more than I can possibly explain. (What am I meant to say when I see Jordan? Should I try to find him at lunch so we can talk? Should I sit next to Amina in psych like I always do, even though she never returned my seven thousand phone calls?) But nothing could have prepared me for what I see when I walk past the Year Twelve lockers on my way to maths.

There's a big group of students huddled across the footpath in front of the lockers, which are lined up against the back wall of the canteen, opposite the gym. People are pointing and giving each other these *Oh. My. God.* looks.

When they see me, some turn and whisper to each other, others smirk and shake their heads, some even point and laugh. I push my way through the crush of people and books and backpacks to the front of the group.

And then I see it.

Scrawled across Jordan's locker in big, black, block capitals, is the word FAGGOT. Below it is a cartoon that looks like it was drawn by a five-year-old, of what I assume is supposed to be two guys having sex.

My stomach drops like I'm in one of my nightmares.

"Who did it?" someone asks from beside me, but I already know the answer. There's only one person messed-up enough to do something like this.

Like I've summoned Satan, Gibbo's voice cuts through the chatter from somewhere in the middle of the huddle. "Probably been checkin' me out in the showers for *years*. Fuckin' perv."

My cheeks burn and tears blur my vision. A sour taste rises in my mouth and I go to scream at him to shut the hell up, but then a boy steps out of the crowd and walks up to the lockers.

Jordan.

He turns and sees me standing there at the front of the crowd with tears running down my cheeks. And suddenly, it's like no one else is there. The sound of the students shouting and laughing disappears. My vision goes fuzzy and the schoolyard fades to black around us.

It's just me and Jordan.

He's only meters away, but it feels like we're miles apart, standing at opposite ends of a highway in the middle of nowhere. He doesn't say anything, but he doesn't have to. Everything is there in his eyes.

Anger. Humiliation. Hurt. Betrayal.

He turns back to the lockers, pulls some books out and slams the door shut, before walking off toward the quad. And suddenly I'm on that staircase again.

Falling and falling and falling.

I feel the bones break. I hear them splinter and crack.

One missed step and it's all over.

One missed step. It's as simple as that.

Forty-One

I TELL YOU WHAT, it's virtually impossible to concentrate on Year Eleven practice exams when you suddenly have no friends and everyone you care about thinks you're an awful person.

I have no idea what I can say to Dad to patch things up between us, so we're. both just *existing* in the same house. Like super awkward roommates. Things have never been like this between us. Ever. Talia and Abbey used to go weeks without talking to their mums because of some fight they'd had—usually because the girls were being petty and dramatic—but for me, this is weird. And awful. Like, the worst.

I just don't know how to fix this.

I pretty much fail every single exam. I mean, they're not *real* exams, so I guess it doesn't matter, but the teachers are all like, "You were doing so well lately, Luca," and, "I'm very disappointed in your performance, Luca," and, "Where is your head at these days, Luca?"

I just say I'm sorry and that I'll try harder on the actual exams in a few weeks' time. But then they're all like, "I'm worried about you taking this class next year if you can't handle the Year Eleven units. Maybe you'd be better off choosing something else?"

But there *is* nothing else. These are the only subjects I can bear.

I need Amina. I need her help. In so many ways.

Whenever I see her in class, she looks at me like I'm this awful person. Like she wouldn't dare associate with someone like me. And it's only now that I realize how enormous the difference is between having *one* friend and having *zero* friends.

When I walk past our old spot on the benches between the portables, Amina is sitting there with Bree and Alicia. I know it's just a bench. I know I'm being dramatic. But it's like a dagger through my heart. And I deserve it. I do. I lied to Amina for months and months and let her humiliate herself in front of the boy she's been madly in love with since primary school. I get it. But it still hurts.

So, I sit by myself up the back of the canteen in the corner everyone avoids because it kinda smells like pee. I spend most of my lunchtimes with my head in my hands, trying to figure out the point of this whole thing. This whole fucked-up year. Like, what is the *point?*

Dad always says everything happens for a reason, that the Universe has it all planned out for us. Well, if anyone can find the "plan" in the absolute shambles that is my life right now, I'd love to hear it.

I mean, I fall down a flight of stairs, shatter my foot, lose the one thing I love most in the world—along with the future I'd worked so incredibly hard for every single day of my life—

then get kicked out of school, lose all my friends, and have to start from scratch. That's a whole bunch of shit, right? But sure, the Universe has a plan, so just keep going, Luca. So, I start at a new school, make new friends, learn new things, and realize, "Hey, there's actually more to life than ballet!" then fall head-over-heels in love with the most beautiful, wonderful boy I've ever met, and we live happily ever after, right? The End. *Right?*

WRONG!

"Kidding," says the Universe. "Just wanted to make you feel like *maybe* everything would be okay so that when I messed everything up for real it would be heaps more dramatic. Now get this: your dad doesn't like you, you have zero friends, no prospects in life, *and* you ruined your only chance of ever being with the boy of your dreams."

Awesome. Thanks, Universe. That's just fucking perfect.

I really need to talk to someone. Actually, I need to talk to *three* people. But none of those people are talking to me. Which makes things kinda difficult. But then I have a brilliant idea . . .

It's Saturday morning. I pull on some shorts and a T-shirt and head to the bus stop. It's hot and dry outside, and my back starts sweating almost instantly. I should probably call first, but I know she'll say no if I ask. I figure if I just rock up, there's no way she'll be able to turn me away. Not in my current emotional state.

I hop off the bus and walk the couple of blocks down to the Ballarat Allied Therapies, feeling like I've definitely made the right decision. Sami always knows what to say. I always leave her treatment room feeling lighter and happier and more in control. She just *gets* me. She's like, my fairy godmother with a mean set of elbows and a killer pair of heels.

As I head up the ramp, memories come flooding back to me. Jordan strutting into the waiting room. Jordan crying in front of me. Jordan and I standing out here swearing at each other, saying awful things we didn't mean, things I thought we'd never be able to get over. But we did. And now this.

"Hi," I say to Shelby the receptionist, who is nodding along to the waiting room music as always.

"Oh, *hi*, Luca," she replies, smiling wide. "How are you? It's been so long!"

Like that's a bad thing.

"Um, is Sami here? I know it's super last minute and she's probably booked up, but I need to see her. It's . . . kind of an emergency."

Shelby smiles with no teeth. "Sorry, hun. Sami's not in today."

"What? She always works Saturdays."

"Not this one! She's away. Early Christmas with Julia's family."

I feel the energy drain right out of me. My shoulders slump and I look down at my shoes.

"I can book you in with Mark in an hour?" Shelby says. "He just had a cancellation."

"No, it's okay." I shake my head. "Don't worry about it."

I turn and walk out the automatic doors.

"Bye, Luca! Nice to see you!"

I scuff across the ramp and sigh out whatever tiny amount

of hope I had left. There's no one else to turn to. No way to fix this mess. Emotion bubbles in my chest as I grab the railing and look up to the clear blue sky for answers.

What now?

And then, as if the Universe actually heard me, the answer comes to me like a spark of electricity. I suddenly feel awake. Aware. Like someone flicked a switch inside my brain.

I smile up at the sky as I set off across the car park, my heart beating double time.

I know what I need to do.

Forty-Two

SO HERE I AM. Standing outside the glass door to the Gwen Anderson School of Ballet. I timed my bus trip so I'd arrive when the afternoon classes had already finished. I've been out here on the street for the last fifteen minutes, just staring through the glass at the staircase that ruined my life. About five times now, I've decided this is too much and that I should just go home. That there's no way in hell I could ever dream of walking up those stairs again. But then, here I am, still standing outside the door.

I need to do this.

I put my hand on the long metal door handle, force a breath out through tight lips, and pull the door open. I step inside and gaze up to the top of the stairs. I can still hear Abbey calling out to me from the waiting room. Grace crying in the exact spot where I'm standing right now. Talia swearing from the other side of the door.

I shake the memories from my mind and place my good foot on the first carpeted step.

They're just stairs. They're just stairs. They're just. Fucking. Stairs.

And in my head, I know that's true. I've been going up and down the stairs at home for *months* now. But this feels different. It feels like so much more than that. An overwhelming surge of emotion swells up inside me, and I have to steady myself on the handrail. I grip the wooden rail tightly, taking deep breaths to slow my racing pulse.

I wish Sami was here to coach me up the stairs. I need her standing beside me, smiling her brightest smile, saying, *You got this, Luca. Let's go! One foot in front of the other!*

I take another deep breath.

One foot in front of the other.

I can do this.

One foot in front of the other.

And without another thought, I climb straight to the top of the stairs.

When I step into the waiting room, I don't know if I want to laugh or cry or scream or jump up and down. But then a door creaks open behind me and someone says, "Luca?"

I whip around to see a blonde girl standing in the door to the girls' change room in a leotard and trackies. She looks like she's seen a ghost—which isn't that far off, I guess.

"Grace?" I reply. "What are you doing here? Class finished like, half an hour ago."

"Hello to you, too," she scoffs.

"Sorry, I—" And I don't know what it is—maybe seeing a familiar face, maybe just being here at the studio in the first place—but tears start flooding down my cheeks, completely out of my control.

"Oh my gosh, Lu." Grace runs over and wraps her arms around me. I rest my head on her shoulder and let it all out.

"It's okay."

I'm crying so hard now that I'm actually making noises. Like, those gross, snotty, gasping-for-air crying noises.

"Lu, what is it? What's wrong?" Grace pats my hair like Mum used to do after she tucked me into bed. Or is that just another made-up memory, hijacked from some corny kids' movie?

"I ruined everything," I say, looking up.

"What do you mean, 'everything'? Did you hurt yourself again?"

"No," I reply, though I do feel like I've been punched in the stomach. "Just like, everyone I care about."

And then I collapse into her arms again. I don't know why she's being so nice to me. She's one of the people I hurt the most. But she just hugs me and lets me cry.

When I eventually pull away, I'm almost shocked to see that it really is Grace standing there. I'd forgotten how pretty she is. In my mind, I've been picturing her as that little girl who shrank away behind her bitchy friends, who couldn't even look me in the eye while Talia tossed racist comments around like confetti. But here, now, Grace looks pure and beautiful. Angelic. It's the Grace I know. The Grace I love.

"Okay," she says, sitting me down on one of the wooden benches that run along the wall of the waiting room. "Lay it all out for me. Tell me everything."

And there's nothing I want to do more than fill Grace in

on the last however many months it's been, to explain every painfully awkward detail, every lie, every wrong step, and ask her what the hell I should do to fix it all. But that wouldn't be fair to her. Not in this moment. And I refuse to be a shit friend for a single second longer.

"Grace, I'm sorry."

"Don't be sorry, you're obviously upset, I just—"

"Not about this," I reply, gesturing to my wet and splotchy face. "I mean about everything. Everything that's happened since I broke my foot. I turned into someone else. Someone awful."

"You're not awful," Grace replies, but it has that tone of like, *You're not* awful, *but you're certainly not great, either.*

"I shouldn't have ignored you after my accident, I shouldn't have deserted you when I changed schools, I shouldn't have let our friendship get completely ruined by my own shitty situation. I'm sorry."

"It's okay, Lu."

"It's *not*," I press. "It's definitely not okay, Grace. And I know I'll never be able to make up for what I did, but I was broken. My life was in literal pieces and I didn't know how to act any more. How to be a good friend, how to be . . . I dunno . . . how to be *me*."

"I know."

"I know you know, but I just want you to understand that if I could take it all back, I absolutely would. We've been friends since we were two and a half years old, Grace. We had something really special. You never did anything to hurt me, not once, not ever. And I just abandoned you because *I* felt like shit and couldn't handle it."

"You didn't do it on purpose."

"No, but . . ."

"And it's not all your fault," she says. "I'm partially to blame, too."

"You're *not*, you—"

"I *am*, Lu," she says, her expression pained. "That day when we bumped into you and your friend from North . . . I will never forgive myself for that."

"You didn't do anything, it was—"

"*Exactly*," she interrupts. "I didn't do anything. I've never been able to stand up to Talia, but the things she said that day . . . I should have defended you. I should have defended your friend. I should have told Talia to shut her fucking mouth and grow the hell up."

Grace never swears, and it feels like daggers being thrown when she does. When she finishes speaking, her cheeks flush and she runs a hand over her slicked-back hair.

"I haven't spoken to either of them since then," she says quietly.

"Abbey and Talia?"

She nods. "I can barely look at them without screaming."

"What about at ballet?"

"They pretty much pretend like I don't exist. Which is fine by me. My god, you should have seen their faces when Miss Gwen gave me the solo in the Open Classical for the end-of-year recital."

"What? You got the solo? Grace, that's amazing!"

"Thanks. It's pretty incredible."

"I wish you'd told me all this."

"Well," she says, pulling her mouth to one side, "I did try to call you. Once. But you didn't answer, so I convinced myself you didn't want anything to do with me. Which would have been perfectly understandable."

I think back to Jordan's caravan in Ocean Grove. The missed call from Grace. I wonder if everything would've turned out differently if I'd just called her back . . .

I sigh and let go of the thought. "I'm sorry I wasn't there for you."

She smiles, her blue eyes a little watery. "I'm sorry, too."

We sit in silence for a long moment. Maybe I'm imagining things, but I swear I can feel a year's worth of awkwardness slipping away into thin air around us.

"Wait, so why are you still here?" I ask. "It's so late."

"I had a private with Miss Prue," Grace replies, fishing her phone out of her bag. "It was supposed to be on Thursday afternoon, but it got rescheduled. She's still in the studio if you want to say hi?"

I nod, feeling a hot rush of nerves.

"I have to go," Grace says, standing up. "Mum's waiting downstairs in the car. Are you good here?"

"I'm good," I reply, and even though I don't mean it that way, the words really sink in.

I *am* good. I'm okay.

"Text me?" Grace says.

"Of course."

As I open the door to the studio, I'm greeted by the all-too-familiar smell of vinyl flooring, hairspray, and sweat. I close my eyes and breathe it in deeply, feeling like the scent alone is enough to send me back in time to the day I broke my foot.

"Luca?" Miss Prue calls out from the opposite side of the room. "Luca Mason, is that you?"

I wave, feeling self-conscious and out of place all of a sudden. "Hi, Miss Prue."

She gracefully trots over to me and pulls me into a tight hug. "It is *so* good to see you, Luca. How have you been?"

"Okay, I guess," I reply as she lets go. "How are you? How's Miss Gwen?"

"We're fine," she says, swatting at the air. "How is your foot? Oh, Luca, I was so, *so* sorry when I heard you wouldn't be coming back to the studio. Miss Gwen was absolutely *devastated*."

"She was?"

"Oh yes," she replies, before leaning in and whispering, "Don't tell any of the girls, but you were always Miss Gwen's favorite."

I can't help but laugh. Turns out I was Mr. Favorite, after all. I wish Talia was here right now so I could rub it in her jealous face.

Miss Prue lets out a deep sigh. "You had so much potential, Luca. You were a truly gifted dancer. One of a kind. Honestly."

Hearing those words is like getting slapped on one cheek and kissed on the other at the same time.

"Thanks," I say, because what else am I supposed to say. "Um, Miss Prue," I add, glancing around the studio. "I was wondering if I might be able to ask a favor?"

"Of course."

"Would you mind if I used the studio for a minute? Um . . . alone?"

She smiles, her lips pressed together. "Certainly, darling. You're always welcome here, you know that."

"Thank you."

She looks down at her watch. "I do need to get home to the kids, though, so I'll have to leave you to lock up. Is that all right? Do you remember how?"

I nod.

"Okay, well—" she gives my shoulders a gentle squeeze "—it was *so* good to see you, Luca. You have no idea how happy it makes me to see you back at the studio. Stop by whenever you like, okay?"

"Will do," I reply. "I'm sure I'll see you again sometime."

"I'm sure you will," she says, before slipping past me, grabbing her handbag from the front desk, and dancing down the stairs.

I wait until I hear the glass door close behind her before I slip off my shoes and step into the studio. The second my feet touch the cold vinyl floor, my chest tightens, and my eyes start to blur. I blink away the tears, and slowly—as if I'm walking on glass—make my way to my usual spot at the barre, where the afternoon sun always shone through the window like my own personal spotlight.

It's been two hundred and ninety days since I last stood here. I counted on the calendar before I got on the bus.

Two hundred and ninety days.

I pull my phone out of my trackies and click into Spotify.

I hit Play on one of my old ballet playlists, put the phone on loudspeaker, and put it down on the floor beside the wall.

I gently place my right hand on the wooden barre and, as soon as I touch it, a shiver travels up my arm and all the way down my spine. I twist my neck from side to side until the joints pop—old habits die hard, I guess.

I close my eyes . . .

Take a deep breath . . .

And start the first exercise.

Pliés. Where we always began. Every single class.

And it feels like coming home.

I keep my eyes closed, slowing bending and stretching my legs, my arms floating through the air around me. I try to ignore the fact that my left ankle doesn't bend far enough, that I can't rise up onto my toes properly, that I can barely point my left foot. I try to ignore it all and just let myself *move*. Because dancing isn't about thinking. It's about *feeling* and *knowing*. It comes from the heart, not from the head. And my body knows exactly what to do.

I don't open my eyes until I finish the full set of barre exercises, all the way through to *grand battement*. When I stop, I'm already out of breath and dripping with sweat. I mean, I knew I was out of shape, but this is something else. I wipe my forehead with my T-shirt, then leave my phone on the floor and walk into the middle of the studio, planting myself right on center stage. The place where I've felt more comfortable than any other in my entire life. I lock eyes with myself in the mirror, hardly recognizing the boy staring back at me. I place my bad foot behind me in fourth position and prepare for a *pirouette*. I bend my knees

327

and hold my arms out, feeling the energy coil up inside me like a spring wound tight. I take in one last breath, then release the tension, rising high onto the toes of my good foot, turning and turning on the spot like a wooden spinning top.

And suddenly, the walls around me disappear. Miss Gwen's studio vanishes into thin air, and I'm sailing up through the sky past the clouds.

Spinning and spinning and spinning.

Soaring all the way up to the sun.

When I eventually float back down to earth, I rest my hands on my knees and gasp in a long, shaky breath, sweat and tears dripping down onto the floor beneath me.

And I smile.

Because for the first time in two hundred and ninety days, I finally feel like *me*.

Forty-Three

THE YEAR TWELVES FINISH their exams, which means they're finally free. There are a couple more assemblies and events for them to attend, but they're basically done. Thirteen years of schooling, over. Just like that.

Which means Jordan is one step away from being out of my life forever. We still haven't spoken, not since Gibbo's party. As much as I desperately wanted to send him nine million apology messages, I thought it was probably a good idea to give him some space, especially while he was in the middle of exams. The last thing I wanted to do—after everything I'd already done—was make him fail high school.

I still haven't spoken to Amina, either. But on Monday afternoon, I put on my backpack, get the bus to Woolies for supplies, then head across town to her house. I have no idea how this is going to go down, but I've got everything I need to give it its best possible chance of working.

I step up to the door, pull out my phone, and press play on Spotify. I knock on the door in the most cheery way I can think of and—luckily—Amina answers.

"What the—" she almost jumps out of her skin. "What are—who—*Luca?*"

Here I am, standing on Amina's doorstep, wearing the cardboard Harry Styles mask I printed out at home, with the chorus of "What Makes You Beautiful" by One Direction blaring on loudspeaker on my phone, a Woolies green bag swinging in my hand.

"What on *earth* are you doing? You're going to get me in trouble."

But I just groove along to the music like we're in some cheesy pop film clip, while the 1D boys tell Amina how she lights up their lives like nobody else.

She doesn't know what to do with herself. I can tell she's trying not to smile at my incredibly awkward dancing, but eventually, a laugh escapes her. Feeling like I've managed to break the ice, I click pause on my phone and push the Harry Styles mask back onto the top of my head.

"Hi," I say.

"Hi?" she says, like it's a question.

"Amina Ahmad, welcome to your official apology."

I do a big curtsy, and she says, "Luca, this is absurd."

"I come bearing gifts." I hold up the Woolies bag and reach inside. "Because no apology is complete without . . . Apology Pie!"

Amina looks stunned. "You're bribing me with a halal pie?"

"I wouldn't say *bribing* . . . It's a gift. A peace offering."

She narrows her eyes at me. "How did you even know I like Garlo's pies? That is so random."

"You told me at lunch one day. Ages ago."

"Did I? How on earth do you remember that?"

"You did a twenty-minute monologue about it, it's not something I was ever going to forget."

She twists her mouth to the side to stop herself from smiling. I hand her the pie and she takes it, giving me a suspicious look.

"I also brought . . ." I sling my backpack off and pull out a pile of schoolbooks, holding them in the air like baby Simba.

"Your biology homework?"

"Got it in one! And also my maths homework and my psych homework. Because I almost failed every single one of my practice exams, and if there's one thing I know you love doing, it's helping me study."

She glances down at the pie then back up at me. "Let me get this straight," she says. "You thought that if you came to my house in a Harry Styles mask, did a little dance, gave me a pie, and asked me to help you study, I'd forgive you for lying to me for months and letting me completely humiliate myself in front of TJ?"

"Yes," I reply matter-of-factly, "that is exactly what I thought."

She holds out the pie. "Take your stupid Apology Pie. It's not going to work."

"But *also*," I say, pushing the pie back toward her, "I thought that if I actually *apologized*, that might help too?"

She looks up to the sky. "Luca . . ."

"Amina, I'm sorry. Truly. You are literally the most beautiful person I've ever met, and you have been *nothing* but kind to me since the day you gave me a personally highlighted timetable."

She looks down at the welcome mat and says, in a quiet voice, "It's easier to read that way."

"You took me under your wing and helped me in more ways than you will ever know. You didn't deserve to be lied to. I was in an incredibly awkward position—not to mention the fact that I was going through the shittiest time of my entire life—and I swear I wanted to be honest with you, but it wasn't my secret to tell. But I'm not here to make excuses. I messed up. Me, and only me. I take full responsibility for everything."

I put the Harry Styles mask back on and get down on one knee.

"Amina Ahmad," I say, my voice muffled by the mask.

"Oh, for goodness' sake."

"Will you accept my apology?"

There's this moment that stretches out for an eternity where I'm certain she's going to say no. And I don't have a backup mask.

She furrows her brow. Shakes her head. Rolls her eyes . . .

"Fine."

I jump up off the doorstep and wrap my arms around her.

"Thank you, thank you, thank you," I say, bouncing her up and down.

"Okay," she says. "O*kay*. Just come inside before the neighbors think I'm being attacked."

We cover Amina's dining room table with schoolbooks. I mean, you can't see a single centimeter of wood once we've laid everything out. Seeing all my school stuff like this makes me more anxious than I thought it would. I need to learn all of *that* by Monday.

"How did you do so badly on your practice exams?" Amina asks. "You've been doing so well."

"Uh, a little thing called 'being distracted by the fact that I had no friends.'"

Amina purses her lips. "Well, I didn't put in *that* much effort with you all year for you to fail everything now."

"How did you go?" I ask. "Are you still on track to be Dux of the World?"

She snorts. "I don't know. I think Alicia and I are neck and neck. She beat me on the chemistry practice exam by one percent. I was mortified."

"What did you get?"

"Ninety-eight."

I click my tongue. "Yes, I can see how getting ninety-eight percent on a practice exam must have been absolutely *mortifying*."

"Shoosh," Amina says. "I cannot let her beat me. You know that speech is everything to me."

"I told you once, and I'll tell you again: You could take Alicia in a fight."

Amina laughs. "No violence necessary. We're going to do this the pacifist way. Me, you, and a good old-fashioned study party."

"Just because you add the word 'party,' it doesn't make it fun. You know that, right?"

She raises one eyebrow. "You've clearly never been to one of *my* study parties. You think Gibbo's eighteenth was big? You've got no idea what you're in for, Luca Mason."

I laugh, still baffled by how Amina can be *such* a nerd but *so* adorable at the same time.

"Meanwhile," she says, "can we just take a moment for the fact that you have a *boyfriend?*"

There's this awful sinking feeling in my chest. "Well, *had*, I think."

"We'll fix it," Amina replies. I tell you what, she's handling this whole situation about a billion times more maturely than I ever would've been able to. "That was so horrible what Gibbo did to TJ's locker. I'm so glad he got suspended."

"Yeah, but it was my fault."

"Luca, it was not. It was *Gibbo's* fault."

"I guess," I reply. "I don't know. I'm just . . . trying to respect Jordan's space at the moment."

"We'll fix it," Amina says again. "I promise. You both deserve to be happy."

To be honest, I don't know if I *do* deserve to be happy after everything I've done. But it's nice to hear someone say that. Especially Amina.

"Actually," she says slowly, "I think I have an idea."

"Oh?"

But then her mamah calls out, "Pie's ready!" and Amina jumps out of her chair.

"Apology Pie first, brilliant idea later?" she asks, her eyes sparkling with excitement. And I mean, a meat pie shouldn't bring someone *this* much joy, but for the first time in months, I feel like I've finally done something right.

Forty-Four

WHEN WE WALK INTO the gym on our last day of school, I could not be more proud of my best friend. I feel like love hearts are shooting out of my eyes every time I look at her. She did it—not that I ever thought she wouldn't. Amina Ahmad: Dux of Year Eleven at Ballarat North Secondary College. Straight A+s in every subject.

It's worth mentioning that I managed to pass all my exams too. English was my top subject—my first A in the history of the world—followed by drama and health (both Bs). I got a D for biology—those damn phenotypes—but Cs for psych and maths, which was way better than I expected.

I sit there in the audience at the Year Twelve farewell assembly, biting my nails and tapping my foot. When Mr. Fennel finally calls Amina up to the lectern at the front, everyone claps half-heartedly, but I whoop and cheer uncontrollably.

And Amina's speech is everything. I mean, I knew she was a genius, but damn can that girl give a good speech. She's funny, inspiring, profound, moving. People aren't into it at first—everyone hates this kind of pointless assembly—but by the end, I kid you not, you could literally hear a pin drop. When she finishes, everyone stands and applauds. I look around me. Some of the Year Twelves are wiping away tears—as are all their parents up in the back—and the little Year Sevens have stars in their eyes, like they've seen, for the very first time, a future where anything is possible. Her whole speech is flawless, but there's this one line in particular that sticks in my mind in a way that I just know I will never forget:

"How are we to know who we are, when we've only just begun?"

Mr. Fennel thanks Amina for her "rousing" speech and invites all the Year Twelves up onto the stage (aka the front of the gym underneath the basketball ring). Standing there in their casual clothes, they look like they're halfway between kids and adults, like they don't quite belong here anymore, but like they don't belong anywhere else, either.

I find Jordan standing at the back of the group, smiling and whispering to Macca beside him. He looks relieved. He looks . . . happy. Which kind of kills me.

I place my hand over my pocket to check that the folded piece of paper is still inside. Like it could have somehow crawled out on its own while I've been sitting here in the gym. But it's there. My stomach twists at the thought.

I go to look for Gibbo in the audience so I can actively hate him for ruining everything, but then remember he's not here. He ended up getting suspended for the rest of the term, and apparently, he might not be coming back next year at all—I can only dream.

I don't know if Jordan has spoken to him, but I'm guessing not. Calling your mate a "faggot" and a "perv" is not really something you can come back from. Rightly fucking so.

When it's time for everyone to file out of the gym and go home for summer, I dash straight over to Amina. She sees me coming and puts her hands over her mouth, the happiest and most overwhelmed I've ever seen her. And it's not like she doesn't get overwhelmed on a daily basis.

"You. Are. Incredible," I say, pulling her into a hug.

"Really?"

I let go. "I know I wasn't here for that other girl's speech that you loved—"

"Sarah Peters?"

"—but she's got nothin' on you, girl!"

"Stop," she replies, blushing hard.

"I'm serious, Amina. You are the literal queen of speeches. That's going to go down as the single greatest speech in the history of Ballarat. You'll be an urban legend."

"Urban legends are stories that aren't true."

"Whatever." I hug her again. "I'm so proud of you."

"That was a wonderful speech, sayang," a stern voice says from behind me. I turn to see Amina's mamah and papah standing together, looking as adorable as always. It's only the Year Twelves' parents who are supposed to come to the assembly, but they refused to miss Amina's speech. I stand aside to let them hug their daughter.

"Wasn't she amazing?" I say, taking in the perfect family portrait.

"It was very moving," her mamah says, her round face beaming.

"We are very proud," her papah says, with one arm still around Amina. "Very proud, indeed."

And because I literally can't stop myself, I say, "And this is why Amina is going to make an incredible teacher."

"Luca," she warns, the mood instantly changing in the air around us.

"A teacher?" her papah says, letting her go. "My little girl is going to be a doctor." He nods once like it's the final word on the matter. End of story.

I give Amina a look that says, *This is your chance.*

She tugs on the edge of her hijab and says, "I'm not, Papah. I'm going to be a teacher."

"But you—"

"Please," she interrupts. "Just listen for a sec?"

Her papah's face is like ice all of a sudden. Her mamah bites her lip.

"I know you only want the best for me," Amina says, her voice calm and collected, "and you want me to have every opportunity in the world, but I am not even remotely interested in medicine. It doesn't make me happy. Not like I know teaching will."

"Amina," her mamah says, "you need to listen to your papah. He knows what's best."

"But she's amazing at this," I say. "Can't you see? No one else could stand up there and give a speech like that. These kids—" I flap my arms around at the gym "—do not listen. Our assemblies are usually mosh pits with added fart noises. But everyone listened to what your daughter had to say. They actually cared."

I glance at Amina, whose mouth is hanging wide open.

"Do you have any idea how much she helped me this year?" I go on, because it's too late to stop now. "I would have failed every single subject without Amina's help. She's better than any teacher I've ever had, and she's only in Year Eleven. I mean, we all know she's a genius, but is there anyone else in the world who could explain how to solve linear equations through a game of charades? Seriously, the girl deserves an Academy Award. She is born for this. I know it."

Amina looks down at her feet and wipes her eyes. Her mamah looks to her papah, who turns to glare at Amina.

"It makes her happy," I add, knowing I've already said too much.

But then her papah's face relaxes. "We will talk properly about your options another time," he says to Amina, and she looks up, surprised. "You should both go and talk to your friends now. We don't want to keep you."

They turn and walk toward the exit and Amina stares at me, her eyes sparkling with tears, like I just bought her tickets to a private show with old-mate Styles.

"Thank you," she replies, her voice catching a little.

I shrug. "I mean, it's not like I owe you or anything."

Forty-Five

MR. FENNELL ANNOUNCES THAT we need to clear the gym for the cleaners, and Amina and I are ushered outside with the rest of the students. It's one of those stunning spring days—warm, with a soft breeze, and a crystal-clear blue sky—that makes you forget how awful the Ballarat weather is ninety percent of the time.

The Year Twelves are all hugging and crying and signing each other's school shirts in permanent marker. Out of the corner of my eye, I spot Jordan standing with his mum and dad under a tree at the edge of the quad, and my stomach ties itself into a knot. And then that knot ties itself into five more knots.

I slip my hand into my pocket and run my thumb over the edge of the piece of paper, wondering why the hell I ever let Amina talk me into doing this.

Then I realize I'm staring, and that Jordan's mum is waving at me. I'm honestly surprised she recognizes me when I'm not a hungover, sweaty mess, but I smile back and give her an awkward wave. Jordan glances over, and his eyes meet mine.

And my heart almost splits in two.

"It's time," I say, turning back to Amina.

She grabs my hand and gives it a squeeze. "You'll be fine, Luca. Just do it like we practiced."

But I just stand there, nodding, trying to convince myself that this isn't going to be a total disaster.

She nudges me with her shoulder and whispers, "Go."

"I'm going, I'm going," I reply. "I just need to . . ." I take in a deep breath and shake the nerves out of my hands. "I got this."

Then, as casually as I can manage—which is clearly not casually at all—I walk over to Jordan and his parents.

"Hi!" I say, trying to sound cheery and not terrified.

"Hey," Jordan replies, his expression completely unreadable. "Dad, this is Luca. Luca, this is my dad, Steve."

His dad—who I can't help but notice has Jordan's hazel eyes—reaches out to shake my hand. "Nice to meet you, mate."

"Nice to meet you, too."

"And," Jordan says, "I believe you've already met my mum?"

"Please, call me Yuko," she says, with a nod.

"Hello again," I reply. "Um, Jordan, can I talk to you for a sec?"

"Sure," he says, then turns to his mum. "I'll be back in a minute, okay?"

"Take your time," she says, and his dad gives me a weird, nervous grin.

Jordan struts off into the quad without another word, so I follow a pace behind, my heart rate increasing with each step. He stops when he gets to the circular brick flowerbed in the very middle of the quad where he hangs out with his mates at lunchtime. Well, *used* to hang out with his mates, I guess, since he won't be coming back here after today.

He turns to me, a heavy frown on his face. And before he can tell me I'm a terrible person and he never wants to see me again, I yank the piece of paper out of my pocket, unfold it, and start to read:

"Jordan," I begin. "When I first—"

"What is *that?*" he interrupts. "Did you write me a speech?"

"No," I reply, thinking back to the four hours Amina and I spent together in her dining room perfecting every single word. "Well, kind of, but it's not a *speech* speech. It's just . . . something I need to say. I didn't want to forget anything."

Jordan stares back at me. I wish I knew what he was thinking right now.

I clear my throat and start again. "Jordan. When I first met you, I instantly knew that you were going to be an important person in my life. I . . . I—"

But I stop myself. Because this isn't right. As perfectly constructed and beautifully written as this speech is—all credit to Amina, obviously—this isn't how I should be doing this. Because *this*—whatever this thing is between me and Jordan— is like dancing. It needs to come from the heart.

So, before my brain can convince me not to, I shove the speech back into my pocket and say the only words I can think of that will do even a shred of justice to how I feel right now . . .

"I love you, Jordan."

And as soon as I say it, I feel lighter than air.

"And that might not be enough for you," I go on. "That

might not fix us. But it's true. I love you. And that's all I really wanted to say."

For what must be a whole minute, Jordan stares down at the concrete, kicking at the little stones at our feet.

"I wanted to hate you," he says, finally looking up.

I don't know what I'm supposed to say to that, so I don't say anything at all.

"I really did. I wanted to be angry at you and blame you for everything that happened. I told myself that if you hadn't broken your foot, if you hadn't gone to the OT, if you hadn't moved to North, if you hadn't been at Gibbo's party, if you hadn't called me that morning, if you weren't so damn beautiful in the first place, I never would have been in this position." He takes in a deep breath and runs a hand through his hair. "But none of this was your fault. People were going to find out about me eventually, whether I told them or you told them or they found out some other way. And I know us being together is nothing to be ashamed of anyway, so why the fuck should I care what anyone thinks? I just had this really clear idea in my head of how I wanted to tell people, of how I thought the whole thing should go down. I wanted to be in control of my own story, you know?"

I suddenly remember something Sami said to me on the day I officially became a "free man" and walked out of her treatment room wearing only one shoe.

"We always think the biggest, most important moments in our lives are going to go exactly how we want them to," I say. "But they never do."

Jordan smiles with one corner of his mouth. "No. They sure don't."

"I'm sorry." I feel like I've been saying that a lot lately, to a lot of people.

"You don't need to be sorry. I shouldn't have asked you to lie for me. I just . . ."

"You weren't ready."

Jordan gently shakes his head. "I wasn't ready."

"I didn't mean to tell Gibbo . . ."

"I know," he nods. "Gibbo can fuck off, anyway. I don't think all friendships are made to last."

Silence.

Then Jordan says, "I told my parents."

"What?"

"I told them about you. The day after Gibbo's party, after I went to get my phone. Mum said you came to the house and I just told them. Right then and there in the kitchen. Like it was the most normal thing in the world."

"But you . . . Why didn't you tell me?"

He shrugs. "I don't know. I guess I had to process it myself first. And then all the shit went down with Gibbo at school, and I thought you hated me, and—"

"Are you kidding?" I laugh. "I thought *you* hated *me*. And you had exams. Like, really important, one-shot exams. I didn't want to ruin your life any more than I already had."

Jordan takes a step forward. "You didn't ruin anything."

"And . . . how did it go?" I ask. "Telling your parents?"

"Fine," he replies. "Good, actually. Mum cried a little bit but said she loves me no matter what. And Dad said he doesn't care who I date, as long as I'll still have a beer with him at the footy."

I laugh. "I'm glad."

"Me too."

"And . . ." I swallow. "What exactly did you tell them?"

"I told them I have a boyfriend."

"Have a boyfriend? Or *had?*"

"*Have*," Jordan replies. "If that's okay with you?"

I snort.

"What?" he says.

"*If* it's okay? Jordan, in what universe would it *not* be okay that you still want to be my boyfriend?"

"Good to know," he chuckles. Then he takes another step forward. Looks into my eyes. Takes a breath. And says, "I love you too, Luca Mason."

And I mean, I'm playing it cool on the outside, but on the *inside*, the cheerleaders are back, and this time, they've brought the whole damn marching band with them.

Jordan leans in and kisses me, and I swear to god, my feet lift right off the ground.

When he finally pulls away, he holds out his hand and says, "You want to get out of here?"

I stare down at his open palm, wondering if he has any idea how long I've been waiting for this impossibly perfect moment.

"Sure," I reply, having to blink back tears.

I reach down and take his hand in mine, and just like that, we walk back across the quad together. In front of the whole school.

Holding hands.

Me and Jordan Tanaka-Jones.

Forty-Six

JORDAN INVITES ME TO a party with the Year Twelves that night, but I tell him it's probably better if it's just him and his friends, and that there's something important I need to do anyway.

"Just so you know," he says, "we're hanging all day tomorrow. Just you and me."

"It's a date," I reply, not bothering to pretend like the word "date" doesn't give me butterflies.

When I get home, I call out to Dad.

"Up here!"

I jog upstairs and find him in his bedroom, a huge pile of clothes all laid out on the bed.

Mum's clothes.

"What are you doing?" I ask, flicking on the light.

"Oh, thanks," he replies, laying a floral blouse on top of the pile, "I didn't even realize it was getting dark in here. I thought I'd finally get some of this stuff ready to take to the Salvos."

"You're not doing this because of me, are you? Because of what I said?"

He brushes some dust off his hands. "No, Lu. I'm doing it because it's the right thing to do."

"But . . . all those things you said about moving on being different from forgetting. You were right. I was wrong. That's why you're the adult and I'm the stupid little kid."

He tilts his head to one side. "You're not stupid, mate. Don't ever say that."

I shift from one foot to the other.

"Dad. I'm sorry. For what I said about Mum."

"I know you are."

"But you're still mad at me."

"I'm not mad."

"But you . . . you don't talk to me anymore. Not like you used to."

"Luca," he replies, "I've been a teacher for twenty-five years. And I learned a very long time ago that there are some things you can't teach people. Sometimes you need to give them the time and space to learn things on their own."

"So, what are you saying?"

"I'm saying I was just giving you time and space."

"To learn my lesson?"

"That's not how I'd put it, but sure."

"This isn't *Sesame Street*, Dad. This is real life. You know that, right?"

He shrugs. "It worked, didn't it?"

We're quiet for a moment, and then I say, "I went to the studio last week."

His eyebrows perk up. "Oh?"

"Now, you don't need to get all 'I told you so' or anything—"

Dad pretends to zip his lips "—but it felt really good to be back in the studio. And hard. Like, incredibly hard. But it was . . . good." Before he can get too excited, I add, "And I stand by the fact that I'm never going to make it as a ballet dancer. But . . . I also don't want to forget that I ever was one."

Dad smiles. "I'm very glad to hear that, mate."

I glance over his shoulder out the window. The sky is streaked with pink and red. It reminds me of this rhyme I think Mum used to say: *Red sky at night, shepherd's delight.* It meant it was going to be a beautiful day the next day.

"Grace was there," I add. "At the studio. I think we might . . . hang out sometime."

"Well," Dad nods, "I'm very glad to hear that, too."

"And . . . I should probably warn you . . . you'll be seeing a lot of Jordan over the summer. I mean, if that's okay?"

Dad's grin widens, just a little. "Sounds good to me."

My eyes drift back to the window. To the fiery red sky.

"Dad."

"Yes, Lu."

"You know how I said I don't remember Mum?"

He nods once. "I do."

"Well . . . I don't know if that's exactly true."

"What do you mean?"

"Sometimes I have these weird flashes of memory. Of her. But I don't know if they're real, or if I made them up, or if I saw them on TV or something."

"You've never told me that," Dad says, his forehead crinkling.

"I know. I was . . . embarrassed to ask."

"Why would you be embarrassed?"

"I dunno. In case I was making them up. Like, I wasn't even three when Mum passed away, how could I remember anything about her? Sometimes it didn't feel like I was allowed to remember."

"Oh, Lu. Of course you're allowed, she's your mum. What do you remember?"

"Little things," I say, staring down at her old clothes. "Silly things."

"Like what?"

I take a breath. The air smells kind of musty in here. I guess all those clothes have been in Dad's cupboard for almost fourteen years . . .

"Like . . . how she had that rhyme about the sunset?"

"'Red sky at night' and all that?" Dad asks.

"Yeah. And how she used to play 'This Little Piggy' on my toes?"

Dad grins.

"And how she'd stroke my hair until I fell asleep? And rub little circles on my back if I hurt myself? And how, this one time, she made me eat pea and ham soup, and I spat it out all over my highchair?"

"You remember that?"

"I didn't make it up?"

"No, mate," he says, walking around the end of the bed. "You didn't make any of that up."

He wraps his arms around me, and I sink into his chest.

"I can't believe you remember the pea and ham soup," he laughs. "You would have only *just* turned two."

"It was so gross."

"Your mum loved it." He's all sniffly now. "God knows why, it was bloody awful."

We both laugh and he lets me go.

"You don't have to get rid of all her stuff," I say. "Not if you don't want to."

"I'm gonna keep some of it," he replies, wiping his eyes. "Like this . . ."

He picks up a long, paisley skirt and holds it to his waist like he's measuring it for size.

"I don't think it's gonna fit, Dad," I say with a smirk.

"Shut up, you. This was the skirt she was wearing when I proposed to her."

"What? No way."

"Yep," Dad replies, swishing the skirt from side to side. "Over twenty-five years ago now."

"And she still had it when she . . .?"

"She did. She wore it all the time. After we got engaged, she called it her 'good luck skirt.' She always looked so beautiful in it." His voice breaks on the word beautiful and tears fill my eyes.

"Well, you should definitely keep it then," I say. "You wouldn't want to forget something like that."

"Mate," he says, clearing his throat. "I couldn't forget this skirt in a million years."

Forty-Seven

I CLICK INTO MY messages and open our Harry Styles Is Our Savior group chat.

Jordan: **Happy Birthday beautiful xxx**

Grace: **Happy bday Lu! See you soon!** Purple love heart.

Amina: **Selamat ulang tahun! Happy Birthday, Luca! (Also, PLEASE can we change the name of this chat already?)**

The four of us have been hanging out a lot since school finished. It all started when Grace invited me to Miss Gwen's end-of-year ballet recital, and I made Amina and Jordan come with me for moral support.

And I mean, holy shit. I can't tell you how hard it was to sit there in the auditorium, when the last time I was in that theatre I was up on stage, standing front and center, doing my thing. But it didn't hurt like I thought it would, like when I watched my old ballet DVDs after my surgery, and it felt like pouring disinfectant on a fresh cut. This was more like the ache of an old sprained ankle when it's really cold outside. Painful, yes. But distant. Dull.

And it honestly made me so happy to see Grace dance.

I didn't realize how much I'd missed that. She was *flawless*. I introduced her to Jordan and Amina at the stage door—even though she'd technically already met Amina, which Grace apologized for about nine hundred times in three minutes—and then we all went and got pancakes. I know, right? How very Disney Channel of us.

I saw Talia and Abbey too, but they didn't even say hi. They walked past when the four of us were all hysterically laughing about the tiny tots' routine—this one little girl just ran laps of the stage in a monkey costume, yelling, "Where's my banana?" over and over again—but they wouldn't even make eye contact. To be honest, I was kind of glad.

Miss Gwen and Miss Prue were so happy that I came. Miss Gwen said I looked like I'd put on weight, but Miss Prue said I looked "healthy." They asked if I'd come and teach some classes for the younger kids next year, but I don't know if I'm ready for that—physically or emotionally. I said I'd think about it.

Honestly, I'm kind of okay with not knowing where I'm heading at the moment. I always had such a clear path to follow. One direction, my whole life. But right now, I think I'm happy not knowing what's around the corner. I think . . . I dunno, I guess I realized that once you're forced to step off the path, you can go whichever direction you like. Which is kind of cool.

Jordan got his results back last week, and his scores were easily high enough to get into his first preference architecture course at Melbourne Uni. He hasn't had an official offer yet, and we haven't talked about what we're gonna do if he moves to Melbourne, but we'll deal with that when we have to, I guess.

"Here we are, Birthday Boy," Dad says as we pull up at

the Botanic Gardens at Lake Wendouree. "Seventeen years old, hey? Honestly, it feels like yesterday that—"

"Dad," I say, unclipping my seatbelt, "can you *promise* not get sentimental in front of my friends?"

He smiles. "I love you, Lu."

"Yes, Dad. I love you too."

We jump out of the car and walk into the gardens. It's a beautiful day. Like, the sun is shining, birds are chirping—it's literally that kind of vibe.

"Happy Birthday!" Amina squeals when we find her. She's set up a full picnic feast on a bright-pink floral rug. There are cakes and lollies and chips and cheese and crackers and chocolates and what I think is some kind of animal fruit sculpture. In true Amina style, it's totally over-the-top and absolutely perfect.

"Yayyyyy!" someone cries, and I turn to see Grace running over to join us. "Sorry I'm late. Mum had to drop my brother at work."

"It's fine," I reply, "we just got here."

"Happy Birthday, Lu," she says, planting a kiss on my cheek.

"Thank you." I check my phone. "Have you guys heard from Jordan?"

"He's coming with your present," Amina says. "It's from the three of us."

"What? You guys, I said no presents."

"Yeah," Grace snorts, "like we were ever going to obey that ridiculous rule. Wait—" she pulls her phone out of her Gucci handbag. "I think this is him. Hello? . . . Yep, he's here . . . Okay, no worries . . . Yep . . . Bye!"

"And?"

"Close your eyes," she replies, but before I even have a chance to shut them, her hands are around my head like a blindfold.

"How long do I have to keep them closed?"

"Just wait," Amina says.

After like, a lifetime, Grace says, "Okay, we're ready!"

She takes her hands away and I open my eyes. When they finally adjust to the light, I see Jordan standing there on the grass, looking as beautiful as ever. You'd think the effect would have worn off a bit by now, but he legitimately still takes my breath away.

"Tada!" he says, holding out his arms. "Happy Birthday!"

Standing in front of him is a brand new, shiny, turquoise bicycle, with a cute little wicker basket on the front. He dings the bell twice for effect, a big, dopey grin on his face.

"You have *got* to be kidding me."

Dad laughs. "About bloody time."

"Isn't it cute?" Grace says with a little golf clap. "I picked the color."

"Do you like it?" Amina asks.

I literally don't know what to say.

"Come give it a go!" Jordan says. "Try it out for size."

Shaking my head in disbelief, I walk over to him.

"I can't believe they told you I don't know how to ride a bike," I say quietly, so only he'll hear me. "I'm like, *mortified* right now."

"What, like not being able to ride a bike is a deal-breaker?" He pats the seat. "Come on, what's the worst that can happen?"

I look down at the bike, like it's a dog that might bite my hand off if I try to pat it.

"Don't worry," he says. "We got you."

I glance over my shoulder. Grace and Amina are smiling like we're on our way to Disneyland, and Dad looks like he's about to cry. I turn back to Jordan and kiss him on the lips.

"I know you do."

Acknowledgments

IT'S NO SECRET THAT it takes a village to publish a book, and I have been supported, encouraged, and inspired by the most incredible bunch of people imaginable.

To my incomparable agent, Claire Friedman of InkWell Management, thank you—this book would not exist if it weren't for you! From the minute we spoke on the phone, I knew you were the perfect agent for me in every way. I trust you implicitly, your editorial insights are golden, and your support is unwavering. Thank you for making this happen.

An enormous thank you to my stellar U.S. publishing team at Page Street Publishing. I am overjoyed that my book is joining the diverse and beautiful Page Street YA list! Thank you, thank you, thank you to Lauren Knowles and my brilliant editor, Tamara Grasty, for believing in Luca's story. Tamara, your notes and suggestions have been essential in making this book the best it can possibly be. Thanks to Lizzy Mason, Heather Taylor (my wonderful U.S. copy editor—apologies for all the Aussie slang!), and to my U.S. cover designer Kylie Alexander for making the book look so incredibly beautiful.

Thanks also to my amazing team at Penguin Random House Australia. Zoe Walton, your enthusiasm for Luca's story melted my heart, and you've made this nervous little debut author feel completely comfortable at every step of the publishing process. Thanks also to my brilliant editor Mary Verney—who knew copy edits could be so fun?—Tina Gumnior, Tijana Aronson, Laura Hutchinson, Benjamin Fairclough, and everyone at Penguin Teen Australia. You are all superstars and I'm so lucky to have you in my corner!

To my first readers—Poppy Nwosu, Holden Sheppard, Sophie L. Macdonald, Jade Arnold, and Hannah Andrews— thank you! It feels like a hundred years ago that you read one of the early drafts of this story, but this book wouldn't be the same without all your incredible feedback.

Annie McCann, my dear friend and fellow book nerd, thank you for helping me bring Amina to life. Your openness and generosity and willingness to share during our many chats and Messenger back-and-forths has been truly astonishing. Amina honestly wouldn't be the girl she is today without your invaluable insights, so, from the bottom of my heart, thank you!

Thanks to Reece Carter for being the best Hype Boy a guy could ask for (but seriously, thank you); to Ayaka Hornsby for your detailed and considered feedback on Jordan's character; to Brodie James for answering my incredibly random but incredibly specific ballet questions; to Rachel O'Loughlin, my self-proclaimed biggest fan (lol); Jeremy Lachlan, for the coffee debriefs and helpful advice; to my Bloomsbury Australia family, the entire #LoveOzYA community, Bookstagrammers far and wide (special shout-outs to Robby Weber, Jacob Demlow, Kai Spellmeier, Jodie Robertson, Jenny DuRoss, and Sam Evans), and everyone in the world who messaged, liked, shared, commented, retweeted, boosted, and supported me in any way, at any point in this process.

I'm sure it's no secret (after reading this book) that I think teachers are kind of awesome, and I was lucky enough to have some brilliant teachers as a teenager, so I'd like to give a special mention to some of them here. To my childhood dance teachers—Trudy and Lisa Harris, Ashlea Pyke, and Fred Fargher—thank you for lighting a fire inside me and setting me on the most wonderful path in life. (The "Little Shop of Horrors" U16 Jazz routine will live rent-free in my mind for all eternity.) And to my high school English teachers—Mr. Coish, Mrs. Keable, Mrs. Smith, and Mr. Maiden—thank you for always encouraging me to write. Teachers like you are not easy to come by, and I appreciate everything you did for me over the years (even if I did talk through most of your classes and distract all the other students . . . sorry!).

To the Assettas, thank you for welcoming me into your family. Your constant support truly means the world to me. (And Chiara, if this is the only book you ever read, I hope you liked it!)

Ash Collins . . . You were the person who was there, one random day in 2015, when I decided I wanted to write a book. You put up with me babbling on about writing all day, read my (terrible) short stories, and told me—without a hint of doubt— that I could make it as a writer. But long before that, you were my best friend in the world, and by far the best thing about high school. I honestly don't know who I'd be if we hadn't met. I'm sorry I kicked you in the chin that time in Year Eleven dance class, but it was the meet-cute you know we deserved. May the Lord and Lady of Marmara Drive continue their reign for many a glorious year!

My big brother Judd. Thank you for always encouraging me when I need encouragement, debating with me until the early hours of the morning when I need to be challenged, making fun of me when I need to be brought down a peg, and loving me unconditionally. And to Nina (and little Kira), thank you for always being fully present and interested and supportive—it means more than you know.

Dad. Peter. You'll never get to read this book, but there is a piece of you in everything I do. You loved books and libraries more than anyone I know, and I have you to thank for my love of the same. I love you, and I miss you dearly, but your memory will live on in my thoughts and words forever.

To my beautiful mum, Vicki. I honestly don't know what I would do without you. You taught me to read and write, to be silly, to always shop for bargains, to be curious, to laugh, to love. I always say that I'm turning into Vicki Madden the Second, but if I end up even half as incredible as you, I will be very, very happy. You're truly one in a million, and so much of what I've done and achieved and experienced in my life is all thanks to you. I love you.

And finally, my husband Daniel, who read the first draft of each and every chapter of this book the second I'd written it. My Love, without you by my side, none of this would have been possible. You inspire me beyond belief, you make me laugh, you force me to relax when I'm stressed and overwhelmed and I've buried my head in a pillow, and you show me every day that dreams really do come true. I love you more than words can say. I truly am the luckiest man in the world.

(Oh, and thanks to Ollie for being endlessly adorable, even when you want to play and I'm on a deadline.)

About the Author

ORIGINALLY FROM BALLARAT, TOBIAS worked for ten years as a dancer, touring Australia and New Zealand with musicals such as *Mary Poppins*, *CATS*, *Singin' in the Rain,* and *Guys and Dolls*. He now lives in Sydney with his husband, Daniel, and their Cavoodle, Ollie. In 2019, Tobias edited and published *Underdog: #LoveOzYA Short Stories*, which featured his first published work, "Variation." He also co-wrote the cabaret show *Siblingship*, which played to sold-out audiences around Australia. Tobias is a passionate member of the #LoveOzYA and LGBTQ+ communities, and he currently works full time for a major independent publishing company.